COLTER'S *Revenge*

OUTLAW LOVERS

JAN SPRINGER

ELLORA'S CAVE
ROMANTICA PUBLISHING

An Ellora's Cave Romantica Publication

www.ellorascave.com

Colter's Revenge

ISBN 9781419960758

Edited by Mary Moran.
Cover art by Syneca.

This book printed in the U.S.A. by Jasmine-Jade Enterprises, LLC.

Electronic book publication May 2006
Trade paperback publication June 2010

COLTER'S REVENGE

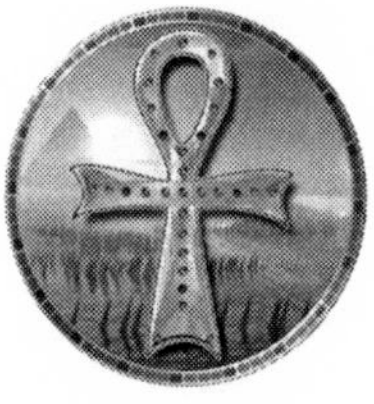

Dedication

For Mary Moran – a wonderful editor and a great friend.

And for my nephew Colter.

Thank you both for all your support!

Trademarks Acknowledgement

The author acknowledges the trademarked status and trademark owners of the following wordmarks mentioned in this work of fiction:

Boy Scouts: Boy Scouts of America, The

Jeep: Daimler Chrysler Corporation

Prologue

The Terrorist Wars
Baghdad, Iraq
General Black's Mansion
Spring, 2016

"How's it feel to have two cocks buried inside you, Starry Eyes? Does it live up to your ménage à trois fantasies?"

Ashley Blakely shivered at Dr. Colter Outlaw's soft question. Trembled at the unbelievable fullness of having his massive length impaling her soaked pussy and his friend Blade's thick, lubed cock nestled deep inside her rear.

She wished she could answer him, but the erotic way Colter's finger rubbed against her engorged clit made it really hard to concentrate on answering. Not to mention her wrists burned beneath the silky scarves holding her hostage and her shoulders were beginning a seductive ache at being strung up by the arms.

"She's at a loss for words," Blade chuckled from behind her.

His hard chest pressed firmly against her back. Steel-like muscular arms encircled her torso as his long, eager fingers busily pulled and squeezed her sensitive nipples until she cried out from the pleasure-burn.

Colter's gaze met hers. In the depths of his green eyes she recognized the fierce love. The raw hunger for her. The look always made her catch her breath and her heart race.

The last thing she'd ever expected was for the ruggedly handsome soldier Dr. Colter Outlaw to take her seriously when she'd shyly answered his question a couple of days ago regarding what her number one sexual fantasy would be. She'd admitted it was a ménage à trois.

Having only met him several weeks ago when he'd come to live at the mansion and attend to the general after he'd suffered an almost fatal gunshot wound, she'd been shocked at the sizzling attraction that had quickly cumulated between her and the doctor. With the general temporarily out of commission, she'd had a meager strand of freedom available to her, enabling her to talk with the doctor about the advances in the medical profession concerning the X-virus.

He'd been surprised when she'd admitted she'd wanted to train to be a gynecologist back in the States, but had limited telling him the entire truth of how her stepbrother Dr. Blakely, the man who'd actually invented the original X-virus that had killed so many women, had sold her to the Army because she'd rejected his advances. The general had purchased her and she'd become his sex slave in Iraq. The soldier doctor didn't need to know the horrors of her past. It would only put a damper on things. Especially now that she was enjoying the best sex in her twenty-five years of life.

At first, she'd been stunned when earlier that evening the general had left the compound for the first time in weeks. Colter had also disappeared for a couple of hours only to reappear with the awesomely tall, darkly tanned stranger named Blade. Quite a looker, almost too beautiful for a man to be. He had sensitive eyes the color of chocolate pudding and short golden blond hair.

The sexual hunger brewing in Blade's eyes had just about made her come on the spot. It hadn't been hard to allow both the stranger and Colter to make her fantasies come true.

When she'd been sold into slavery, she'd learned quickly to live on the edge. To take each day as if it could be her last. And that's exactly what she'd been doing since the soldier doctor had come into her life.

"I want you to come away with us, Ashley," Colter whispered in her ear as he began a slow, erotic plunge that made her quivering vagina wrap tighter around him. Her heart picked up a frantic beat at his words. She belonged to one of the most powerful generals in the United States Army. It would be a death sentence for both Colter and Blade if she went with them.

"She's so unbelievably tight," Blade hissed as he started a perfect thrusting rhythm that had her moaning at the powerful way his cock stretched her anal muscles, muscles that had been well maintained by the general's butt plugs and sadistic toys.

"We can get you out of here, Starry Eyes," he was whispering so low she could barely hear him.

"I…I…can't. The general…he'd kill you."

She winced at the pleasure-burn as Blade's hard erection slammed deep up inside her ass again.

"He'll never know."

"He'll know. He owns me. I can't simply go with you," she cried, desperation mixing with the wonderful fullness of Blade's hard cock nudging deeper into her anal channel.

As if disappointed with her answer, Colter's thrusts became harder, harsher, more desperate. More arousing. Blade seemed to sense his friend's change in mood and became gentler with his own seductive plunges.

"I don't care. I want you with me."

"He'll know you took me. He'll kill you both. God! Don't talk about this now."

She could barely stand. Without the silky scarf restraints holding her arms up, she would have melted to the floor by now. She was literally exhausted from the shattering orgasms the two men had blessed her with through the night. Perspiration dripped from her forehead. Tremors laced her aroused body. Erotic shivers made her wonder if she would ever be able to go back to her life of sadistic sex without orgasms with the general.

"We'll all be safe," Colter ground out between clenched teeth. She could feel his body tightening, sensed his time was near. Felt the blossom of yet another violent climax taking root deep inside her belly.

She hated the general more than anything and she wanted to be with Colter so badly it hurt. Wanted him to take her from this horrible life of being a sex slave to a sadistic American general.

But the last thing she wanted was for Colter, or anyone else for that matter, to be hunted down for stealing her. Deep inside her heart she knew she would never be able to live the same way after her experience with this ruggedly handsome soldier doctor and his friend.

The orgasm snowballed. Excitement roared through her. Her fingernails dug painfully into her palms.

Oh, my God! This one was going to be the biggest of them all!

"Come with me, Starry Eyes. Please say yes." The desperation in his voice, the excitement at the proposal of being free roared through her and tangled with the pleasure, snapping her hold on common sense.

"Yes…yes… I'll come with you," she hissed against his tasty mouth.

Colter's nostrils flared wildly at her answer and a most erotic smile tipped his lips.

"Fuck! You are so beautiful, Starry Eyes," he ground out, and his succulent mouth warmly captured hers, sending her spiraling into the splintering orgasm.

He took her hard. Harder than he'd ever taken her during the times they'd secretly been together. She cried out as he plunged his huge, thick cock so deep inside of her vagina, it unleashed a torrent of erotic sensations that slammed into her like she was on a roller coaster of pleasure-pain.

She found herself stiffening with erotic fervor then convulsing against the two men. Pumping her hips frantically against Colter's thrusts and bucking backward into Blade's rock-hard cock.

The scent of their sex spun beneath her nostrils. The sounds of flesh slapping against flesh drifted past her ears and intermingled with the grunts and groans of the two soldiers.

She became lost in her carnal delirium. Barely felt the two thick cocks sliding in and out of her as both men frantically attained their own satisfaction.

Panting for air, she held on for dear life as the sensual euphoria gripped her and dragged her under.

Chapter One

Outlaw Farm
Maine, United States of America
April 2021

"That's a hell of a way for a medical doctor to make a living."

The woman's familiar voice drifted through the late morning mist, making Dr. Colter Outlaw stiffen with anger. Elbow-deep in cold mud, he'd been working all morning on getting the tractor wheels unstuck from the field he'd been tilling. The last thing he needed was for his former S.K.U.L.L. chief and commander Bev White to show up and start throwing jokes.

"I'm finished with the Terrorist Wars, Bev. Get lost."

"That lovely S.K.U.L.L. tattoo nestled just above your gorgeous cock and balls says different, sweetheart."

"You know why I got it. A reminder never to trust you or S.K.U.L.L.," he said, allowing the anger to brush through him. "Now you'd better make yourself scarce, Bev. The Wars are over. As far as I'm concerned, the special permission you had to hold rank over me doesn't wash in this country. A woman alone has no rights in the States anymore. You could be Claimed right here on the spot. Lots of sexually starved men around."

"Speaking about yourself?"

Bitch! She knew him too well. "Go away, Bev. I'm busy."

"Not that it's any of your business, but I've got my minimum four husbands waiting right at your farmhouse.

Your brothers and a certain pregnant lady are keeping them entertained so we can talk."

"What do you want?" He kept his gaze glued to where his wrists disappeared into the mud, not wanting to give away the burst of excitement ripping through him that a woman stood mere inches away. A woman he'd fucked on a weekly basis as per mandatory US government regulations for the soldiers participating in the Terrorist Wars. She'd been one of those very rare women who'd received special permission to hold rank over men during the Wars, only because she'd had the connections in very high places enabling her to keep her position when the Claiming Law had come into effect. Yes, she'd been his boss, but she'd also been a woman. A woman who'd been ordered to have sexual relations with her men. She'd made it no secret she enjoyed sex and had eagerly spread her legs.

"S.K.U.L.L. needs you for one more assignment," she cooed from behind him.

"Fuck off. I'm retired."

If he were lucky she'd take the hint and leave. Obviously today wasn't his lucky day.

"Why don't you turn around and let me try and change your mind?"

He didn't dare turn around. The last thing he needed right now was to see Bev and her trim, muscular, feminine body. It would just remind him of the steamy sex they'd shared. Sex he hadn't had in a while.

He kept his concentration to the tractor tires and continued to scoop away the mud.

"I quit S.K.U.L.L. and you. I'm quite happy working on the farm."

"And quite happy not fucking your wife on a daily basis, as per Claiming regulations?"

Her words stung. "That's none of your business."

"I could very easily make it my business if you don't at least hear me out."

He didn't like the cool tone in her voice. Apparently, she was serious. With her connections, she could follow through on her threat. All the government needed was one complaint and he and his brothers would be required to perform sex with their Claimed wife, visually, on a daily basis, via a live video feed to the government to prove she was being used properly to alleviate her husbands' sexual tensions.

"She's what? Seven months pregnant?" Bev continued. "Word through the grapevine is you haven't fucked her in several months now. The Claiming can easily be revoked."

"My brothers and I Claimed her legally. We're all satisfied with the arrangement. And you can take your grapevine and shove it right up your—"

"I'm sure you don't want to annoy me, Outlaw."

Bitch! "What do you want, Bev?"

"What would you say if I told you that you could have your very own pleasure slave during this assignment?"

"I'd tell you again to fuck off."

"And if I told you there was enough money in it to help get the Outlaw farm out of debt?"

Colter swallowed at the surge of hope. Dare he trust her? She'd nailed him quite nicely when he'd asked for S.K.U.L.L.'s personal help in finding Ashley when she'd suddenly disappeared after the ménage with himself and Blade. They'd point-blank refused him. Blade had tried to help find her, but he'd come up empty-handed.

"Sorry, hon, once a back-stabber, always a back-stabber."

By the sharp inhalation of her breath he'd hit a sore spot.

"I can't trust you, Bev," he continued. "You proved it when you refused to help me."

"It's against government regulations to use our organization for your own personal benefit. You knew that coming in."

"And you made damn sure I knew it going out."

"Oh come now, Outlaw. Don't be so sensitive. We trained you better than that."

He closed his eyes as her warm, feminine fingers gently curled over his naked shoulders. The welcome warmth of a woman touching him, rubbing her bare knees against his naked back, had his cock growing hard and his balls swelling tight.

He didn't have to be a brain surgeon to know she had come to him totally naked.

Dammit! He hadn't been with a woman in months. Not even with Callie, the woman he and his brothers had Claimed in order to protect her from the government. Ever since he'd discovered she was pregnant he'd opted not to participate in the ménages. Up until then he'd thoroughly enjoyed their sexual relations, but it hadn't meant anything to him except alleviating his sexual needs. What he really wanted was a woman to look at him the way Callie looked at his brother Luke. What he wanted was unconditional love not just sex.

He'd seen the look he craved in another woman's sparkling blue eyes. A woman he could never have.

He jerked as Bev's feminine fingers slipped down his sweaty chest to latch onto his nipple rings. She pulled gently and he clenched his teeth as a sweet bite of pain flamed through his buds.

"On top of all that money plus your very own sex slave there is an added bonus of why you should take this assignment."

"If fucking you is one of them, I want no part of it."

"Oh, Outlaw, I would have thought you'd miss our weekly mandatory sessions. I've always told you that you're my favorite lover. Believe me, you'll want to take this S.K.U.L.L. assignment."

She pulled a little harder on the nipple rings and he gasped at the pleasure-pain.

"I'll be the judge of whether I need to accept the assignment—not you," he ground out. Wet heat from her pussy splashed against the back of his neck as she ground herself into him. A moment later, her bare legs came around to his sides.

Holy crap! She was going to straddle him.

"Bev..." he warned, not knowing if he could keep himself from giving in to the delicious lust her touches were creating.

"Don't move, sweetheart," his former chief and commander whispered as she gyrated her hips against the top of his head. "I want to fuck your head and then your other head, and then we'll talk."

"Talk now, Bev. Or I'm out."

She let out a quaking breath and continued to ride him, the musky scent of her arousal slamming into his nostrils making his cock pulse hotter.

"All right... I figured you'd be very interested for a couple of reasons."

Shit!

"You're a doctor who's available at such short notice. And you once expressed an interest to me in pursuing research for the X-virus cure. Why didn't you?"

"I decided family doctoring was a higher priority these days," Colter lied. Truth be told, financial reasons had been the stumbling block. He couldn't afford to leave his brothers high and dry on the farm. It had been easier to set up a doctor's office at the farm and help with the chores between patients.

"Your assignment involves the widow of Dr. Blakely. I believe you remember the scientist? He's the one who invented the X-virus and almost killed your Claimed wife and your brother Luke a few months back."

Oh he remembered that creep, all right. If he and his brothers hadn't shown up at the farm when they did, Luke would be dead and Callie and her unborn child would be the mad doctor's guinea pig. She'd most likely be involved in ménage à trois with the evil scientist and his wife. Thankfully, things had worked out differently.

"Go on." He held his head still as Bev moaned and gyrated her hips faster, pressing her hot, wet pussy harder against him. His cock hardened painfully and he couldn't stop the groan from escaping his mouth as the thought of another woman entered his mind. A dark-haired, blue-eyed beauty named Ashley. Ashley instead of Bev. Standing behind him, her heavy breasts dangling like ripe fruit above him, elongated burgundy nipples inches from his mouth, her bare legs on each side of his shoulders as she fucked his head with her bare, hot pussy much the same way as Bev was doing to him now.

"Dr. Cheri Blakely has a convention booked at the nearby Pleasure Palace. Word has it she'll meet with several doctors who are representing drug conglomerates…oh yes! Your head feels so damned good, Outlaw. Just like the old days."

She began to pant, the weight of her body pressing heavier on his head.

"Why is she meeting with these doctors?"

"She claims to have an instant cure for one of the X-virus's less lethal mutations. If you can get S.K.U.L.L. that cure…ohh…God…yes!…"

She was grinding her hips harder now, soaking his flesh with her hot juices, making his neck sticky and ache like a son of a bitch. The sultry sound of Bev's erotic moans made his teeth clench as visions of Ashley sliced through his brain. Visions of her wrists being tied above her head. The erotic way her sparkling blue eyes glowed when he made love to her. The cute way her full lips parted in a sensual gasp as his hard, thick cock sank swiftly into her sweet, wet pussy. The tightest pussy he'd ever encountered in his life. If he ever got his hands on Ashley again, he'd exact the sweetest revenge. He'd brand her. Brand her so she'd never forget what she'd lost out on by doing what she had to him.

And then he'd let her go and never look back.

"Oh yes! Oh beautiful!" Bev's lusty shouts split the air. He held himself still until her moans died away.

"Are you interested?" she finally puffed as she climbed off him.

"No." Although the farm was mortgaged to the hilt and it was only a matter of time before the bank foreclosed, there was still a chance they could make payments with this year's crops, and if need be, they could sell off more of the Outlaw land. Selling, however, would be a last resort.

"Oh and before I get to your other head…there's the other incentive for you to accept the assignment."

The smug, confident tone of her voice made him pull his arms from the muck and stand. He would have told her where to take her assignment but stopped short when he turned and saw the thrust of her pert, naked breasts with the small pink nipples and the hot, sassy, shaven pussy he'd always enjoyed fucking during the Terrorist Wars. Had enjoyed until he'd met Ashley, a conscripted sex slave for one of the American generals stationed in Iraq.

He'd be lying if the sight of a naked woman didn't make him hot and horny. Any red-blooded American male would be turned on. Especially one who hadn't had sex in several months.

"If you think seeing you naked is the incentive, think again," he lied.

"S.K.U.L.L. knows where your missing brother is being held."

Holy Shit! Had he heard right?

"If you bring us Blakely's cure for the X-virus, S.K.U.L.L. will reveal Tyler's exact whereabouts. Maybe even bring him home."

"We've already got a plan in motion that will see him released in a couple of months."

"We know all about you blackmailing the Barlows. That you have threatened to tell the government they don't have the required number of husbands for Laurie."

"Where the hell did you hear that garbage?" Shit! How had she found out?

"Don't bother denying it, sweets. Sorry to tell you this, but you lost the blackmailing angle a few days ago when the Barlows secretly took on another man and legally reclaimed Laurie with another Claiming. They have no reason to keep your brother alive. He's been turned back over to the terrorists who used to hold him. He's not in the States anymore. He's been moved back overseas. You know how much terrorists love to torture Americans these days. It's only a matter of time before he's used up or killed. If you tell me you'll accept the assignment, we can keep him alive. If you bring us Blakely's cure, S.K.U.L.L. will bring your brother home. If not…"

* * * * *

Pleasure Palace, Maine
Two days later…

Dr. Colter Outlaw tried hard to contain his anger as the armed guards at the gate motioned them through onto the property where the meeting with Cheri would take place.

Gazing out the side window of the sleek white limousine S.K.U.L.L. had supplied him with, he could easily make out the newly erected three-story white marble hotel called Pleasure Palace. The lush property contained hundreds of acres of pine forests, rocky cliffs, gentle streams and beautiful meadows. Land once owned by the Outlaws. Now it belonged to the Barlow brothers who'd been quick to erect the bordello for the numerous sex-deprived men who craved to fulfill their sexual fantasies in a world where women were rare, most having been wiped out by the mutated versions of the X-virus.

It was bad enough that this had once been Outlaw land, but now that he actually had to come there and see what they'd done with it, he could literally feel the tension ripping through his shoulders, making the expensive monkey suit he wore fit too snug. He reached up and adjusted his bright blue tie, trying to loosen the stranglehold from around his neck. Why S.K.U.L.L. had insisted he wear this business outfit was beyond him. He would have preferred to break into Dr. Blakely's widow's suite and search for the cure, grab it and clear out. But S.K.U.L.L. had gone to great lengths to create an elaborate, foolproof, fictional cover for him as a doctor who worked for a research facility. They'd also supplied him with a fake ID, had arranged for anyone who might recognize him there to be away on business. S.K.U.L.L. had also arranged for him to have a private cabin along with a private sex slave to cater to his every whim while he was there. How the hell could he turn down his own slave? He'd have to be mad to do that, wouldn't he?

Colter frowned. There really was only one black-haired, blue-eyed woman who held any appeal to him. Unfortunately, he didn't have a clue where she was, and she'd made it perfectly clear she didn't want him anyway.

"We're here, Dr. Van Dusen," said the limo driver.

Pleasure Palace looked even fancier close up, Colter mused as he stepped out of the vehicle and quickly gazed around. Red ceramic tiles covered the multi-peaked roof. White marble walls sparkled in the bright sunshine and blood-red shutters adorned the numerous barred windows.

A moment later his driver was quickly ushering him past the heavily armed guards and inside to a main foyer.

The place looked utterly extravagant. Crystal chandeliers hung everywhere, the floors were pink marble and plush, red velvet furniture adorned the lobby.

Colter felt his mouth literally drop open in shock when he noticed a fully dressed man sitting on a couch in a side foyer casually reading a newspaper while a naked woman with an obviously just spanked, flushed red ass knelt on her knees in front of him. Her large breasts jiggled as she busily shined his shoes.

Unbelievable.

"Dr. Colter Van Dusen?"

A woman's soft voice snapped him from the shocking scene and he turned around to face a beautiful brunette of about fifty with sparkling brown eyes. He recognized her instantly from the pictures S.K.U.L.L. had asked him to memorize.

Dr. Cheri Blakely. This was the widow of the scientist he'd killed.

Now that he was meeting her in person, it was hard to imagine this gorgeous woman having been married to the mad doctor who had almost wiped out the female race by selling a submissive virus to the DogmarX, a group of terrorists who believed all women should be submissive to men.

"Please take care of the doctor's luggage, driver," she said to his limo driver.

When the man left to do her bidding, she extended her elegant hand to him. Her fingers, laden with diamond and sapphire rings, felt velvety warm against his palm. Her wrists were adorned with an array of gold bracelets that clinked as they shook hands. He didn't miss the extra squeeze she gave him just before they parted.

"I recognized you from the portfolio your company Lamp Light Research sent to me. I'm Dr. Cheri Blakely. I'm pleased you could take the time out of your busy schedule to make it for the conference."

"I'm pleased to be here," he lied. "My company is very interested in purchasing the cure for the X-virus mutation C."

"My, you do get down to business rather quickly, don't you?" she chuckled. "Didn't anyone tell you that all business and no pleasure makes for a very boring convention?"

Before he could answer, she clicked her fingers.

Two burly, bare-chested men came down a nearby hallway with a barely clothed, very young woman walking between them.

Sweet Jesus. The woman looked absolutely stunning.

Another roar of heated blood coursed through his veins at the sight of the black leather halter-thong teddy. Her young, curvy body was barely concealed beneath a delicate mesh cloth. It left little to his imagination.

Her head was bowed in a subservient pose. Long strawberry blonde bangs were draped over her forehead and tangles of silky hair dropped over both her shoulders.

A ball and gag held her mouth captive.

When Bev said he'd get his own sex slave he hadn't quite pictured one this young or presented to him quite this way.

He remembered not to swear with anger and demand her immediate release.

Beneath the sheer mesh her pussy was partially shaved, the remaining curly pubic hair in the shape of butterfly wings. A small opening in the cloth allowed shiny, delicate golden butterfly weights to dangle brilliantly from labia rings. Her pierced belly button contained a tiny gold butterfly that hung from a gold ring with a short one-inch chain.

He noticed red marks lashed across plump breasts and giant nipple rings adorned too-small red nipples and too-big butterfly weights dangled off those rings.

"By the frown on your face I take it Reena does not please you, Dr. Van Dusen?" The surprised tone in Dr. Blakely's voice made Colter's head snap away from the young pleasure slave.

How the hell could he take this young woman to his room and enjoy sexual relations with her? She was barely out of her teens.

"She pleases me."

"Good. I'm glad to hear it. Reena is as yet an unClaimed woman. She was recently captured in the Maine Woods. She's rumored to be part of the growing Resistance. Sexual torture among other things hasn't proven useful in getting information from her and so the government has given her to Pleasure Palace to put her to work here satisfying men. I'm sure you've heard about the Resistance? A group of unClaimed women along with some sympathetic men who've banded together and are using illegal means to try to bring down the Claiming Law?"

At her comment Colter's heart picked up speed. Yes, he'd heard there was a group calling themselves the Resistance. His brother Cade, who was now a bounty hunter, had mentioned them. He'd also mentioned that capturing members of the Resistance and turning them over to the government could be a very lucrative enterprise.

Colter eyed the woman with renewed interest. Could she be a member of the Resistance as Cheri had said?

"She's been fully trained as a pleasure slave now. Her need for independence squashed. She is eager to please."

Despite a shard of shame flashing in her eyes, she lifted her head for a quick peek at him. He noticed a roar of defiance in the way she held her shoulders back. It was quite obvious they hadn't broken this woman. He stifled an inner smile of encouragement and suddenly realized he couldn't take advantage of her.

Cheri's gaze dropped to the area between his legs. "She's looking for a well-hung man such as yourself to show what she's learned during her training. I'll have her sent to your cabin."

"For me, business always comes before pleasure. I won't be partaking in any until the business aspect of my trip is over and I win the bid for the X-virus C cure."

"You'll have a long wait then," a familiar woman's voice curled through the air and Colter couldn't help but stiffen with both dread and excitement. He smelled her fresh, clean scent a split second before she stepped into his view.

God! Was he hallucinating?

She looked so different than the last time he'd seen her. She'd been a beauty when he'd bedded her years ago. But now she was even more beautiful. The buttery chandelier light made the luxurious black hair piled high on top of her head absolutely glow. Delicate silver ribbons were beaded intricately through the lush black curls. A couple of sexy tendrils hung down on both sides of her face.

Tiny silver chain necklaces draped around the long column of her neck and he didn't miss the single sliver of silver metal trailing from the necklaces to drop between the luscious swells of her generous breasts. Breasts pushed up high and pressing hard against the tight, glittering silver dress that boldly hugged her curves. To his irritation, he found himself intrigued with the possibilities of where that single strand of chain led.

"I didn't expect you until later, Ashley." Cheri's cold voice sliced through Colter's shock. But try as he might, he just couldn't seem to tear his gaze from Ashley. He noticed the paleness to her skin, the nervous way she smiled at him and then the quick way her eyes darted back to Cheri.

"My bodyguard was able to push through all the checkpoints quickly with the bribes the general gave me to use."

"Bribes by the general are most impressive," Cheri commented. "I trust you have the general's document giving you permission to be here and to act on his behalf?"

Ashley nodded.

Colter noticed her fingers tremble as her dainty hand dipped inside her glittery silver purse. She withdrew a document and handed it over to Cheri.

He could just kick himself for continuing to stare at Ash like some dumb, love-struck teenage boy. But he just couldn't help it. She looked so sophisticated, more hauntingly beautiful than he remembered. Was it any wonder the general had kept her hidden, preventing him from finding her and exacting his revenge?

Conflicting emotions raged through him, happiness at seeing her again, burning anger that of all times for her to come back into his life this was the most inopportune. Obviously S.K.U.L.L. had had no inkling she would be here or they would have prevented her from coming. She could easily blow his cover. He had to eliminate the problem. Pronto.

She turned her dark blue eyes upon him again and heated blood surged into his cock at the memories of them together. Of her soft whispers, her hungry touches upon his flesh, her cries of arousal every time he'd made her orgasm. He could literally feel his member growing, thickening, pressing hard against his pants—wanting to escape. Wanting to bury itself deep in Ashley's ultra-tight channel.

The tightest, warmest, wettest channel he'd ever encountered.

An odd emotion he couldn't quite put his finger on glittered in her eyes. If he had to venture a guess, he'd say she looked relieved to see him.

"I'm glad to see the general allowed you to attend the convention in his place, Ashley," Cheri said coolly. "I, of course, will need to speak to him and get verbal permission for you to be here."

"I already told you over the phone he's out of the country on his latest quest for an art collection. When he calls, I will tell him to call you."

"You make sure that you do."

"The general, of course, is concerned for my safety. I trust this document will ensure it until he has a chance to get in touch with you?"

"It looks official enough," Cheri said, giving the paper a cursory glance. Her eyes narrowed and her voice lowered so that only the three of them could hear. "As to that other matter we discussed over the phone. I trust your hysteria has been resolved and I will get what I want when the general returns?"

A look of utter fear flooded Ashley's face and Colter couldn't stop the pang of uneasiness from gripping him.

Something was wrong.

Terribly wrong.

Ashley rebounded quickly, plastering a bright smile on her luscious lips, making Colter wonder if maybe his instincts were incorrect.

"Yes, the general has made it quite clear that I have nothing to say on the matter."

What matter? He wanted to ask the question but forced himself to center his emotions. He couldn't allow Cheri to get an idea that Ashley and he knew each other, and he could only hope she wouldn't blow his cover.

"Good."

"But the general did say he is most interested in obtaining the cure for your husband's virus, Cheri. I intend to make sure he gets what he wants."

"I bet you always give the general whatever he wants," Colter couldn't stop himself from commenting dryly.

He noticed Ashley bristle at his remark. Ouch, sore spot?

"You two know each other?" Cheri Blakely cocked a curious well-manicured eyebrow at the two of them.

"Actually—" Ashley began.

"No, we don't," Colter quickly cut her off. "I'm Dr. Colter Van Dusen. My company is Lamp Light Research. And I aim to get them the cure."

He extended his hand.

She hesitated a moment before slipping her warm fingers against his palm.

So soft. So fragile.

Both concern and arousal coursed through him as he shook her hand. He didn't miss the traditional slave chain jewelry on her wrist, fragile strands that reached out and encircled each of her fingers. Nor did he miss the nervous way her long, black lashes fluttered as her eyes once again darted from him to Cheri and then back to him again.

Instincts about something being wrong kicked in again. Big time.

"Well, Dr. Van…Dusen. It looks as if we want the same cure. Perhaps I should quickly eliminate my competition?"

Colter stiffened at her remark. Was that a threat? Would she divulge to Cheri Blakely his real identity and screw his chances at getting the cure and exchanging it for his brother?

"Perchance we should meet and discuss this over drinks?" Ashley said. "Maybe I can change your mind about acquiring the cure?"

He was just beginning to register the big six-feet-seven-inch-tall, burly, bald-headed man standing behind Ashley. He was the same bodyguard who had allowed Ashley and himself many spontaneous rendezvouses while he'd stayed at the general's mansion in Iraq. He remembered that the man couldn't speak due to his tongue having been cut out by the general and he'd also been castrated among other things to ensure he would never take an interest in Ashley.

The man was eyeing Colter with a rather intense scowl of hatred. Despite his inability to speak, he knew instinctively this guy would break his cover if Ashley gave him the word to do so. He forced himself to take a deep, calming breath and returned his attention to Ashley. A lusty happiness edged away the nervousness in her eyes as she gazed back at him.

Rest assured, he'd make sure that look changed to one of pleasure-pain soon enough.

"If your…bodyguard will allow you?"

"He won't mind. I would be honored to meet you at shall we say five? At the bar?"

"I'll be there."

"Well, I'm glad to hear there will be a little healthy competition going on for the cure," Cheri Blakely cooed. "Just remember there will be three other doctors who will bid, Ashley. You may have to spread your legs for them also."

At Cheri's comment, Colter's self-control slipped a notch.

"I'm sure you'll get to them before I do," Ashley said cheerfully as if it were an everyday occurrence for both women to spread their legs for men.

Fuck! Who was he kidding? Ashley had done exactly that for Blade and him at the general's Iraq mansion. He forced himself to bite back a scalding retort that was sure to grab unwarranted attention.

"I must get a move on and check myself in. I'll see you later, Dr. Van Dusen."

The intense way Ashley looked at him made his balls swell even harder. Now that he had access to Ashley once again, revenge plans quickly formulated in his thoughts.

The big bald-headed bodyguard followed close behind the woman Colter had fallen in love with during the Terrorist Wars. Her cute, rounded ass shimmied against a tight silver dress that hugged her every delicious curve as she headed to the check-in counter.

"Take Reena back to the dungeon to await another customer. When Dr. Van Dusen decides he wants to be serviced by her, be sure she is quickly made available for him," Cheri instructed the two muscle men who had brought the pleasure slave forward for him.

Colter forced himself to stifle the flicker of concern when the men roughly grabbed onto the young woman's pale upper arms and quickly ushered her back down the hallway. He'd have to mention her to S.K.U.L.L. See if they would extract her based on the rumor of her being with the Resistance.

"Come with me, Doctor, I'll introduce you to a most wonderful shoeshine while we await for your turn to check into Pleasure Palace." Cheri chuckled as she linked her arm through Colter's elbow and led him toward the room where he'd seen the naked woman polishing the man's shoes.

Just before he entered the side foyer, he allowed himself a quick glance over his shoulder. A glance that allowed him another breathtaking view of the only woman he'd ever wanted to spend the rest of his life with.

Chapter Two

Ashley couldn't stop her trembling even when she spotted guest cabin 23 nestled beneath a team of weeping willow trees. The white saltbox-style wooden cottage with burgundy shutters and white picket fence looked utterly adorable. White French lace curtains adorned the numerous windows and she gratefully slid the electronic key into the slot in the door. A beep zipped through the air and the door opened. To her surprise, she discovered her suitcase and her bodyguard's duffel bag had already been delivered. They sat just inside the door of the luscious Pleasure Palace two-bedroom cabin they'd given her and her bodyguard for their stay.

Thankfully she was alone. At least for a few minutes.

She didn't think she could deal with her bodyguard right then. Especially at the sympathetic way he'd been looking at Reena. Ashley had wasted no time in writing a note and telling him to go back for her and pretend that Ashley wanted the pleasure slave for herself over the course of the next few days.

It was a shame that the general had done so many horrid things to her bodyguard Mike just to ensure he wouldn't be attracted to her. Despite that fact though, the general didn't realize Mike still found immense pleasure in pleasing women, Ashley included. In the end, what the general hadn't known hadn't hurt him.

Now that she was alone she could concentrate on herself. Concentrate on the familiar sexual hum racking her body. The intense lusty cravings she had to live with on a daily basis compliments of being infected by one of the mutations of

Blakely's X-virus, the virus of which she was there to obtain the cure for.

She hadn't expected Colter Outlaw to be here. Hadn't expected to ever see him again. Especially since their last sex-fest together had been under such false pretenses. He'd been the one man whom she'd dared allow herself to fall in love with. The one man she'd allowed herself to trust. The one man who'd ultimately betrayed her.

Ashley blew out a confused breath.

So if he'd betrayed her, then why was she reacting like this toward him? Why did her breasts feel so tight beneath her dress? Why were her panties soaked?

It had to be the X-virus kicking in. She was due for her medication soon. Thankfully the mutated version she'd contracted didn't make her pass out or kill her if she didn't take her medication on time. This mutated version of the virus allowed her some leeway. The virus made her horny. Horny and, despite not wanting to, she occasionally became submissive to men, especially when under stress. But she definitely had to take the medication within a certain timeframe or the virus would begin to attack her brain, altering signals and eventually making her a permanent sexual submissive.

And that's one thing she'd never allow.

A quick survey of the small main room gave her a feeling of warmth, which edged away a little bit of her tension. The walls were painted a plain peach. Light golden brown wooden beams laced the ceiling and a large sofa sat against one wall. She noted some eight by ten black and white photos hanging on the walls, pictures of several men and a woman in naughty ménage poses.

Explicit poses that made her suddenly feel too hot as visions of her ménage à trois with Blade and Colter suddenly sprang to mind.

Oh dear. She'd better find her vibrator and she'd better do it quick.

Blowing out a quick breath, she grabbed her suitcase and entered the bedroom. It was similarly decorated as the other room except with a huge king-size bed and a cabinet against one wall. Flinging the suitcase onto the bed, her thoughts immediately strayed to the erotic way Colter had looked at her in the foyer. So much pent-up passion waiting to be unleashed. So much lust raging in his eyes. Lust she knew all too well. Lust she'd never been able to forget.

But there was something different about him now. No trace of the laughter or gentleness she remembered. That sexy five o'clock soldier shadow he'd worn on his handsome face was gone in favor of a hot, clean, business look.

Her pussy quivered and creamed harder as she remembered how wide and muscular his shoulders had felt beneath her searching fingertips all those years ago. How hard and powerful his thighs had felt against her soft flesh as he'd slammed his hips against hers, fucking her, thrusting his gorgeously long cock into her over and over again.

God! She couldn't go out there meeting Colter for drinks and tell him his identity was safe with her with her pussy all sopping wet and bothered. She needed relief, for heaven's sake. Relief first, and then later, to take the lusty edge off, she would take some medication. Then she'd be okay to meet with him. She hoped.

She unzipped her suitcase and her trembling fingertips fell upon her makeup bag. A warm, fuzzy feeling slammed into her as she opened it and touched the long, slender plastic item she used on a daily basis to bring herself relief.

A nice, hot shower would be the perfect atmosphere to shake off her lust and to fantasize about what life could have been like with Colter Outlaw.

* * * * *

From the window of the quaint cottage Colter had managed to get himself assigned to he watched anxiously as Ashley's big bodyguard walked the beautiful pleasure slave named Reena past his building toward Ashley's little cottage with the white picket fence.

"She's a gorgeous creature," Blade whispered from beside him. "I wouldn't mind being alone with her for a few months. I could probably teach her a few new tricks she hasn't been taught yet."

"Just make sure the bodyguard disappears. He can ID me," Colter said to the S.K.U.L.L. member. Blade was an excellent gynecologist and had always been a solid, dependable backup. His devilish good looks, wavy blond hair and chocolate-colored eyes, however, were a detriment. His looks got him too much attention and that's why S.K.U.L.L. usually made him work behind the scenes, never giving him the juicy assignments he craved, such as the one Colter had just been given.

"Who is that guy anyway? He looks familiar. Like I've seen him somewhere before."

"Let's just get him out of the way, shall we?" Although Blade had only seen the bodyguard once and at a distance, he'd figure out soon enough why the man looked familiar. And when he did, all hell would break loose.

"Okay, but the slave will have to disappear too. Can't leave behind any witnesses saying the man you wanted removed was actually kidnapped," Blade whispered, a wide grin on his face.

Colter knew that once the S.K.U.L.L. team members had her in their possession they would probably see if the pleasure slave would be receptive to them. They wouldn't force her, but they wouldn't leave her in peace either.

"Just make sure the boys don't harm her. She's too young to be in a place like this."

"She's a pleasure slave, Colter. She probably doesn't even remember her life before being one. If her training was effective, she probably needs sex on a continuous basis just to keep herself from going mad. And if she's with the Resistance as rumored, then she's probably forgotten about them too. But we can try to debrief her and see what we can come up with. So what about this Cheri Blakely chick? Have you got any info on the cure she's selling?"

Irritation nibbled at him and he couldn't stop himself from snapping at his friend, "What's with all these questions? I just got here, Blade. We haven't discussed it yet."

"Hey, man. Take it easy, bro. You'll get the cure, don't sweat it." He nodded out the window. "Looks like S.K.U.L.L. is on the move."

Colter watched as a small band of men dressed in camouflage fatigues laden with deadly assault weapons quickly and quietly emerged from the clumps of nearby bushes behind Ashley's bodyguard and the pleasure slave. The slave's head lifted as she detected they had company. Her eyes widened at the men bearing down on her and the bodyguard. The ball gag in her mouth prevented her from crying out in alarm.

Before the bodyguard knew what had happened, he was unconscious and being dragged back into the bushes. The pleasure slave kicked and punched fruitlessly as one of the team members hoisted her tiny frame over his wide shoulders and disappeared into the pristine wilderness.

"I'll report back to Bev that you've made contact," Blade said as he headed for the door. "And I'll check back with you at our scheduled time."

"Sure thing."

With his heart hammering violently against his chest, Colter followed him outside. He watched him disappear into the nearby woods where Blade would keep an eye out to make sure Cheri didn't leave the compound without him knowing about it.

When he was sure Blade wouldn't see him, he headed toward Ashley's secluded cabin. It wouldn't be too long before she discovered she'd just lost her bodyguard and inherited a heap of revenge from an old lover.

* * * * *

The hard spray of hot water pulsed wonderfully against Ashley's aching breasts. Needles poked and sliced into her flesh and she smiled at the way her nipples reddened and elongated. Her pussy heated as she sank the thin, long, waterproof vibrator deep inside her vagina. Sensual vibrations ripped through her. She cried out at the violent impact.

Oh yes! Horny was an understatement. She was so aroused she couldn't stop the shudders of pleasure from washing over her in a gush of maddening waves. She enjoyed the way her wet vagina clenched the long, thin intrusion. Loved the way her hips gyrated as if with a mind of their own. The erotic tremors sliced wonderfully into her engorged flesh, making her moan and mewl into the steamy shower. Lodging the vibrator deep inside her pussy, she allowed the clitoral seducer free rein.

It slid and bit and licked.

Oh yes!

Sucked and breathed and heated.

Oh my!

She could almost imagine Colter's presence there with her. His big hands holding her hips steady as he pushed her against the wall. His fingers sliding over her inflamed clitoris. Rubbing her there. Rubbing her hard.

Another climax washed over Ashley and she cried out Colter's name, wishing him there. Wishing him to step inside the stall. To have his broad shoulders beneath her eager hands, her fingertips moving over his pierced nipples, grabbing tightly onto his nipple rings, holding him captive as he thrust that big, massive cock of his into her tight channel.

From the corner of her eye she thought she detected a shadowy movement on the other side of the frosted glass enclosure, but she didn't care. She was too far-gone enjoying her Colter fantasy to care that her bodyguard had returned with Reena the slave.

They'd hear her masturbating. She didn't care. She had to do it on a constant basis anyway, compliments of the X-virus.

Each stroke of the vibrator filled her, but not full enough. The state-of-the-art piece of machinery the general had given her had never been able to totally fulfill her X-virus-induced lust.

Nothing had. Only Colter. And Blade.

The two of them holding her. Making her suck their cocks. Stretching her arms up over her head and tying her, making sure she couldn't run away while they did naughty things to her. Things she'd loved.

When the second climax finally ebbed away, she sighed and shut off the vibrator. Her climaxes had barely taken the edge off.

The only thing that would permanently get rid of this constant lust was getting that cure Cheri was toting around. And only then could she start living life like a normal woman.

* * * * *

Colter quietly closed the door behind him, thankfully escaping the overheated bathroom.

Whew! If that frosted glass hadn't been there, he would have stepped right into the shower and taken her right then and there. The sensual outline of her shadow and the erotic sounds of her mewling and moaning had just about made him lose his well-planned control. And the sultry, desperate way she'd screamed out his name had made his legs buckle. He'd been lucky the toilet seat hadn't been up when he'd sat down.

Oh man! His revenge plan might not be as easy as he'd thought.

* * * * *

Ashley didn't know how long she'd slept or what alerted her to the feeling someone was lurking around in her room. After masturbating in the shower and discovering her bodyguard and Reena hadn't returned, she'd felt so tired from the day's travels and the tension of getting through all those security checkpoints along the freeways that she'd drawn the drapes in her bedroom, set the alarm and promptly fallen asleep.

But now as she sifted through the layers of sleep, alarm bells were ringing inside her head.

The strong scent of man drifted beneath her nostrils, making her very aware of who he just might be. Before she could so much as open her eyes, a strong, hard hand clamped over her mouth. At the same instant, one of her wrists and then the other were quickly held captive.

Fear crushed her and she screamed into the intruder's hand, struggling against the tight embrace.

"Shh, Starry Eyes. It's just me," Colter whispered against her ear. His face was so near she could feel the stubble of his shadow brush against her cheek. She found herself remembering he had to shave twice a day because his hair grew so quickly. God! She'd forgotten that fact over the years.

She stopped struggling. Past experience had shown her trying to escape his hot hold was useless.

"I'm going to lift my hand off your mouth so we can talk. Don't scream or you'll suffer the consequences, is that clear?"

She nodded against his hand.

The moment her mouth was free she parted her lips in order to alert her bodyguard, but Colter was quicker.

His hot mouth slammed over hers in one scorching motion. The brutal fierceness of his sensual attack ripped the breath clean from her lungs and shattered her control. Heated sensations rocked her. His strong, hot tongue invaded her mouth, sending erotic shivers straight through her right down to her toes.

Somewhere at the back of her mind she noted an odd softness melting around her neck followed by a quick snapping noise. Before she could register what that sound could be, Colter broke the scorching kiss and pulled away.

The delicate sound of something tinkling crushed her passion.

Opening her eyes, Ashley cursed loudly when she discovered he'd snapped a collar around her neck. From the collar she also noted a sturdy chain that led to a nearby bedpost ring.

"Just like old times, Starry Eyes," Colter whispered. She felt the mattress move as he stood and glared down at her.

There was no warm "like old times" look in his gaze. Only cold, hard anger. An anger that matched her own.

"What the hell do you think you're doing? You can't get away with this."

He grinned cockily. "I already have."

"I'll scream. Once my bodyguard hears—"

"Scream as much as you want. Your bodyguard has been removed. The cabin is secluded. I made sure I obtained the only other cabin within shouting distance."

No! This wasn't happening! He was going to ruin her plans!

"Why are you doing this?"

"I can't have you running around threatening to expose me."

"I wouldn't hurt you."

His eyes flashed cold anger. "Your earlier hint says you will. Not to mention Cheri's insinuation that you would get rid of the competition by spreading your legs in order to get the cure."

"That's Cheri's petty bitchiness tactics because her husband couldn't get me and—" she cut herself off before she said too much. That was a part of her past she'd rather not let him know.

"Oh do tell. I'm curious to hear why the general wouldn't share you with her and her late husband Blakely. I hear the Blakelys enjoyed ménages. Just like you do..." he said his last sentence so softly Ashley found herself shivering with unwanted excitement as erotic memories of him and Blade crashed into her.

She flung the thoughts aside, allowing anger to seethe through her. The son of a bitch wasn't going to get away with this nonsense.

"Get this collar off me, you bastard."

"I love it when you call me names."

"Colter, I'm serious."

"So am I. That collar stays on you until I say otherwise."

His eyes darkened dangerously. She swallowed at the tightness in her throat. Shit! The guy wasn't kidding. Damn him! He was going to screw her plans!

"I don't have any time for your games, Colter. I need that cure, and I'll do anything I can to get it. Even...killing you if I have to," she lied.

"When I'm finished with you, you just might want to, Starry Eyes."

"Don't call me that." It reminded her of a time she'd rather forget.

"Why not? Don't you like my nickname for you anymore?" he purred softly. Too softly, as if they were intimate lovers, as if they'd never been separated for years. For an instant, that warm look she'd fallen in love with melted the hardness in his face. Then it quickly vanished.

"That was another time. I'm not in the Terrorist Wars anymore," she whispered.

"But you're still fucking the general," he replied coldly, a muscle twitched angrily in his cheek. Did she detect jealousy in his voice? Or maybe it was just wishful thinking on her part?

"What do you want from me?"

His eyes narrowed. Fear slithered up her naked back. If looks could kill, she'd be dead. "I'm going to keep you out of the way so you won't blow my cover."

"I'd never do that. I would have told you that very fact over drinks."

"Like hell."

The cold way he said it slammed into her gut like a punch from his own fist.

"What? You don't trust me?"

"You haven't earned my trust, Starry Eyes."

What was that supposed to mean?

"And until you do, I want you at my mercy."

In response, he reached over and yanked the white sheets off her nude body, displaying her to him.

Oh, my God! The heated way he looked at her almost made her self-combust!

"What the hell are you doing?" She was about to grab a nearby blanket when his next words stopped her cold.

"Don't you dare cover yourself from me, Ashley. Ever. Or you will suffer dire consequences."

Excitement and anger rolled into one and she closed her eyes against the raw hunger splashing in his eyes.

Did he think he could simply pick up where they'd left off? Any other time and she'd give him a second chance, if his explanation for leaving her in Iraq were a suitable one. Now, however, was not an option. She needed to get her hands on the cure and she couldn't do it by staying here...as his plaything.

Okay, just relax. You can handle this.

"I told you, I'm not in the Wars anymore—"

"Stand," he instructed.

"The hell I will. Get out of my room!"

God! The ravenous way he glared at her made her tremble with hardcore lust. Made her want to submit to his will. She could literally feel the urge to surrender to him washing through her veins and her stomach twisted in shock. She'd forgotten to take her medicine!

Shit!

"Colter, I need—" How could she tell him she needed her medication? How could she reveal to him she was infected by the X-virus? Pride told her to say nothing. Past experience told her she still had time before the full effects of the virus took hold, before she actively became his plaything...not that it sounded like a bad idea. She wouldn't mind reliving what they'd shared back in Iraq.

"I said stand."

The cold, fierce way he said it gave her the distinct impression he wasn't kidding around. He was serious. Deadly serious. And if she had any hope of getting away from him, she'd best do his bidding. Besides, if her bodyguard really were out of the way, it meant she was totally at his mercy in this luxury cabin. Totally under his control.

Damned if that thought didn't turn her on.

Reluctantly she did as he demanded.

Standing at attention, she forced herself to dangle her arms at her sides. It wasn't as if he hadn't seen her naked before, and it wasn't as if she'd never wanted him to see her naked again. She just hadn't imagined it to be quite this way.

Instead of covering her nudity as she wanted to do, she boldly stared straight at him. Damned if she was going to show him she was afraid of what he did to her body.

His Adam's apple bobbed wildly as his gaze swept over her curves. She could literally feel the heated burn of his eyes as they caressed her generous breasts. Silently she cursed herself at the way her breasts swelled, the intimate way her nipples beaded.

"Cup your breasts."

"Go to hell," she found herself saying softly. Found her nipples suddenly aching with the need to have his fingertips brush across their hardening tips.

She couldn't stop the shivers from coursing through her as she saw the thick bulge pressing against his pants. The lusty need to submit to him grew within her. She could literally feel the last remnants of resistance shatter.

Damn her! Why hadn't she taken her medication? It would have been easier to protest. To resist him.

"I'm warning you, Ashley. Do it now."

God! His voice sounded so cold and yet so hot. But what about her medicine…she should tell him.

"I—"

"Do it!"

Her pussy creamed at his sharp command. She did as he ordered, holding her breasts in her hands, feeling their heaviness, reveling in how swollen and tight they felt.

"Colter—"

"Do not speak unless I ask you a question."

Oh, God! Her brain began to fog over at the command. The need to submit began to take hold. The X-virus was kicking in.

Shit!

"Stay that way until I say otherwise."

Again she wanted to tell him to get her medicine but even that thought was lost as she watched him turn his broad back to her. The tips of her fingertips tingled as she remembered digging her hands into his hard shoulders all those years ago. Feeling the hot ripples of his muscles as she held him against her, his long, thick cock sliding deep inside, stretching her, plunging into her very core.

She breathed out an aroused breath and watched as he headed toward a nearby cabinet she hadn't had the chance to explore yet. But she'd read the brochures of Pleasure Palace and knew what that cabinet would contain.

Her heart pounded frantically as the door creaked open. The first thing she saw was the arrangement of butt plugs of varying sizes. The second thing she noted was the assortment of vibrators and dildos. The third thing she noticed was the raw hunger flashing in his eyes when he turned to face her.

She swallowed back the unwanted excitement rushing through her.

"Keep holding those breasts. Hold them out. Nice and high," he said. His eyes narrowed slightly as his gaze dropped to her breasts.

She swore she saw the bulge between his legs growing, pressing harder against his pants.

"Tell me...how do they feel? Do they ache to be touched? Crave to have my lips suckling those big nipples?"

"Yes," she found herself whispering, hoping he would touch her.

"Good." He turned his back to her and began to inspect the cabinet.

His voice sounded so cold and so hard it brought a spring of hot tears burning against the back of her eyes.

God! What had turned him into such a cold bastard? She wanted to ask him when he suddenly whispered, "Here's something of interest."

She didn't like the satisfaction lacing his words, but she held her ground, determined not to watch what he was reaching for. In the end, she found herself caving in to the need to know and strained her neck to see over a gorgeous set of broad shoulders. As he moved his arms to sift through the sex toy cabinet, she couldn't stop her breath from backing up at the way his biceps bulged against the dark suit.

A tearing sound ripped through the air.

"Shoot!" he spat.

She couldn't help but laugh as the suit seam across his shoulders literally ripped apart, showing the pale blue shirt beneath.

He swore softly, shrugged out of the jacket and placed it on top of the sex toy cabinet. Then he swore some more, untied his tie and shoved it into the jacket pocket.

When he turned around, she caught his long fingers working open the top three buttons of his shirt, allowing her to get an intoxicating peek at his curly chest hairs and then his dark frown. To her surprise, a gentle wave of erotic fear shuddered through her. He looked absolutely riveting when he was pissed off. It was an interesting side of him she wouldn't mind exploring.

"You've still got the most beautiful breasts I've ever seen, Starry Eyes. And those nipples… I wonder if they still taste so delicious."

In contrast to only moments ago when she'd hated hearing her nickname, her knees now melted at the intimate words he'd picked out for her.

Oh, God! This was just happening way too fast!

"But that's all you are to me. Just breasts. A hot cunt. A luscious ass. And you are just a woman. A woman in a long string of fuck fantasies. Is that clear?"

She was just a fuck fantasy to him? Anger nudged at her submissiveness and somewhere at the back of her brain a sad voice told her if she'd had any delusions about him being the same man she'd fallen in love with, then the cold finality of his words only confirmed what the general had told her about him. That he'd brought Colter Outlaw to his mansion and made Ashley available to him to use. Colter had filled her with hope then satisfied his and Blade's lust with her, and left her without looking back.

"Now let go of your breasts and clasp your hands behind your back. Make your tits stick out nice and hard."

Despite her slight hesitation to do what he suggested, her pussy creamed with heated liquid.

Stupid X-virus! She was actually being turned on by the horrible way he was treating her. Uttering an exasperated sigh, she reluctantly let go of her breasts and clasped her hands behind her back, pushing her shoulders back, suddenly quite eager to please him.

Yes, she was definitely not a normal woman with this X-virus racing through her. Especially with the frantic way her heart pounded against her chest as he moved toward her. His walk was almost graceful—in a predatory kind of way.

Maybe the word "cocksure" was more appropriate for the way he came at her on those long, powerful-looking legs. Cocksure that she would do what he told her to do without a fight.

But how could he know she'd been infected with the virus? She'd never told him. It made her feel inferior. Hence her overwhelming need to get the cure.

The webs of the X-virus began to ebb from her brain and her thoughts cleared. From past experience she knew she'd only have a narrow window of opportunity of a few minutes before the fog of submission would drape over her again.

She had two choices.

Tell him about being infected and ask him to give her the medicine.

Or escape.

Escape sounded a whole hell of a lot better than revealing her inferiority.

She allowed him to pass her. Readied to attack him.

As if sensing her next move, his hands gripped her upper arms and, with unbelievable ease, he twisted her around, grabbed her wrists and, within a blink of an eye, she heard the cold finality of handcuffs snap around each of her wrists.

"Fuck!" She bit out and tried to kick at him.

With ease he grabbed her by her bare hips, his hot hands branding her flesh as he hoisted her onto the bed and onto her back.

"Stay right there, Starry Eyes, or next time I won't be so gentle."

"Geez, I'd hate to see your violent side," she grumbled, trying to fight the submissiveness clambering over her at his command.

Warily she watched him as he sat down on the bed beside her.

She couldn't help but flinch and turn her head away as he raised his hand. Strong fingers gripped her chin. He held her with calm determination as he twisted her head toward him.

"Easy, I won't hurt you." His voice sounded so calm she almost believed him. Almost.

"You already have."

"I apologize for being brutal. I've forgotten how passionate you can be, but I'm sure I'll remember quickly."

Her heart thundered against her chest and she swore her bared breasts moved with every beat.

"Just lie there and enjoy this, Ashley. And keep your eyes on me the whole time."

Another command. The last of her resistance once again blew away.

She couldn't stop her soft gasp as he placed an odd-looking black suction cup over her left nipple.

"Eyes on me, Ash."

Her eyes darted back to his face. No smile. Only cold, hard determination.

As he pumped the suction cup, the intense suckling on her nipple just about made her scream, it felt so good.

Her mind cleared again. She grabbed at her chance.

"You're doing this for a reason. What is it? Are you in this with Cheri Blakely? Are you both planning to sell me to the Pleasure Palace? The general will come for me. He won't let you get away with this," she lied.

Anger flared in those green eyes. He was furious with her. Not just mad but spine-tingling pissed off. Why? Because of her question? Or was it something else?

"This suction cup is designed to create sensitive nipples," he said coolly. "A ring is placed on the outside edge of the suction cup. As your nipple is sucked into the cup, the ring is dropped over your nipple and hugs it nice and tight, keeping it plump and ultrasensitive."

Ashley bit her bottom lip as it did just what he said, the small, black rubber ring rolling onto her nipple and tightening wonderfully.

"After doing this a few times, your nipples will be so sensitive to my touch, you won't be able to think straight."

"Interesting way to divert the enemy."

"Odd that you should consider yourself my enemy."

"Boy you sure have me fooled if you aren't mine."

"I wouldn't do this to just anyone, Starry Eyes." There it was again. The soft look that drifted in and out of his eyes so fast it was frustrating.

"Then answer my question. Why are you doing this to me?"

"I'll let you ponder about the reason for a while. In the meantime..."

She sucked in a sharp breath as he placed the suction cup onto her other nipple. Pumping it wickedly, she felt the air suck her nipple right into the contraption. God! That felt unbelievably wicked.

"You like that, do you?"

"No." The heat flaming her face made a liar out of her.

He chuckled.

She threw him a dirty look and dug her nails into her palms as the rubber ring slipped over her nipple and held it captive.

"There, that should hold you until I get back."

"You aren't leaving me here like this!"

"Why not?" he tossed over his shoulder, his hand on the doorknob.

"Because someone might come in, for crying out loud!"

"Wouldn't want that now, would we? Can't have tons of men running around Pleasure Palace getting the idea that an unClaimed female was in their midst. They might get the wrong idea. Might think you're here to service them."

Oh boy! He was talking as if he might bring them in here.

"I'm not unClaimed," she hissed.

The instant she said those words she immediately wished she could take them back. He stopped cold. His body tense, coiled with tension. When he turned around, she noticed the paleness to his face. A lack of color that hadn't been there moments ago.

"How many?"

"Five," she bit out.

His eyes darkened with such fierce anger she swore he just might hit her. She didn't know how long he stared at her, but she could tell he was trying to determine whether she spoke the truth or not.

Finally he shook his head. "You're lying. There's no way the general would let you come here with only one bodyguard and a note allowing you to bid on the cure. He would have sent you with at least one of your husbands, not a note."

"They're all very busy men."

"Too busy to make sure their valuable possession won't get snatched? No, Ash. I don't think there are any husbands in the picture, at least not yet. I will tell you what I do think, however. I think you're full of secrets. You were scared when you showed up and handed Cheri that note. Scared of Cheri, yet relieved to see me."

Ashley swallowed at the tightness strangling her throat.

"Why were you relieved to see me, Starry Eyes? Did you think we'd be able to pick up where we left off in Iraq?" His voice lowered into a tight whisper. "Did you think I would share you with Blade again?"

She shook her head, trying hard not to remember their ménage à trois with Blade.

"Do you want me to share you with other men, Ashley? It would be the ultimate revenge for me to watch other men pleasure you over and over again, keeping you on the edge for hours, for days, maybe even years like I've been on the edge just thinking about you."

Oh, God! He'd been thinking about her just as she'd been thinking about him. But why was he so angry? Why was he talking about revenge?

"My Claimed wife didn't think she could be shared. But once she started, she got addicted to ménages mighty fast."

Her heart stopped at the mention of a wife. The mere thought of him being with another woman pissed her off. Made her see red. Made her realize she could never have him again now that he'd Claimed another.

She shouldn't be so jealous, so surprised that he had taken a woman. Colter was a passionate man, a man with fierce sexual appetites. During the few weeks they'd been together, he'd made love to her so many times she'd lost count. He couldn't stay long without sex.

And from the bulge pressing against his pants, he certainly wanted some.

"I've heard many women fantasize about having sex with more than one man at the same time. You'd think this Claiming Law would have women scrambling to be Claimed," he said thoughtfully. "Perhaps I should see about why you're walking around here as an unClaimed woman."

"The general—"

"Fuck the general!" he snapped so harshly she literally jumped on the mattress. "The general is not here at the moment, Ash. Neither are your…imaginary husbands. No one is here to help you. It's just you and me. The sooner you remember that, the better off the next few days will be."

Having said that, he yanked the cabin door open and slammed it so hard on his way out, the windows vibrated.

Next few days? Oh please, God, no. Please tell her she'd heard wrong.

Chapter Three

Colter couldn't stop his hands from shaking as he lifted the tall glass of Terrorist Tequila, a strong alcoholic beverage brewed overseas and shipped to the States via the black market.

He wished the trembling in his hands were due to the powerful drink. It wasn't.

Seeing Ashley naked and vulnerable, finally having her collared and chained to the bed, at his mercy—getting ready to exact his sweet revenge—made him so horny his balls and cock had grown so painfully hard he'd been barely able to walk out of the room.

He should have told S.K.U.L.L. to take her away as they'd done with her bodyguard and the pleasure slave. Should have asked them to keep her tucked away somewhere safe until he could deal with her.

For now though, she was safe with him.

Safe in her room—chained to her bed. Totally naked. Gorgeously naked. Her nipples properly ringed. Red. Tight. Perfect for sucking—for bringing the flare of arousal into her bright blue eyes.

She was probably getting terribly sore by now.

Good. His cock was good and sore too.

But he'd never allow himself to fuck her again. Never allow himself to get lost inside her warm, wet, welcome pussy as he'd done at the general's mansion.

Shit!

The general.

They shouldn't have saved his life. Should have let that son of a bitch get his head blown off and just left him to die. Then again, if he hadn't met the general, he'd never have met Ashley.

Bastard!

Colter lugged back another stiff swallow of the cold drink, trying hard to ignore his trembling hands.

He should have told her the original deal. Should have told her she'd been a gift to him. A gift from the general for saving his scrawny neck. Instead he'd fantasized. Told her he would take her away from her life as the general's pleasure slave. Told her he loved her.

Damned if he hadn't meant it.

"Sulking over your drinks, Dr. Van Dusen?" Cheri Blakely's soft voice curled around him, making him tense, making his guts twist with irritation. "I thought you were meeting with Ashley? Did she stand you up?"

"She had…another commitment."

"Her loss is my gain. May I join you?"

"Please." At this precise moment, the last thing he wanted to do was to talk to Cheri, especially with Ashley's nipples ready to burst beneath those rings he'd put on her. She wouldn't suffer too greatly if he waited a few more minutes. It would just make her ultrasensitive for the next step in his plan.

"I'll have a shot of absinth, please," Cheri gestured to the nearby bartender. "And get one for Dr. Van Dusen also."

Colter downed his tequila and smiled tightly as he felt Cheri's hand sliding up his inner thigh.

"I'm sorry, Cheri, but like I said, business before—"

"Please, let me indulge myself, Dr. Van Dusen. It might be in your favor when the time comes to bid on the X-virus C cure."

"Of course, the cure." He needed to keep his mind on the cure, not Ashley.

"Already so aroused?" Cheri murmured as her hand cupped his clothed bulge. A bulge that had grown painful as he'd brooded over his drinks while thinking about Ashley and the revenge he had planned for her. A revenge that should be frivolous compared to what needed to be done in order for him to get the cure.

"I tend to react quickly when a beautiful woman has her hands on me," he tried to keep his voice steady and smooth even though he felt like bucking his hips in an effort of getting her hand off him.

Despite the fact he could hear his zipper lowering, could feel her ring-laden fingers slide into his pants, he forced himself to keep his gaze on her. Forced himself to keep his lips smiling at her.

"I can make you a generous offer right now for the cure of the X-virus. I can have the money transferred into your account within minutes," Colter said softly.

"Ah, darling, I'm afraid the cure isn't here."

Shit!

He clenched his teeth as her fingers found his swollen rod.

She smiled. Her red lips parted. Her eyes glazed. Cripes, it looked as if she might get herself off just by touching him.

"When will the cure be arriving?"

"When all the other doctors are here."

Can you be a little more specific? he wanted to ask, but he winced in pain as her sharp nails scratched along the side of his left ball. A burning sensation quickly followed.

Shit! That hurt! He found it hard not to shift uncomfortably.

"Try the absinth I ordered for you," she purred, and nodded to the green liquid shimmering in the shot glass. He hadn't even noticed the bartender having placed it there.

"I'm fine, thanks."

"Oh but you must at least try. It is my favorite. Just like scratching a man's balls is a favorite hobby of mine."

Great.

He winced as her sharp nails scraped along the tender skin encasing his right testicle.

"Hurt?"

Shit, yes.

"A little." He forced his voice to remain cool, steady.

She pouted.

"I can make a man stay on edge for hours just by scratching his balls."

"I'm sure you can," he took a sip of the absinth, pretending disinterest. The bitter herbal taste of the liquid, however, was hard to ignore as the flavor melted over his tongue.

"Especially after he's gotten drunk on absinth."

Lovely.

He took a couple more sips for good measure and tried to ignore how his balls pulled up and tightened harder beneath those fiery fingernails. The buzz of the alcohol zipped along his veins. Just what he needed to take off the edge of tenseness at having this woman groping him.

"At Pleasure Palace they don't make absinth as they normally make it elsewhere," she purred. "Of course, they still use the traditional wormwood, star anise, fennel and herbs, but they also add a secret ingredient."

Who cares?

"They've doubled the wormwood, therefore doubling the thujone. Thujone is the principal narcotic found in the wormwood plant. It's also a main ingredient found in my cure for the X-virus."

Now that got his attention. His heart picked up speed at an alarming rate. Whether it was from the tasty, bitter drink or her willingness to talk about the ingredients in her X-virus cure, he wasn't sure.

He played with the condensation on the side of his suddenly empty glass, trying to act cool, a direct contrast to the frustration gnawing at him at not being able to ask questions. It would only make her suspicious.

"How interesting."

Cheri giggled like a schoolgirl. Her cheeks flushed brightly and that glazed, lusty look in her eyes deepened. Her fingers were now scratching up the sides of his cock, leaving such a burning trail of hurt he hoped like hell she wasn't using razor blades on him.

"You let me suck your cock right here and now and I just might tell you a little bit more about the cure."

"Might" being the operative word. He could sense she was a woman who played her cards close to her chest. No way in hell was she going to give away too much. But there could always be that chance she might say something important. Something he could use and give to S.K.U.L.L. to work with.

He was quite ready to do anything to get the information he needed to get his brother released from wherever he was being held. S.K.U.L.L. said they knew where and, if he could trust them, his brother would be back home within a week.

Desperation slammed into him. He needed to get the cure from Cheri and give it to S.K.U.L.L. It was the only hope Tyler now had.

"No one is stopping you," he said tightly, tensing himself against the assault of thinking about her mouth against his cock. The only mouth he wanted on his cock was Ashley's. Not this bitch's.

He caught the surprise and then the pleased look splashing over her face at his agreement to have her go down on him.

She'd been expecting him to deny her. Why? Did she already suspect he wasn't who he said? Although S.K.U.L.L.

had reassured him Pleasure Palace only hired a select, highly trained pleasure crew and that no one he knew worked here, there was always that chance someone, perhaps another customer or the owners—who he knew personally—would show up, recognize him and rat him out.

Had Ashley's bodyguard informed someone before S.K.U.L.L. had taken him out?

Colter had been at the check-in desk when Ashley's bodyguard had appeared and presented a note from Ashley requesting the use of the pleasure slave named Reena. Her bodyguard had thrown angry scowls at him, making it very obvious he didn't like Colter being there. It was a direct contrast to the friendly way he'd behaved toward him at the general's place in Iraq.

The instant Colter had checked-in, he'd refused the offer of being escorted to his cottage and headed outside where he'd been able to stake out the bodyguard while immediately calling his backup for help. Although the bodyguard wasn't able to speak and tell anyone his true identity, he could still write a note to anyone and blow his cover. On top of that, he needed the bodyguard out of the way so he could have access to Ashley. A couple of minutes later when Blade and a S.K.U.L.L. member had turned up, he'd instructed the member to take over surveillance, allowing he and Blade to head over to his cottage.

Maybe Ashley had said something?

No, for some damned, unexplainable reason he sensed she wouldn't hurt him. But she may have said something inadvertently. He'd have to question her when he returned to the cabin. It was imperative he kept his cover. Cheri would drop him like a hot potato if she discovered he was the one who'd broken her husband's neck months ago.

"Alas, I wish I could take your gorgeously swollen erection into my mouth, Dr. Van Dusen. I believe yours is the biggest cock I've ever had the pleasure of scratching, but I have to leave Pleasure Palace tonight. I have an appointment I cannot miss."

An odd relief poured through him at her words.

"Seems like it's my night for getting stood up."

"Don't despair. I will return."

"With the cure, I hope. My company is quite anxious for the bidding war to begin."

"The cure will show up when the time comes, Dr. Van Dusen. Not to worry."

Having said that, she kissed him full on the mouth. Her lips were cold as they slid over his and he barely kept himself from gagging before she broke off.

"That should hold you, *mon ami*. Ta-ta." Waving as she left, Colter slumped with relief into his chair the instant she cleared the doorway.

Shit! His balls and cock were on fire. He'd have to check out the damage. But first he needed to get back to Ashley.

* * * * *

Ashley gritted her teeth against the pleasure-pain slicing through her sore, tight nipples. They felt swollen and raw, looked an angry red and needed some tender, loving care pronto.

Colter was right when he'd said her nipples would get sensitive. Son of a bitch. How dare he do this to her?

She wished she could take the rubber rings off, but her hands were firmly cuffed. She'd tried to rub her nipples against the soft edge of the blanket, but the delicate friction grating against her rock-hard nipples had just made her horny.

An edge of nervousness zipped through her. What if Colter didn't come back?

God! Where was that son of a bitch? Why was he so angry? What had happened to the tender, possessive man she'd fallen in love with?

The sound of the doorknob twisting made her catch her breath. As it flung inward, she saw him walking in, and with him came the unmistakable odor of alcohol. He'd been drinking.

His hot gaze immediately grazed over her nudity. Shimmers of delight raced up her spine at the lusty way he looked at her. It almost made her forget he'd tied a collar around her neck and cuffed her.

The bastard knew her fetishes. Being collared and cuffed was one of them. He remembered her weakness of loving to be dominated sexually…unfortunately that's the only way she wanted to be dominated.

"How are my nipples doing?" he asked.

He was breathing heavily. His stare hot. Intense. He must have been gone only about twenty minutes, but he seemed different now. The curve of his jaw looked darker with stubble, his voice hoarser as he came toward her. "Are they sore?"

Her pulse roared at the sight of the big bulge pressed against his pants. She might ask the same question about his balls. She held her question back and tore her attention from his pants to find his smoldering gaze drifting to her shaven pussy.

She creamed wonderfully.

Irritated at her reaction, she forced anger into her voice. "When are you letting me go?"

"When I'm finished with you," he replied. Softness splashed into his eyes. Once again he was looking at her as he'd done in the past. Tenderly. Hungrily.

She swallowed at the sound of his zipper lowering.

"Would you like a little relief?" he asked her.

Her heart hammered as his hand slid inside his pants.

"First you have to bring me relief." His last two words slurred.

"You're drunk."

"As a skunk," he laughed.

Her eyes drifted to his pants, to that luscious cock he slid out and held in his hand. She frowned at the sight of the fresh scratch marks etched along his swollen balls and hard shaft.

Bastard.

"You've been with Cheri."

"You jealous?"

She didn't answer, but she could now smell the other woman's perfume wafting through the air. The sweet scent sickened her. Infuriated her.

"How do you know I've been with Cheri? Her obvious fetish for scratching a man's balls isn't something she'd tell just anyone."

She could barely manage a glare at him despite the overwhelming urge to answer his question.

"Would it help if I told you nothing happened?"

"I'm sure those scratches are a figment of my imagination? That's how she brands her next man. She wants you, Colter. You won't have a choice in the matter. She always gets what she wants. Don't think for a minute sleeping with her will give you a better chance at obtaining that X-virus cure."

"I have no interest in bedding that woman. But I do have an interest in your hot, little mouth relieving the pain she's inflicted. If you remember, I'm not into pain, but I can exact it on someone who is, if she really wants it."

Her tummy clenched wickedly at his words. A side effect of the X-virus C mutation was a heightened enjoyment of the sexual things a woman enjoyed when she was normal. When she'd been uninfected, she'd enjoyed a little pain with her sex. Now she craved a lot of pain with her pleasure.

But to be turned on by a man who'd stolen her heart, abandoned her and was now treating her like shit. It just wasn't normal. Thankfully the fog of submissiveness was lifting again. There was still time to get him to do her bidding.

Bastard!

"Undo my cuffs."

He shook his head. "I want you on your hands and knees, Ash. You, as my pleasure slave. Your luscious mouth sucking my cock. Just like old times. Then we'll talk."

She couldn't stop herself from licking her lips. She wanted to taste him. Wanted to remember the silky hardness of his cock in her mouth. To feel the masculine power of his heated length sliding into her throat.

But she needed to stick to her principles. Giving into Colter Outlaw would enslave her heart again, and the last thing she needed right then was another complication in her life.

Damn Colter Outlaw for thinking he could just pick up where they'd left off without so much as an explanation as to why he'd never taken her away from the general as he'd promised.

His gorgeous cock loomed closer. The bright red lashes of another woman's claw marks looked angry and raw as they mingled with the pulsing web of blue veins. His shaft needed to be comforted. Soothed by a woman's tender mouth. Her mouth.

"I'm waiting, Starry Eyes," he said impatiently, his fingers stroking the massive length.

Oh...heavens. She could barely form a coherent thought anymore. Right then all she wanted...no, all she needed was to taste him. To feel his engorged cock in her mouth, sliding down her throat. Needed to remind him how it had been between them when they'd been together. It was the only way she could think of to keep him away from Cheri Blakely.

Her breath hitched in her throat as he grabbed her by her arm and helped her up.

"On your knees, sweetheart." Pleading gripped his voice.

Sexual tension rippled through her pussy at his command and she sank to her knees onto the warm, plush velvety carpet. Her mouth watered yet again at the sight of the dark silk arrow of hair aiming down to a thick thatch cradling two swollen spheres and his long, thick cock, which was only inches from her mouth. The angry purple mushroom-shaped head pulsed, a drop of pre-come appeared in the slit.

She could smell him. Hot, fresh male ready to be devoured.

Heart hammering wildly in her ears, she parted her lips and, with the tip of her tongue, gave the tip of his smooth, fat head a long luxurious swipe, sucking the salty dot into her mouth.

Delicious. Absolutely delicious.

His cock twitched. He groaned. Her nipples tingled in response.

"Bend your knees a little," she whispered. He did as she asked and she sat up on her knees where she leisurely brushed one nipple and then the other one against his hot cock head, gasping at the pleasure sparks the gentle friction created. She watched as her bound, aching nipples grew even longer, harder, and the intricate web of veins in his shaft pulsed thicker, became engorged as she continued her seductive touches.

Then she nudged her breasts away and leaned her mouth closer, placing gentle kisses here and there, relishing his increasingly louder groans. When she reached his thick root, his hand fell away and she took one swollen, scratched, velvety-hard ball into her mouth, sucking gently, tenderly at the scratches with her tongue.

He sighed his thanks and moaned with her every ministration.

When she was finished sucking and soothing both his balls she let him go, kissing her way back up along the pulsing, hot length to find another bead of pre-come waiting for her.

"God, woman, you are the starry-eyed devil herself," he whispered harshly as he placed his hand back on the root of his cock and aimed it toward her open mouth.

His words warmed her. The instant his silky, hard flesh touched her lips she could feel his tense need, the coiled desire in his cock.

From then on her instincts and pleasuring experience took over.

Opening her mouth, she allowed his silky, hard cock to come inside. For a split second she thought of escape, of sinking her teeth into his thick, juicy flesh, of hurting him as she'd been hurt by him.

That thought disintegrated as he said her name again, this time in an almost painful moan. As if his heart were being twisted, broken in the same way hers had been shattered.

He said her name again. This time a plea for her to continue. She hadn't even realized she'd stopped. She pulled her head back, allowed his erection to slide almost all the way from her mouth before she pulled her head forward again, allowing him to sink back into her mouth all the way to the back of her throat.

Instantly she felt the rapid pulse of his cock and began a steady rhythm that matched it. Strangled moans ripped from him as she bobbed, allowing her tongue to caress the length of him, sucking her cheeks inward to fashion the same wet tightness of a woman's channel.

His breaths grew ragged. The groans higher. His hips bucked against her in a frenzy. His cock grew tighter and suddenly he cried her name once again in warning and she smiled at the warm gush of salty stream sliding down her throat.

Greedily she accepted his liquid, her mind bringing her slowly back to the other times she'd done this to him. Times filled with passion.

A sharp, hot, tingling arousal knotted deep inside her belly. It spread outward, slid into her pussy as she remembered the tender way he'd touched her, had made love to her during those long, hot nights in the general's palace.

Her warm thoughts shattered as he pulled his limp flesh from her throbbing mouth and he slumped onto the bed.

His breaths ragged through the room, his eyes were closed, sweat glistened on his forehead.

Her nipples burned, screamed to be released from their rubber restraints. To be soothed by his loving, hot mouth. Her pussy pounded with wicked anticipation he would in turn go down on her, her clit felt so engorged she knew a few hard rubs and she'd climax violently.

She had to get the cuffs off. Bring herself relief. Get her medicine before the next wave of submissiveness hit.

"I won't allow you to make a slave out of me. I'm not as stupid and naïve as I was the last time we were together."

Puzzlement slashed across his face. His eyes popped open. A fierce frown draped his full lips. He looked as if she'd just insulted him.

"I don't think you're stupid…or naïve," he said softly.

God! She'd forgotten how sensitive he could be beneath that confident exterior.

"You sure are acting like it. A woman doesn't want to be collared and used by a man she—" she was about to say "a man she once loved" then quickly changed her mind. He'd only laugh at her. "A man she hasn't seen or heard from in years and used as if she's just a piece of meat, a vessel for his own lust."

She could hear his breathing slow. Could sense the tenseness between them begin to subside. If only a little.

"Forgive me, Starry Eyes."

Halleluiah!

"I should be thinking about your relief too. Come closer so I can take off those rubbers from your nipples."

Oh darn.

"You can un-cuff me. I'll take them off." The last thing she needed was for him to touch her with those gorgeous hands.

"Now you're acting naïve," he chuckled.

"Oh come on! I have things I need to do."

"You mean doctors you need to fuck so you can get a chance at the cure. Maybe even have a go with that bodyguard I took care of."

"He's not my bodyguard. He's one of my husbands," she lied, hoping he'd get pissed off enough to let her go.

"The man's been castrated and he doesn't even have a tongue to pleasure you with."

"There are other ways…and I might add he's quite good, better than some men who are whole."

That same shocked, horror look she'd seen earlier when she'd told him she was Claimed raced across his face, making her want to tell him the truth. She almost did, but another plan began to formulate. Something that would ensure she could have a better chance at getting the cure.

The best part was he'd never know she was using him. She just needed to get to her medication first and then she'd be able to go through with his planned sexual torture in one piece. She'd little doubt she couldn't. After all, the past five years of knowing Colter had betrayed her had been enough torture to last a lifetime.

"You seriously didn't think I wasn't Claimed, did you? I already told you that I was," Ashley said as she took advantage of his shock.

"Sorry, Starry Eyes, I didn't buy it then and I don't buy it now. Besides the general is a very powerful man in the Army and he's got important connections in the government. I think he'd pull strings to keep you all to himself."

"He has power but not that much power," she lied. She kind of liked the look of jealousy flooding his face. Served him right for chaining her up without her permission.

"He has enough power to do whatever the hell he wants. Obviously he wanted to make sure he kept you. Do all those imaginary husbands keep you satisfied?" he growled. "I remember you as being very passionate, almost insatiable."

"A lady never kisses and tells."

"You'll tell me." His voice was now as soft as velvet, and she went as still as a board as his large hand reached out. A soft gasp escaped her lips as his fingers feather-brushed the aching nipple of her left breast.

Her nipple pulsed and beaded even harder in reaction.

He did the same to her other glass-peaked nipple, brushing it with featherlight touches with the tips of his fingers until she couldn't stop herself from arching toward him.

"You never could resist my touch."

"You're an arrogant son of a bitch," she whispered. *Please, don't stop doing what you're doing.*

"Your nipples are so damn beautiful. Like tiny, delicate rosebuds."

She cried out as he used a small gadget to pry the rubber ring off her sore flesh. When her nipples were free, they pulsed and screamed with pleasure-pain as the blood rushed back. Colter was quick to come to her rescue. He sat up and curled his hands around her waist, pressing his face into her swollen breast, sucking one aching nipple at a time into his wonderfully hot mouth, the velvety yet abrasive texture of his wet tongue ravishing her flesh, flaming an erotic line of fire through her tender globes, which subsequently erupted between her thighs, deep inside her pussy.

"Let my hands loose," she whispered, desperation roaring through her. She wanted to wrap her hands around his neck and push his face harder against her breasts. Wanted to feel the bristle of his sexy five o'clock shadow rake her nipples.

"Not on your life."

"Colter, please..." His caressing mouth was burning her alive, making her think naughty things, making her forget why she'd come to Pleasure Palace in the first place.

The way his teeth nipped and bit made her breasts flame. Oh, God! His luscious mouth would be the death of her.

When he finally pulled away, it was all she could do to whimper her distress.

"That's enough for now, Starry Eyes."

For now?

"Time to get ready for bed."

Her eyes popped open.

Bed?

"First, a shower."

Her breath backed up in her lungs as she waited for him to grab her arm and lead her into the shower with him. Disappointment roared through her as, without looking back, he headed into her bathroom and quietly shut the door behind him.

* * * * *

Colter pressed his back against the bathroom door, wiped the perspiration beading his forehead and closed his eyes as the familiar lusty need churned through him. The need to dominate her. The need to brand her for his very own. To never let another man touch her.

His grip on revenge was sinking fast. He couldn't go through with it. At least not without remembering how good the sex had been between Ashley and him. Maybe he should forget about revenge and concentrate on getting the X-virus cure. Maybe he should just leave Ashley here. Forget about her.

He should be sucking up to Cheri Blakely. Following Cheri Blakely—fucking her until she handed over the cure. He could grab it and never look back. Do it before he did something with Ashley he might regret.

Despite her saying she didn't want him, he could read the sexual hunger devouring her eyes, felt the lusty tension in the eager way her satiny lips had melted around his cock.

He hadn't planned on having her go down on him. Hadn't planned it until he'd entered the room and seen her sitting on the bed, her hands cuffed, her generous breasts thrust out like sacrificial offerings with those two red, plump nipples that looked like cherries, her long legs hiding her pretty little pussy from his view. Her pretty lips parted in that familiar look of lust whenever she looked at him.

The erotic sight had made him hot.

Too hot to think clearly.

Merely touching her hard nipples then sucking the sweet buds into his mouth, feeling her burning flesh press eagerly against his tongue…it had pretty much caved in any resistance he had. He'd wanted to fuck her tight pussy right then and there.

The erotic sight of her luscious curves had clouded his thinking. Had made his cock ache and tighten so painfully the only immediate way he could allow himself relief was from her pretty, pouty mouth.

The blowjob had been…well, mind-blowing. Spectacular to say the least. Better than anything he'd ever remembered experiencing in his life. The cute way her head had bobbed as she'd handled his thick, pulsing cock had ignited a fierce warmth inside his heart for her.

She could have hurt him dearly if she'd wanted to. Her teeth were sharp. His parts ultrasensitive from Cheri's scratches, but Ash hadn't done anything to indicate he'd made her do something against her will.

Instead, her warm tongue had intimately caressed and tended to the burning scratches on his balls. Had touched and explored and sensually licked the entire length of his cock before expertly taking him into her hot mouth. The way she'd been able to take his large cock down her velvety throat without gagging had been awesome. But then again the general must have taught her that aspect of lovemaking and many other things.

His fists clenched in anger and he fought against the stabs of jealousy raking through him.

Man! He needed a cold shower. A really ice-cold shower.

Or perhaps he needed to find out what else the general had taught her?

Chapter Four

He wasn't taking a shower or a bath, and it was awfully quiet in there. What was he doing? Thinking up new ways of sexually torturing her as he said he'd do?

By the time the door opened and he stepped out of the bathroom, her heart banged so hard against her chest she thought it would come right out.

He wasn't naked as she'd expected him to be, but he wasn't fully dressed either. Clad only in a sharp pair of black suit pants, he looked absolutely stunning without his dress shirt.

Warmth scuttled through her veins and her face heated as her eyes zeroed right in on his silver nipple rings.

"Looks like those imaginary husbands of yours haven't been keeping you as satisfied as you'd have me believe."

He held something up in his hand.

Oh shit! Her vibrator. The one she'd used earlier today while she'd showered and fantasized about him.

To her shock, her face flamed with embarrassment.

"Didn't you know that a man's cock, if used properly, is better than a vibrator? Or have you forgotten that fact?"

She watched warily as he walked over to the sex-toy cabinet again.

"Perhaps I should punish you for lying to me about your husbands. A woman with so many husbands wouldn't need a vibrator, nor would she latch onto my cock so quickly and so hungrily, acting as if she hadn't had one for quite some time."

"I haven't lied to you," she lied, squirming uneasily on the bed as she watched him sort through the many items Pleasure Palace had stocked in the cabinet.

"If you were my woman, I'd forbid you to use sex toys when I wasn't around. I'd want you hot and ready, on edge and eager to be fucked whenever I was in the mood."

"A woman has needs too."

Shut up, Ashley!

"I can see you have many needs…and if I remember correctly, many fetishes. Ah, here's what I'm looking for."

He turned around and her eyes widened at the items he dangled from his fingers.

"Clit clamps were a favorite of yours. You know I'm surprised the general didn't outfit you with clit or nipple rings. He could have hung weights off them. Kept you aroused 24/7. Now I wonder why he'd allow you to wander around with a vibrator," he pondered, and bit his bottom lip thoughtfully before turning around and looking through the cabinet again.

"Ah, here we are. Oh! And these too. Fantastic!"

Jesus! What was he getting all excited about?

Ashley swallowed at the wickedly tight throat, wishing she could have a glass of water or, better yet, another taste of his cock.

The sound of plastic ripped through the air and she noticed he was holding something in his hand. What it was she couldn't tell.

But the lusty, smug kind of way he was looking at her just about made her come right on the spot.

There was something else he was holding in his hand as well. Velvety straps.

"Oh no, you don't," she cried out as he walked toward her.

"Oh yes, I am."

"Colter. Don't—"

His hot arm curled around her naked belly, pulling her right against him.

It took him only a split second to yank a pillow down from the top of the bed and hoist her belly first on top of the fluffy pillow.

Before she could even think, he'd removed her cuffs and strapped her wrists to the spirals on the bed. With her hands secured and her face down, she couldn't get a good look at him, but when she kicked out with her free foot, she connected with something solid.

Yes!

He swore violently, grabbed her ankles, and bound and tied them too.

A sharp slap to her ass followed by a harsh chuckle made her freeze.

Another chuckle. "I knew that would get your attention. Brings back memories, does it?"

She shivered at the softness etching his voice. Remembered how her ass had burned so beautifully that weekend compliments from all the spankings he'd given her. Spankings that had made her so aroused she thought maybe she was some sort of sex maniac for loving everything Colter did to her. Then and now.

God! Stop remembering! Ashley stiffened as the blindfold came over her eyes and everything went black. Her heart was hammering so hard with excitement it just about came out of her chest.

The sound of plastic crinkling drifted to her ears.

"This is nice and fresh. They must have just put it into the cooler."

Fresh? What was fresh? What cooler?

"What are you doing?"

He chuckled softly. "You'll see."

She heard the soft crackle of the plastic draw near her ear and a whiff of an odd aroma drifted beneath her nose.

"Can you guess what it smells like?"

It smelled like ginger. But why would he have ginger? She inhaled deeper, trying to figure out what else it could be.

He smacked his palm against her left ass cheek. She blew out a breath at the trailing burn. He slapped her other ass cheek until it also burned. Her pussy clenched wickedly.

Dammit! She couldn't stop reacting so wonderfully to those ass slaps.

"Colter…" *I need my medicine!* No! She couldn't tell him.

Ashley clenched her teeth together as he continued to smack her ass, leaving an unbelievable flushed feeling zipping through her buttocks and deep into her vagina. He'd tire of this nonsense sooner or later, and then she'd figure out a way to get to her suitcase. All she had to do was be brave.

And enjoy.

Yes, she sure was enjoying the pleasure-blaze splashing through her bottom. When her ass burned so hot and she couldn't stop herself from crying out, he finally stopped. A moment later she heard the water in the bathroom running. Twisting her head around, she tried to peek out from the bottom of the blindfold. She saw nothing but a thin line of light, which gave her a cockeyed view of the white bedding beneath her. Dammit! How the hell could she get him to let her go?

"Did you miss me?" he whispered, when a moment later she heard his feet pad against the carpet.

Yes, a naughty little voice whispered in the back of her mind. *Yes, I've missed you like crazy over the years.*

She felt the bed move as he sat down beside her. Ice-cold hands smoothed over her burning cheeks, sending shivers of delight shooting through her. That felt so beautiful.

"I've never forgotten how soft and curvy your ass is, Ashley. Never forgot you," he whispered.

Then why did you leave me? She wanted to ask him. Ached to ask that burning question. But she wouldn't. Pride prevented her from knowing. Besides, she didn't want to hear his excuse. Didn't want to know why he'd fucked her so passionately for all those weeks while the general had recuperated, or why he'd asked her to come with him then suddenly disappeared, leaving nothing but a note telling her he'd changed his mind. He'd already explained in the note. Why rehash it?

"Now, I'm going to show you what you've been missing all these years, Starry Eyes."

Before she could question him as to why he was making this all out to be her fault, a generously lubed finger nudged between her ass cheeks and lodged against her sphincter muscle.

"Oh!" She found herself tensing, crying out in surprise.

"Easy, Ashley. You just keep yourself calm and quiet."

Another command. The submissive feeling washed over her again. This time she didn't bother to fight it. She needed all her strength to do what he'd just told her to do.

Steadying her breathing, she discovered she couldn't wait to find out what he was going to do to her next.

"You're not allergic to ginger, are you, Starry Eyes?"

"No," she answered quickly. Why the question? She didn't dare ask her master.

"Good. Then we shall proceed."

His lubed finger prodded against her hole until her muscle gave and he slipped inside.

"Ahhh." What a wonderfully tight feeling of pain. She remembered it well.

"You like?"

She nodded as bitter tears of remembrance sparked memories. Memories of Colter's soft finger caresses as he'd explored her rear channel, whispers of gentle endearments into her ear as she'd cried out from the pleasure-pain.

Just as he was doing now.

"I've missed this part of you, Starry Eyes. So sweet. So easily aroused. And you're still so unbelievably tight. Don't your…husbands take you back here?"

"No," she shook her head, clenched her teeth, as her asshole flamed full of desire. She cried out as a second lubed finger slipped inside and prodded around.

"I wish I could take your pretty little ass, Ashley. Wish I could have it again."

Why don't you take me? A voice somewhere deep in the back of her mind urged. *Please take my ass. Please don't sound as if you don't ever want me again.*

As her ass muscles began to relax beneath his soft yet insistent prodding, she found herself drifting away, relaxing, and focusing on the pleasure-pain sifting along deep inside her and the flames that continued to lick her freshly spanked ass cheeks.

All too soon the wondrous pleasure-pain disappeared and she opened her eyes to find the blackness of the blindfold staring back at her. She could hear him breathing, the sound fast and harsh. Aroused. Would he take her in the ass now? Would he put out the fire he'd started in her?

The sound of plastic came again. She found herself lifting her head, orienting herself to the noise.

"Settle down, Ashley. No need to be afraid."

His voice soothed her, sucked her into a wall of security she loved. She didn't even flinch when she felt a strange, cool item penetrate her ass. At first she thought it was a butt plug, but he didn't insert it. Just left it poised in her opening.

Involuntarily her butt muscles clenched around it, tried to suck it in, it wouldn't come inside. Then she felt the pressure as Colter slid the item deeper. Her sphincter muscle constricted.

"There, that should hold you for a bit while I see what other little surprises I can give you." She didn't miss the amusement etching his voice.

The mattress shifted beneath her.

She could hear him walking toward the sex-toy cabinet and found herself wondering how she must look with her bare ass, all flushed and red, propped up on the pillow with whatever it was that was sticking out of her ass, sticking out of her ass.

The cabinet door creaked open again.

"I could give your cute little ass a sound whipping. Before long you'll be begging for it."

Begging? What?

It was at that moment Ashley felt the slow burn between her buttocks. What in the world was it?

As if sensing her question he chuckled and spoke. "The juice of the root has the ability to create incredible horniness."

Juice? Root?

Oh, God! What had he shoved into her ass?

Bucking her hips as much as she could against the restraints to get rid of the item, Ashley quickly discovered her movements only increased the burn, which was rapidly heading into a fire.

"How's our ginger root doing?" He was closer now. Too close.

She cried out as his hands curved over her buttocks again. The instant he touched the root, fire consumed her anus. She shivered as a finger dipped downward and touched her clit.

An immediate burn began there as well. Made her clit swell. Made her pussy clench. Made her cry out.

"Please! It's…burning me alive. Please help me…put…put out the fire."

"You'll have to beg a little harder than that, Ashley."

God! She was starting to feel so unbelievably horny. Her pussy was quivering, anxious to be penetrated. This must be the sexual torture he'd mentioned earlier.

"It won't hurt you, Starry Eyes. Unless you lied about not being allergic and I know you don't have sensitive skin."

Fire licked her buttocks as the unmistakable lash of a whip snapped against her tender flesh. Her muscles clenched the item tighter, the burn got worse.

Perspiration popped out over her skin, chilling the heat.

"You shouldn't have come here, Ashley. Shouldn't have come and reminded me of what we had."

Another sharp lash.

Her buttocks clenched harder. The burn in her ass from the ginger made her gasp.

Oh, God!

Another lash, the fiery pleasure-pain made her forget the burn. Made her want more.

"I remember how you craved Blade's cock up your ass while I whipped your breasts. Do you remember Blade?"

Another sharp snap. She cried out as her buttocks clenched around fire.

Her pussy was on fire now too. A wonderful horniness that begged to be satisfied.

"I asked if you remember Blade?"

"Yes," she whimpered. The coldness in his voice made her wonder once again if he'd been jealous of Blade fucking her.

"Did you enjoy the things he did to you, Starry Eyes? Did you enjoy them as much as I enjoyed watching?"

Oh sweet heavens! She was on fire.

"He's here, y'know. With me. He talks about you sometimes. How much he enjoyed pleasuring you, like I plan to do to you while you're my pleasure captive."

Ashley whimpered at his words.

His finger was sliding against her clitoris, bringing her quickly toward what she knew would be a wicked orgasm.

She'd enjoyed the sex with Blade, but she didn't love him. It had been a fantasy she'd been thrilled to try out at the time. She'd been living day by day back then under the sadism of the general, not knowing if she would be alive from one minute to the next. Having Colter living there with them had turned the general into a docile lamb toward her, had made her wary and on edge waiting for him to recuperate and start in on her with his perversions. The intimate caresses of Colter and then Blade had been an oasis in her otherwise world of fear.

"I…I don't care about Blade," she found herself confessing.

The finger sliding against her clit stopped briefly then started again.

"Maybe I should call him in here? Maybe I should watch him fuck you again, Starry Eyes."

"No, not like this…not with this anger between us."

He sucked in a sharp breath. His finger stopped rubbing her clit.

"No! Don't stop…please."

"You want relief? Maybe I should fuck you, Ashley?"

"Please…" Yes, she wanted relief. She wanted Colter. Had ached for him for years.

Her ass flamed in protest as he removed the ginger root and removed the bindings from her ankles and wrists. Warm hands cradled her waist and he turned her over. She couldn't stop herself from eagerly spreading her legs wide, from arching her hips to him.

The darkness of the blindfold only increased the erotic sensations. She imagined the lusty fire burning in his eyes as he gazed down between her thighs. Imagined how she must look. Her pink petals plump. Her clit engorged—puffy and purple with arousal. Wetness oozing from her slit.

She cried out in protest as he inserted not the hot, thick cock she craved but the thin vibrator that never totally satisfied her. The hum of it split the air. The item lodged deep inside her vagina and the clit stimulator pulsed softly against her ginger-burned clitoris.

She came apart.

The sensations were brutal, beautiful. Crashing against her in harsh pleasure waves. Making her scream with approval as he thrust the vibrating plastic in and out of her spasming pussy.

Oh yes!

The climax seemed endless.

She groaned as her muscles clenched the rod.

"Oh, God. Yeah," Colter hissed roughly. "That's it, sweetheart. Moan for me. Keep those hips moving."

She cried out again as the clit stimulator pressed harder against her throbbing clit. More brutal sensations. More cries. More pleasure waves. Her ass burned from the ginger.

"Breathe into it, sweetheart. That's it. Let's ride this figging nice and hard." His strangled, aroused voice was like an aphrodisiac. Melting over her mind like sweet caresses. Making her believe he really cared for her.

He thrust into her harder, deeper. Powerful strokes that encouraged yet another climax to rock her senses.

She cried out, bucked harder. Her mind spiraled.

The scent of her sex hung heavy in the air. The sound of his harsh breathing raked against her ears.

The awesome touch of his palm coming down and pressing onto her lower belly made the enjoyment sharper.

She was bucking in mindless pleasure now. Trusting him to guide her through it.

She couldn't help but cry out his name. Couldn't stop herself from begging him to plunge his massive rod into her.

"Shit! Ashley…you're so damn beautiful."

His hoarse voice ripped through her needs, making her realize she was begging. She didn't care anymore.

She just wanted Colter.

Erotic shivers crashed over her again making her cry out.

She was heading into the beauty. A pleasure so beautiful, so breathtaking she didn't want to come back.

More convulsions. Hot. Searing. Her vagina clenched wickedly. She cried out at the splintering pleasure-pain.

Then he was cradling her, caressing her heated flesh, bringing her slowly from her sexual euphoria. Bringing her back to him.

"Man, that was awesome," he said. "I've forgotten how gorgeous you look when you come apart like that, Starry Eyes." He held her so tenderly she couldn't stop herself from melting into his welcome warmth.

She missed him so much. Had missed him so badly she'd thought her heart was broken. But it wasn't. She had proof at the way happiness slipped into each and every fiber.

Colter was back in her life. It was incredible. It was something she'd never truly dared to hope for. Yet here he was.

"Sleep, Ashley. Sleep. When you wake up, we'll continue."

She trembled in his arms and allowed the engaging blackness to push away the excitement of his words. She found herself relaxing for the first time in years.

The burning pleasure in her ass dimmed and the tiny remaining spasms racking her pussy vanished. Sweet oblivion wrapped around her. It pushed away her fears. Fears that

Colter would find out she was an infected woman. That she wasn't whole. And that he'd find out her other secrets.

She slept.

* * * * *

"My slave is pregnant." The general's sharp laugh snapped through Ashley like a fissure of lightning that made both her and the visiting gynecologist jump. She'd expected him to be angry, to beat her with his fists. He didn't. He just looked at her naked pussy, an odd smile on his face as he thoughtfully stroked his dark beard. As if he weren't the least bit surprised.

"How far along is she? Four months?"

Oh, my God! He knew?

"Yes, about four months along," the doctor answered as he slipped his rubber gloves off and placed them on the mattress between Ashley's widespread legs.

How had the general known? She stifled the urge to start bawling. It wasn't easy to keep her emotions in check, especially now that her hormones were all over the place.

She'd suspected she was pregnant. Had known it when her period stopped. Had kept it a secret. Knew the general would not approve. Knew that he would know the baby would not be his.

"Yes, I'm pregnant." She forced herself to keep the crispness out of her voice. Now was not the time to irritate him with her sarcasm.

His gaze zeroed onto her blossoming naked belly and to her surprise, he slowly nodded his head. His eyes twinkled sadistically.

"Perhaps I should punish you and the father of the child."

She remained silent, trying hard not to feel anything for the baby's father, the man who had so easily abandoned her.

"Punishing her is not an option, General." The gyno interrupted. "The baby is a female."

Devastation rocked her at his words.

No! Sweet mercy! Not a girl. Her daughter would only end up like her. At the mercy of sadistic men.

"The child will be highly valuable when she comes of age. You will be quite rich, General. From here on out the slave needs her stress levels lowered substantially. Her blood pressure and blood test readings indicate she is under a great deal of stress. She also needs to be under constant medical supervision. Studies have shown that pregnancy in an infected woman is highly dangerous, both for the mother and the baby."

"The baby…will she be infected too?" Ashley couldn't stop herself from asking the question of the gynecologist, not really expecting an answer. Women of the world, except for those lucky few who had government connections, were recently deemed property—used for sex, breeding children, housework and little else. She was not allowed to speak to an unrelated man, no matter what the circumstances, so she wasn't surprised that the doctor ignored her. Wasn't disappointed when he acted as if she weren't even there lying on the bed buck-naked with her legs widespread for both men to ogle as they wished. But the doctor sure had acted as if she existed when he'd examined her, stroking her clit, plucking at her pussy lips and sticking his fingers into her vagina to feel around in an unprofessional manner, not to mention stroking her G-spot and arousing her right there with the general watching.

Ashley stifled a sob. She had to be brave. Had to figure out how to protect her daughter from the hoards of men who would want her in the future. At that thought, panic gripped her and the sob she'd been holding back wrenched free in a rush.

The doctor frowned and to Ashley's shock, a satisfied smile slipped across the general's lips. The general rarely smiled. And when he did, she knew a devious plan was forming in his wicked, sadistic brain. She swallowed as a tremor of icy fear gripped her.

"Will the girl be healthy?" The general finally repeated her question.

"The virus will not affect her until she reaches puberty. If she gets it and survives the virus, she will require daily medications like your slave. One can only hope a cure has been found by then."

The general's smile widened as he looked down and captured her gaze. Oh, God! The smugness in his eyes made her stomach lurch with sickness.

"What about abortion?"

At the general's question the sour sickness climbed into her throat. Ashley fought it back. She would never let the general have the satisfaction of seeing her so afraid of him that it made her ill.

He was a sadist. It would only arouse him. The last thing she wanted to do was make the general happy. And the last thing she wanted to do was kill Colter's child.

"Unfortunately research has shown all infected mothers who had an abortion the traditional way died."

Both men turned to look between Ashley's legs. Her cheeks flamed. Over the past year of being virtually naked and having the general and his bodyguards seeing her naked, she still felt embarrassed at the way the gynecologist looked at her with lusty appreciation.

"As you know, studies show that an orgasm in an infected pregnant woman will automatically kill the fetus and may be harmful to the mother."

"Interesting form of abortion."

"Under extreme supervision, I can bring her to orgasm."

No! Her mind screamed. No!

The general must have sensed her growing panic. He sent her a stern look that silenced any outburst she might make.

"I've heard that the chances of a woman dying during the orgasmic abortion is more than fifty percent," the general said.

Oh, my God! Would the general make her orgasm just to get rid of her baby? Did he hate the child so much?

"Yes, that is true."

The general nodded. "Thank you for coming, Doctor. I'll see to it she gets the proper attention."

What did he mean by proper attention? Would he try to kill the baby himself?

Ashley could scarcely keep her raging fear in check as the general escorted the doctor out of her room. The instant the door closed she leapt off her bed. She padded barefoot to the door and listened.

Silence.

She needed to get out of there. Needed to protect her child. There was no way she would ever let the general hurt the baby.

Oh, God! Colter, where are you? Why did you leave me? Why? Why?

Turning the doorknob, she pushed against the door. It didn't budge.

Sweet heaven help her! The general had locked her in!

Chapter Five

Ashley opened her eyes to find warm, late morning sunshine splashing away the fear that followed her out of her dream. Cool perspiration dotted her heated flesh and she immediately recognized a searing warmth slicing into her entire right side. Turning her head, she inhaled a sharp gasp at the erotic sight.

Colter Outlaw lay on top of the comforters right beside her. Long black lashes framed his closed eyes, his naked, muscular chest moved up and down steadily in sleep and the rest of him…

Ashley swallowed.

The rest of him…totally and deliciously naked.

Her breathing quickened and her pussy quivered with excitement as she slid her gaze over his well-toned tummy and abdomen, past a fist-sized skull tattoo she'd never seen before nestled just above the dark bush of hair swaddling a huge pair of balls and the most gorgeous engorged cock she'd ever had the pleasure of having buried deep inside her.

"From the look on your face I gather you still like what you see."

Ashley's head snapped up to find such a wickedly delicious grin lifting his full lips that she just about came on the spot.

"What's to like?" she quipped, wrapping the comforter tighter around her.

"You mean what's not to like."

Her tummy did some mighty weird flips as he leisurely stretched his arms out above his head, the lovely bulges in his arms rippling quite wonderfully.

To her shock, or maybe to her arousal, he turned toward her, his elbow casually dipping beneath his neck as he propped his head to look at her. She got another damn good eyeful of his swollen cock and couldn't stop the small gasp at the magnificent sight. The rest of him appeared casual as if they were intimate lovers used to seeing each other naked.

"I've decided to call Blade and have him get you out of here." He said it so casually it took her a few seconds to realize what he'd just said. That's when the anger hit.

"No way. I want the cure and damned if you're going to stop me from getting it."

"I want you safe. With Blade. You won't have to give the cure to the general. I'll protect you from him."

Shit! He'd said those exact words when he'd made love to her that last time they'd been together. He was a man. She couldn't trust him.

"I won't be safe with Blade or any other man, and you bloody well know it. Men can't be trusted. You can't be trusted. You've proved it by locking me in here. Now get the hell out of my cabin."

To her irritation, he merely smiled at her as if she were just a cute little toy.

"Fine then, asshole. Unlock me from this collar and I'll leave."

"I like it when you're pissed off, Starry Eyes. Shows me you've recuperated and that you're ready for more pleasuring."

Her pussy automatically creamed.

"Which is it going to be, Ashley? Going with Blade? Or staying here with me?"

"Neither," she managed to grind out, suddenly wanting to kiss him and damage him at the same time.

Maybe she could kiss him and then grab him by those luscious balls and squeeze until he opened the collar?

Maybe...oh my! He was getting up and his cock was stiff and long and so thick. Her breath hitched in her lungs at the awesome sight. His erection was swollen, so unbelievably thick and so ready.

His grin widened. "I can see you've made up your mind. How about pancakes for our late breakfast?"

* * * * *

"You guys really should have takeout," Colter grumbled as he accepted the bag the irritated maître d' handed him then turned around and quickly left the kitchen.

Apparently Pleasure Palace was just too posh of a place to think that maybe a man just didn't want room service when he had a woman tied to his bed.

Cripes, it had taken him fifteen solid minutes of getting the runaround before the maître d' finally ordered the cook to get him breakfast for two. He just hoped he hadn't brought undue attention to himself by going against their elegant rules of wanting to serve him in his own cabin instead of providing him with takeout and not being disturbed.

Heading back outside into the late morning sunshine, he picked up his pace. The longer he was away from Ashley the more the need to see her grew. Imagining the pure pleasure that must have twisted her face last night when he'd fucked her with the vibrator had been the final nail in his craving for payback.

Sweet revenge would be his. However, pleasuring her without him being emotionally a part of it was starting to be a totally different matter. He wanted to be a part of it now. Wanted to be the one sinking his cock deep into her tight pussy and hearing those cute little gasps escape her mouth as they'd done last night during the figging. Most of all he wanted to make love to her. If he did that, well, leaving her might be a heck of a lot harder than he'd first anticipated.

Strangely enough, it was a chance he was willing to take with his heart.

If he were smart, he'd be calling Blade. Telling him to pick Ashley up. He could take his sexual revenge on her when his job here was done. He could show her how much he'd suffered because he couldn't be with her.

Another question ripped through his brain. Was he simply being stupid and vengeful keeping her there with him, teasing her, sexually tormenting her? Was he acting childish for wanting revenge? For wanting to make her suffer as much as and more than he'd suffered?

Yes, he was being stupid and childish, a wee voice taunted.

You should just tell her how much you want her. How much you need her in your life. How your heart broke when she'd written that note saying she loved the general more than she loved you. How his gut had twisted when she'd also left behind his late mother's antique comb that he'd given her when he'd told her he loved her.

Hell! He couldn't tell her any of that mushy stuff! She'd just laugh at him and tell him where to go. Just as she'd done in that note.

What should he do?

Risk his heart with sexual revenge against a woman who didn't want him? Or give her to Blade and tell him to hold onto her until he got the cure and could exact the revenge on his own?

A familiar low whistle from a slightly open window of his cabin floated to his ears, making Colter stop.

Shit! Blade was in his cabin. He'd forgotten they were supposed to meet there at their appointed time this morning. Hoofing it back to the front door, he slid the electronic key into the door and rushed inside.

"Ah food, I'm starved." Blade licked his lips and made a grab for one of the bags.

"I don't think so, bud."

"What's this? You're holding food from your good old buddy?"

"It's for me and…a lady friend."

Blade let out a low chuckle. "You've got yourself a pleasure slave. That explains why you're half an hour late."

He would have been a hell of a lot later if he hadn't heard Blade's whistle.

His friend grinned wickedly. "I noticed you didn't sleep in here last night. Did you spend the night in one of those sex dungeons they have beneath Pleasure Palace?"

"It's none of your business where I spent the night."

Blade's amused grin only got wider.

"You must have found yourself a real jewel."

Time to change the subject.

"Cheri Blakely said she was leaving for a little while. Why don't you go out and locate her. Then I can strangle the whereabouts of the cure from her."

"We already know where the cure is."

Shit! "So why the hell don't you get it?"

"The security is too tight. A high risk of failure. We don't want to make any attempts to tip her off. After her husband died, she went deep undercover and she's just resurfaced. We have to wait until she brings the cure here where you can step right in and walk away with it. She'll never know she was duped by the good guys. She won't go into hiding and when she comes up with cures, which she will, since she knows the makeup of the virus as she and her husband created it, we can send another undercover S.K.U.L.L. agent in and do this all over again. So, big buddy? Were you in one of those dungeons? You do look a little tired. And where were you going with that food? Obviously not here. It's a good thing I saw you passing by earlier this morning or I would have had to report back that you'd gone MIA. Did you forget we were supposed to meet this morning?"

Colter shrugged.

Blade frowned.

"Well hell, that sure as hell ain't like you. What's going on?"

Here was his chance to tell Blade about Ashley. To ask him to get her out of there. To keep her safe and sound until he could deal with his feelings for her. Yet he couldn't bring himself to do it.

"I've just been snooping around getting information about Cheri and the cure," Colter lied.

"And?"

"No one is saying anything."

"Didn't think so. She's surrounded herself with seven new husbands. They stick to her like glue. She's a hot-looking woman and I hear she's even better in bed."

No one was better in bed than Ashley.

Colter shook the erotic thought away. He should be telling Blade to take Ashley away so he could concentrate on the assignment, but the thought of having her out of his sight just didn't sit right. And for some strange reason he knew she was right about her not being able to trust men or even Blade. Especially the way Blade had talked about that young pleasure slave when he'd first seen her yesterday. From his past experience in the Terrorist Wars, when S.K.U.L.L. men went without sex for too long on assignments, they tended to do things a normal man might not usually consider doing…things like he'd just done with Ashley. Collaring her against her will. Figging her round little ass. Fucking her with a vibrator. Enjoying every minute of dominating her.

Perhaps if he could ease up on his revenge, get her to change her mind and accept her collar and the pleasure he wanted to bring to her, things could be rather pleasant over the next couple of days. Pleasant for both of them.

And when this assignment was over and he had the cure for S.K.U.L.L., he could go back to exacting his revenge on Ashley by simply walking away as she'd done to him.

* * * * *

Ashley slipped the pill into her mouth a split second before she saw Colter's shadow pass the window.

Shoot! Back already.

Slamming the suitcase shut, she twirled the combination lock and propped the case up on the nearby wall. She'd been lucky in getting to the case at all. It had taken an awful lot of cursing and some heavy-duty patience, but she'd managed to use the nearby five-foot-tall lampstand to drag the suitcase within reach so she'd been able to retrieve her medication and throw a cozy robe over her chilling body.

She couldn't stop the tremor of lust from gripping her as she heard the door push open and watched Colter stroll inside holding a couple of large paper bags. She noticed he'd changed into a fresh suit while he'd been gone. It looked similar to the one he'd worn yesterday and she stifled a giggle imagining hearing a sharp rip shredding through the back of this suit jacket just as it had happened yesterday.

"Time to build your energy, Starry Eyes," he chuckled as he plopped himself down on the mattress, whipped off his jacket and started taking metal containers from the bags.

The intoxicating smells of pancakes, eggs and bacon mixed with Colter's sensual scent wrapped all around her and made her stomach rumble wickedly.

At the sound he looked up and caught her gaze. The lusty glaze flooding his eyes made her shiver as tiny carnal sensations rippled through her pussy.

"Come, join me," he patted the mattress beside him. "Or you could just come..."

My God! The man had a way with words.

"I won't be coming at your hands any longer. You will release me from this collar. I'm through playing your games." And now that she had the medicine soaring through her system, she'd be able to resist his sexual touches.

"Ah, so you admit you were playing along."

The aroma of coffee tantalized her nostrils.

"As if I had a choice."

"At the way your pussy was drenched when I touched you during yesterday's figging, it tells me you enjoyed your punishment."

"Punishment for what?" she snapped, anger sizzling through her again.

"I don't like to talk on an empty belly. Eat."

He began sifting through the bags again, bringing out more tin-covered plates.

Damn him! And damn her for giving in so easily. But she was awfully hungry and the food smelled so good.

Sighing in frustration, she plopped onto the mattress beside him.

"How'd you get that suitcase over here?" he asked as he placed a couple of warm tin-covered plates onto the bed beside her thigh.

"What is the problem? Did you think I was too…tied up to be able to get to it?"

"I'd better keep a closer eye on you, Starry Eyes. You seem a little sneaky."

"Me? Sneaky? You're the one who snuck into my room and forced me to be naked in front of you and…"

She stopped. He was frowning now. His hot gaze raking over the pretty pink robe hiding her body from his view. She thought he'd say something about covering herself from him, especially after he'd warned her not to ever hide herself from him last night.

"I didn't realize you were naked until I removed the sheets," he said softly. Was that an apology in his voice? Or guilt?

"Have a go at the pancakes. They smell great." He placed the warm tin on her lap, the warmth searing into her thighs and pussy. "Here, use lots of this." He handed her a canister containing blueberry syrup.

Her favorite.

Coincidence? Or did he remember the blueberry lovemaking session they'd had one morning on their last weekend together in Iraq?

"Coffee tastes absolutely shitty."

Ashley couldn't help but smile. He'd said the same thing about her coffee too when she'd made it for him every morning when he'd been at the general's mansion.

She forced herself to pour the blueberry syrup onto the pancakes and keep her mind off memory lane.

"Any word on when Cheri is throwing her demonstration?" she asked as she dug into the fluffy pancakes with full gusto now that the delicious aroma was sifting deep into her lungs, making mouth water.

"We've got some alone time together before she gets back."

Her heart twisted painfully at the eerie déjà vu words she herself had once uttered when the general had been called away.

Your time with Colter is in the past. It was a setup, Ashley. Don't read any more into it. The general set the two of you up.

Try as she might though, she just couldn't keep her mind off the way Colter had been staring at her during that one morning when they'd met over a pancake breakfast in the dining hall of General Black's mansion and were told the general had left for the weekend.

She remembered the lusty glaze in his eyes as he'd watched her every move while they'd eaten across from each other at the large marble table. He'd looked at her in much the same way he was looking at her now.

Hungry. Fierce. Determined.

She stopped chewing as the pink tip of his tongue dipped out and wetted his bottom lip, capturing a drip of blueberry syrup.

Visions of yesterday's kiss—their one and only kiss—raged through her mind. The erotic taste of his moist tongue smoothing past her teeth. The sensual feel of his mouth sliding across her lips. She almost moaned as her pussy clenched tightly around air instead of the long, hard cock she wished would slide into her.

He kept staring at her as she dug into the crispy bacon and sunny-side-up eggs. Staring and saying nothing. Watching her every move as if he were the predator and she the prey. Her lower belly rippled wonderfully at the thought of being his captive and she fought to focus her attention on getting as much nutrition into her as possible before he decided it was time to play.

Oh! And did she ever want to play with him! To touch him, run her fingers along the hard muscles lining his chest, to finally feel his long, hard cock twitch in her hands when she kissed the smooth head.

Whew! Time to change the subject.

"I was wondering about something," she said as she polished off the rest of her coffee.

"What's that?"

"Isn't Pleasure Palace going to get suspicious if I don't show up soon?"

"I took care of that. As far as they're concerned you and your bodyguard are enjoying the attentions of the pleasure slave named Reena. I've left instructions that you do not wish to be disturbed and that lunch, dinner and tomorrow's food should be left outside your cabin door. Now I don't have to leave the cabin anymore and I can give you my undivided attention."

Oh gosh.

"Are you finished eating your pancakes?"

She nodded, and he gathered up the plates and peeked into the container of blueberry syrup.

"We've got quite a bit of blueberry syrup left and I know exactly what we're going to do with it, but only on one condition."

"What…what's that?"

"You remove your robe."

He could tell she wasn't too sure if she should do as he asked. And he wasn't too sure what he'd do if she didn't take off that robe. He really didn't want a repeat performance of yesterday. Of seeing the anger flare in her eyes when he'd ripped that sheet off and discovered she was totally naked beneath.

The instant he'd caught sight of her luscious body, he hadn't been able to control himself. He'd wanted to look upon her beauty. Wanted to remember what they'd had together that weekend when she'd been so willing to take her clothing off in front of him. Back then, she hadn't been the least bit shy. She'd seemed starved for sex, eager to touch him, explore every inch of him, taste him, just as he'd done with her.

Surprise washed over him when her trembling hands untied the knot holding the robe together. She allowed the robe to part, giving him an erotic view of her curvy cleavage, her slightly rounded abdomen and her bare pussy.

He trembled at the sight. His cock swelled quickly. Thickening, throbbing, pressing against his pants, demanding escape. Demanding satisfaction in her tight little pussy.

Sexual hunger glittered in her eyes and an erotic gasp flew past her lips as he slid his hands inside the robe to cup her full breasts. Silky smooth came to mind as he pressed his palms into her swollen mounds and caressed her firm nipples.

"Uh-uh, if I'm going to be held hostage by you, then this time around I'm going to tell you what I want you to do to me."

Colter suppressed a smile. She was eager and ripe for sex. Maybe this revenge thing was going to be easier than he'd figured.

"And what is it you want me to do?" he queried, quite anxious to find out.

"Kiss me."

Shit!

Kissing wasn't part of the plan. Especially after the erotic longing he'd experienced after their last kiss when he'd first stolen into her room. Hell, he was still recuperating from the heated way his cock had pulsed while his lips had held hers captive. Just as it pulsed and throbbed now as she moved closer to him.

Mischief twinkled in her eyes. "What's the matter? Can't handle a simple little kiss?" Her warm coffee-scented breath tingled against his cheeks. She smelled of delicious woman. Of sex and bacon and blueberry.

"I can handle anything you dish out, Starry Eyes."

She smiled smugly and he got the feeling she was up to something. He doubted it was anything good.

Before he could back off, she pressed her ultra-sweet mouth against his bottom lip, erotically sucking on it. Tasting it. Nipping with sharp teeth before licking away the pain with the tip of her velvety tongue.

Oh man! Her touch was so tender he could literally feel the revenge melting away from his heart.

He growled his approval and captured her sweet mouth. She tasted like heaven, her plump lips like silk, her teeth smooth and straight as he pushed into her mouth. She opened up to him, whimpering when their desperate tongues clashed.

Her soft body pressed into his, and he roared with heat. Hot feminine hands swept over his shoulders like two searing brands. His cock hardened with desperation. Yet something whispered a warning at the back of his mind. A thought telling him he'd better not let this woman go as easily as he'd first planned.

The idea shocked him and he abruptly broke the kiss.

Grabbing her upper arms, he roughly pushed her away in his anger for allowing himself to feel a shred of need for her. Due to his shove, she sprawled backward onto the bed. Her breasts swayed beautifully as she plopped against the fluffy pillows. Her robe spilled open and her legs spread wide, giving him the ultimate view of her pussy.

Starry eyes twinkled back at him. That smug smile rippled across her face again, but it was shaky, as if she weren't too sure about what to do next. Her next words made him inhale sharply.

"I dare you to get on your knees, right here in front of me. Right here between my legs."

A challenge? Did she doubt he wouldn't do what she asked?

And why was he doing it? Why was he actually getting down onto his knees and easing between her legs? Why in the world wasn't he regaining charge over her again?

He would.

Later.

Right now, she was participating beyond his wildest imagination. Giving herself to him so freely. Totally opposite of when he'd first come on the scene. Almost as if she had something planned.

"Stay there and watch." Reaching for a container on the bed, she poured a healthy dose of the blueberry syrup over her pussy, bringing with it the memories.

Oh shit! She was forcing him to remember, to relive the pleasure. Forcing him to…

"Go down on me."

He hesitated. She smiled at him with apparent satisfaction. Dare twinkled in her eyes.

He should never allow her to see how much she affected him. How hard his cock pulsed at the sight of her shaven and pink pussy. How fast he breathed at the sight of the moistness seeping from her opening.

Ah man, he could smell the sweetness of her sexual arousal, the sweet scent tempting his nostrils. His mouth watered. His heart hammered so hard he wondered if she could hear it too.

If he went down on her, he might not be able to keep his heart out of it. It might get harder to walk away. He didn't want to go through the pain and anguish he'd gone through the last time. It might kill him.

He should just get up now. Walk away. Never look back.

Wait a minute! Grab hold of yourself, Colter. What are you afraid of? Let her think she has the upper hand. Let her think she's got you wrapped around her finger again. Make her fall in love with you all over again.

Eat her cute little pussy. Make her remember…

His breath caught in his throat as her long fingers spread her plump, pink pussy folds apart, giving him a bird's-eye view of her engorged purple clitoris.

Man! He could literally see it growing, throbbing with arousal right in front of his eyes.

"Do it," her voice sounded strangled, lusty.

He didn't need any more prompting. He came closer, his mouth zeroing in on her pussy like a heat-seeking missile. His mouth clamped over her delicious cunt in one quick shot that made her buck and squirm in surprise as if she hadn't expected him to do what she'd asked.

Quickly he grabbed her knees, held them firmly apart, held her hostage.

"Oh, God!" she cried out as he smoothed his tongue over her swollen, slippery clit and massaged it. Her whimpers of arousal ripped through the air. The erotic sound spurned him on.

He licked at her plump pussy lips, sucked them into his mouth and enjoyed the taste of her hot flesh.

She leaned forward, her mouth opened in a gasp, her hands sliding over the sides of his head, holding his mouth steady over her steaming pussy.

"Eat me," she moaned. "Oh, God! I've waited so long!"

His heart hammered at her words, at her urgency. He plunged his tongue into her wet channel. Felt the sides quiver, greedily clamping around him.

"Deeper!" she hissed.

Hell! His tongue was only so long!

He managed to pull his head back a couple of inches and thrust a couple of fingers into her tight slit.

She cried out at the impalement and he went to work on her engorged clit, his teeth gently nipping at her swollen piece of flesh as he kept up a slow, erotic thrusting motion.

"Oh, God! Please! Deeper! Harder!"

Shit! Her desperate cries were unraveling him. He wanted to drive into her. Come with her. Make love to her.

The scent of her arousal surged through him. His cock screamed for attention. Twitched and begged to plunge into her tiny slit. But her sweet cream was coming, gushing down the hot channel, thick and tasty as it exploded onto his tongue.

Through her sexual haze, Ashley could hear his breathing grow heavier, quicker. The eager slurping of his mouth on her pussy made her just about explode. It took every bit of her resistance to hold back. To allow him to break first.

She knew he needed relief as much as she did. It wouldn't be long before he took her.

Sweet Jesus! Her plan had to work!

Her hands slipped from his head and landed on his hard shoulders. Taut muscles greeted her and she dug her nails deep into his flesh. She loved the way the thick cords gave way beneath her fingers.

Violent sensations spiraled through her as his mouth made love to her pussy.

"Colter!" she hissed. Her mind was twisting, threatening to give into the carnal pleasures.

"Please! Fuck me! Now!"

His face drew way, his shoulders moved beneath her fingers. At the sound of his zipper lowering her heart picked up a mad beat.

Wild desperation gripped her. She needed to get laid! Now!

For a tense moment he hesitated. Something raw and hurtful tugged at her heart for pushing him like this, but the magnificent arousal splashing through his face made her glad too.

She felt as if she might come out of her skin as she watched him suddenly rip open his shirt, buttons popping around like candies. His eyes darkened. He removed his pants and his underwear. Then he kicked off his shoes and ripped off his socks.

His cock was fully engorged and sticking straight out.

"My starry-eyed devil," he whispered.

The seductive tone of his voice, the spicy scent of man made a fierce hunger gnaw deep inside her empty vagina. She breathed him all the way into her lungs.

Emotions careened through her. Guilt for making both of them lose control. Satisfaction because her plan just might work. Most of all, overwhelming arousal that he still craved her after all the time that had passed between them.

Reaching up, she curled her hands over his thickly muscled shoulders. She loved the damp, solid feel of his silky flesh beneath her fingertips.

"You're mine, Starry Eyes," he growled, and she cried out as his thick cock slid into her wet channel. She gasped as in one solid thrust he buried his shaft right to the hilt.

Sweet mercy! What unbelievable fullness! She'd forgotten how big he was.

He let out a ragged breath. Lifted one hand to gently cup her chin, forcing her to watch him as he began a slow, erotic plunge.

She became lost in the seduction of his eyes. There was an odd darkness there that she'd never noticed before in the past. A darkness that made her think he'd gone through the same hell she'd gone through over the last few years. Could he have missed her as much as she'd missed him?

Her heart contracted at that thought.

If everything went according to plan, then in a few minutes she'd be gone. She wouldn't have to see the hurt anymore. And then what?

Emptiness engulfed her heart. If she escaped, dare she tell the desk clerk Colter Outlaw was an intruder? Especially after she'd sworn to him she would never hurt him. If she did break his cover, then any shred of hope she'd once felt of them getting together would be destroyed.

But she desperately needed that cure!

He caressed the side of her jaw with soft strokes, bringing her out of her momentary doom and gloom. Her arousal was peaking. She could feel the tension zip through her. The fever building.

"Keep your eyes open while I make love to you. I want to watch," he whispered softly.

At his words, tremors suddenly racked her and her body came apart in one long violent explosion of unbelievable pleasure.

Killing pleasure. It wrapped around her like an electrifying blanket.

Moans ripped from her mouth. His hot breath blew against her face. He withdrew and swiftly entered her again, grunting his pleasure.

Her mind reeled at the onslaught.

He withdrew. Plunged harder. Her vagina gripped him tightly, almost refusing to let him go.

He plunged faster, neared his own climax.

His mouth came down, locked on hers. He tasted her. Sucked her as if she were some sweet piece of fruit he couldn't get enough of.

And she couldn't get enough of him either as she held onto him and lost herself in the delicious rapture.

Ashley didn't know how long she slept but when she realized she had fallen asleep, her eyes snapped open and she listened to Colter's uneven breathing.

Sweet heavens, her plan had worked. After having sex, he'd always slept. Yet he'd never been one for sleeping soundly after a fucking session, but this was as good a chance of escape as she was going to get.

Her pussy felt exquisitely sore as she cautiously moved off the mattress. Trying hard to make sure the chain holding her captive made no noise, she tiptoed to where he'd dropped his pants.

She had no idea where he'd put the key to the collar, but he must have it in his clothing somewhere. A quick search of his pants and then his shirt revealed nothing.

Dammit! Where could he have put it?

She gave the room a furtive scan and stopped at the sex toy cabinet. Could he have put the key in there? If he had, she wouldn't be able to get to it.

On the bed, Colter moved slightly. Ashley stiffened. Desperation clawed at her belly.

Would he awaken? Would he screw her plan for escape? She held her breath and waited until he stilled again, her gaze then dropped to the floor where the white sheets lay in a crumpled heap.

A spark of hope gripped her at the sight of his jacket lying there. The craving for freedom grew almost intolerable as she reached down and searched the numerous pockets. Any other time she would have loved to be Colter's sex slave, but not now. Now she couldn't take any chances.

Her fingers touched metal. Wrapped firmly around the key.

Sweet mercy she'd found it!

In a matter of seconds she would once again be a free woman…and then she'd have to decide about Colter's fate.

Chapter Six

"You wanted to see me, General?" he asked as he stood in the doorway of the makeshift tented hospital room of the M.A.S.H. unit. The man in the bed, the top of his head bandaged in white, smiled wearily.

"Ah yes. Dr. Colter Outlaw, is it?"

"Yes, Sir."

"Come in, please. I wish to speak to you."

Colter entered and positioned himself at the foot of the general's bed. He tried hard not to be impressed by the man on the bed and his will to survive. Under the medical circumstances, this man should have died when that bullet slammed into his brain. But he hadn't. He'd been lucky. Very lucky.

"I want to thank you for saving my life, Lieutenant Colonel."

"Any surgeon would have done the same, Sir."

"Ah, but you aren't even a surgeon, are you?"

"No, Sir. No one was available to perform the operation, Sir." Colter held his breath as the man's piercing gray eyes studied him.

He hoped S.K.U.L.L. had done their homework and the general would be grateful he was alive. Unfortunately, it hadn't been his skills that had saved him but another doctor's. But S.K.U.L.L. had seen the general's injury as a way to get a S.K.U.L.L. member into the general's good graces. Colter had been picked.

"Where did you learn your techniques, Doctor? I'm sure digging a bullet out of a man's brain isn't something you were taught in your training as a family doctor."

"I read a lot of medical journals before I joined the Wars, Sir."

"How long have you been in the Wars?"

"About a year, Sir."

"I bet you could use a long stretch of R&R, couldn't you?"

"I don't take time off, Sir."

The general nodded. "They tell me you are very dedicated."

"I took an oath, Sir."

"What would you say if I arranged for you to stay at my palace to take care of me during my recuperation?"

Yes! He was in!

"I'd have to decline the offer, Sir."

"It's not an offer, Doctor Outlaw. It's an order."

Colter forced himself to hide his increasing excitement. Phase one of S.K.U.L.L.'s plan was in full swing. Now all he had to do was get into the general's palace and wait until he could assassinate the general's terrorist son the first chance he got.

When he'd accompanied the general home several days later to help him recuperate, he'd been introduced to the black-haired beauty with sparkling blue eyes. Ashley had made his heart go pitter-patter the instant he'd seen her. It hadn't been long before he'd fallen in love with her and taken her to his bed.

He'd enjoyed many scorching nights and mornings of pleasure with her…delicious pleasure just as they'd shared this morning after breakfast. He'd tried not to give in to the wickedly carnal sensations of lust spiraling through him as he'd sucked the sweet cream from her vagina.

Her desperate cries for relief had broken his control and the fact she still reacted to him so violently during their lovemaking had stroked his ego. Unfortunately for her, it would also hurt her more when he walked away.

Man! Even in his after-lovemaking drowsiness, he could feel his cock hardening with the need to have her again.

Pure pleasure without any interruptions from the Pleasure Palace employees or Cheri or…

Shit!

What the hell time was it anyway? He had to do his check-in with Blade or he would come looking for him…and he'd find Starry Eyes.

At that thought his gut clenched. He wasn't prepared to share Ashley…at least not yet.

In his drowsiness he found himself reaching for her. Emptiness greeted his fingertips.

What the hell?

His eyes snapped open and he immediately noticed things weren't how they should be. Ashley wasn't in the bed. And something soft circled his neck.

"Fuck!" he shouted and quickly sat up. The tinkling sound of chain ripped through the silence. His stomach sank as his fingers touched the collar around his neck. She'd removed the collar from herself and given it to him!

How the hell had she managed to do that without him waking up?

The collar wasn't the only thing he noticed either. His hands were cuffed in front of him and she'd managed to hold his cock captive as well. He swallowed at the lusty shivers shooting through him at the erotic sight. From the base of his cock right up to the tip of his head, a series of metal rings in descending sizes adorned his full length.

Jesus H. Christ! What the fuck was he going to do now?

A giggle from the bedroom doorway caught his immediate attention. His body responded when he saw Ashley standing there.

Fully clothed in a sexy sapphire blue blouse and matching short skirt that hugged her every delicious curve, she looked utterly sinful. She'd done her hair in soft ringlets that cascaded over her shoulders and partially covered her breasts.

"Hello, lover," she cooed as she walked into the room with long, confident strides he found tremendously attractive. He found himself wondering how she'd managed to escape getting the X-virus or one of its many mutations. Hardly any woman had escaped its wrath. In fact, the government was actively recruiting the few who were immune to volunteer to be guinea pigs for a possible vaccine or cure. His Claimed wife Callie had been one of those women. She'd been held against her will in a government lab for five years before finally managing to escape Cheri's mad scientist late husband. She'd eventually been legally Claimed by his brothers and him. It had been the only way they'd been able to protect her from the government because Claimed women were omitted from the government experiments in the hopes they would produce babies, preferably virus-resistant girls for the future.

"Oh if your looks could kill, I'm sure I'd be a dead woman." She smiled at him. A smile that made him believe he wouldn't be able to resist her if she decided to play sex games on him. A strong need to make love to her again coiled inside him. He wanted to hold her. To touch her. To ask her why she'd been gone when he'd come back for her.

"But until then, you're a guest in my cabin, Dr. Outlaw. A guest whom I can do with as I please."

It was then he noticed the little black box nestled in the palm of her hand. Instantly he knew it had something to do with his cock cage.

His instincts, of course, were correct.

Helplessly he watched her thumb work a button on the box. Immediately the rings began to vibrate around his shaft. His teeth clenched as his cock immediately responded to the gentle, seductive, fingerlike caresses curling around his thickening flesh.

The little bitch!

"Come here, Ashley." What he'd hoped would sound like a command actually came out more like a husky plea.

Her eyes widened slightly but she walked closer, allowing him to see that the top she wore had two little holes immediately over her breasts. The holes allowed her plump, burgundy nipples to poke through.

Tension zipped through him. He found himself licking his lips as he remembered the plump, hot feel of her nipples in his mouth yesterday. He'd just about come undone then at the sound of her sexy whimpers.

Her sparkling blue eyes flashed at him with mischief and lust. "What can I do for you? Would you like me to bring you relief?"

She fiddled with the button on the remote control and the erotic vibrations stopped, allowing him a breath of relief.

"Enough, Ashley."

"Uh-uh. I want you to experience first-hand that payback is a bitch, lover."

"Ashley, if I don't make my appointment..."

Her soft fingertips brushed against his lips stopping him cold.

"Quiet, lover. You talk too much."

"Ash—"

Her soft mouth slid across his lips, cutting off his words and short-circuiting all coherent thoughts.

Jesus! She tasted sinfully good. Warm and sweet. Full of restrained, savage desire. He touched her bottom lip with his tongue, enjoying the lush silkiness he found there. The feel of her mouth sliding over his made him think crazy thoughts. Made him think stupid things like how in the hell could he ever walk away from this exquisite jewel?

Breaking the kiss, she sat down on his lap, her legs warm against his thighs, her wet pussy gyrating against the length of his caged cock. She threw her head back in a wanton gesture, her luscious mouth open in a gasp of delight. Her black tangled hair swept all around her and brushed erotically against his chest and shoulders.

God! She looked so damn good.

Revenge, his brain tried to remind him.

Later. Much later.

He brought his cuffed hands up and over her head and down her back, bringing her against him. She splayed her hot hands against his chest, her fingers digging into his chest hairs. He shuddered with need. The remote control fell upon the bed. The feel of her sharp nails burrowing into his flesh made him groan.

To his surprise, she didn't fight to get away from him as he'd expected her to. This was too damn easy. Her body was on fire just like his. He wanted her so bad he could barely breathe. He wanted her…God, did he want her!

But not like this. Not with her in charge. It wasn't part of the plan. He'd only end up getting hurt instead of her. From somewhere deep in his body he barely gathered up the resistance he needed against her.

"Isn't this an interesting twist, Starry Eyes? Should have left when you had the chance," he whispered as calmly and coolly as he could manage.

Fear sparked her eyes at his words.

He didn't care. Let her be scared. She should be.

Especially with the rock-hard erection he had for her.

"Why didn't you leave, Starry Eyes?"

"Go to hell, Outlaw."

The fear flashing in her eyes was still there but something else was there also. Lust. Hunger. A need to be fucked again.

Oh yeah, she definitely wanted to get fucked again. Her gyrating hips proved it.

"I assume you stayed so you could spend more quality time with me."

She didn't need to answer. The sweet way her pussy continued to grind against his restrained cock and the harsh way she breathed, all fast and hard, and her cheeks all flushed pink spoke the truth. She'd stayed because she wanted more.

His job would be done here. Right now. He could deny her more pleasure.

But he wanted more too. Wanted to take her ruthlessly. Take her gently.

First though, he needed to kiss her again.

She knew his intention by the way her blue eyes suddenly flashed with fire. Her nails dug harder into his chest. Whether in refusal or anticipation he couldn't be sure. But he needed to taste her again. Needed it like he needed to breathe. Needed to unleash his own savage desire into her.

"I want to make love to you, Ashley," he whispered harshly against her trembling lips. "Fuck you for old times' sake."

She moaned, ripped free from his kiss. He figured she'd go for his cock and free him.

He figured wrong.

A blade of pain lashed through his cock, shocking him, allowing her to slip free.

Her lips were swollen with passion and he thought he spied hurt flashing in her eyes. Then she quickly looked away and that's when he saw she once again held the control box in her hand, the finger moving over the button and thankfully easing off on the pain, allowing him to feel red-hot anger roar through him.

Bitch! She'd zapped him with that freaking machine.

"Sorry to disappoint, lover," she panted. "I've got something I have to do. I'll see you later."

She grabbed a matching blue wrap and draped it over her shoulders. Just before she walked out the door, Colter grimaced as the cock cage began its slow dance of seduction around his cock once again.

* * * * *

At the front door of Colter's cabin Ashley allowed the tears of hurt to finally burst free. Instead of escaping Colter, she'd decided to turn the tables on him. Give him a taste of his own medicine, so to speak. While he'd slept, she'd carefully outfitted him with the slave gear then she'd showered and prettied herself up for him.

God! She couldn't believe she'd actually done that. Couldn't believe she'd curled her hair, put on the sexy makeup and the seductive blue dress she'd planned on wearing to the bidding for the cure. But the wonderful way he'd made love to her had made her want to do it again.

When she'd walked into the bedroom and found him awake and watching her, he'd looked so sexy with the heavy bad-boy stubble shadowing his face and that slave collar making him all hers, she'd just about come on the spot. When she'd heard his command to come to him, something inside her had just melted and she'd found herself going to him.

All her plans for sexual torture, for payback, vanished the instant their lips had touched. And his comment of fucking her simply because of old times had ripped a painful hole straight through her.

She'd been such a fool to let her guard down. To allow herself, even for a few minutes, to slip back to the old way she'd felt for him. She'd possessed so much passion for him and in the end so much trust. Trust he'd so easily thrown away.

Then and now.

Frowning, she slid the electronic key into the slit. She'd found it in Colter's jacket along with the collar key and had figured it would come in handy. She just hadn't figured it would come in handy so soon.

The beep acknowledging acceptance of the key ripped through the air and Ashley looked around to make sure no one was there before quickly moving inside and locking the door behind her.

The place even smelled of him. A raw mix of his favorite aftershave and his own masculine scent she'd loved so much. His scent brought up a swell of emotions, the most prevalent being anger.

The son of a bitch! Why did he have to come back into her life now of all times? Why had she allowed him to make love to her? Sure it had been part of the plan to have him fall asleep afterward, but why had she enjoyed it so much? Her attraction to him was so damn hard to ignore and really complicated an already very complicated situation.

Taking a deep breath, she scanned the room. It was decorated a little differently than hers. It had a masculine edge. The walls were beige. Dark brown wooden beams laced the ceiling and a large beige sofa sat against one wall. The traditional sex-toy cabinet was nearby, and a gorgeous stone fireplace made of gray boulders and a knotty pine hearth spruced up the cozy room. She noted the tastefully decorated pictures hanging on the walls. Pictures of several men doing naughty things to a woman. If she didn't know any better, she'd think the woman looked like that sex slave Cheri had tried to pawn off on Colter when she'd first spotted him in the foyer.

God! When she'd seen him standing there decked out in a form-fitting expensive suit, his hair shorter than she remembered, his face clean-shaven and eyeing that exquisite slave as though he wouldn't mind having a piece of her, she'd felt a blade of red-hot anger shoot through her.

Her bodyguard had motioned for her to leave, to not allow herself to be seen by Colter, but she'd been transfixed by the man she'd fallen in love with. The man she'd never thought she'd actually see again despite her deep-seated hopes that one day he would come and rescue her from the general.

But he never had.

She'd gathered her courage, presented herself and the forged paper to both Cheri and Colter, hoping to high heaven that if Cheri didn't buy her story of the general sending her to bid on the cure, then maybe, just maybe, Colter would rescue her this time.

It had been an irrational thought in a dangerous situation. She knew that now. Colter was only interested in her for sex. Nothing more. Nothing less. His comment about fucking her for old times' sake had only verified it.

Thankfully, Cheri had bought her fake story and the fear had subsided slightly, allowing those old feelings for Colter to swarm in all around her. Well okay, so maybe it hadn't been because she'd been overdue for her medication that she'd responded to him so erotically in the foyer upon her arrival, but she certainly had responded, and she hadn't missed the appreciation brewing in his eyes when he'd seen her either.

She quickly found the bedroom and spied an open suitcase on the bed. Come to think of it, he'd barely used his cabin. He'd come so quickly to her room to capture her. To make her his sex slave.

Ashley blew out a tense breath as she began to search through the case. She'd come to his cabin looking for answers as to why he was there undercover. Of course, she could simply ask him, but she doubted he would tell her the truth.

She needed to know who he was working for. Who was her competition? What enemy did she have to bid against for that cure of the X-virus C? If she could find something, anything, she could use the tidbit to disarm him.

She searched quickly, efficiently, admiring the expensive suits he hadn't even unpacked. Irritation grabbed her when she found nothing important…that is until she found the antique comb he'd given her when they'd been together in Iraq.

Fresh bitter tears bubbled and a hysterical giggle burst past her lips as she remembered how wonderful she'd felt when he'd presented it to her in Iraq.

It had belonged to his mother, he'd told her. After she'd died from the X-virus, it was all he'd kept for himself as a keepsake. He'd admitted he hadn't been able to come to grips that he might never have a mate in his lifetime, but his mother's delicate, antique brass comb with the faux cameo in the middle and the colorful floral motif surrounded by a spattering of white rhinestones gave him hope he would one day find his one true love.

It was the same hair comb she'd left behind at the general's palace in Iraq when she'd found the note from Colter on her pillow. She hadn't wanted it anymore. Hadn't wanted the reminder of what would have been. Only moments after finding that note, she'd been evacuated from the general's castle due to terrorist threats.

Obviously, Colter had come back for it sometime, why else would he have it?

The sound of the front door opening made Ashley freeze.

Shit! Had Colter escaped? Had he come back here?

Her heart hammered against her chest as she expected him to enter the bedroom and catch her. He didn't.

Whoever was out there wasn't coming into the room. Was it a Pleasure Palace employee coming to clean up?

Ashley eyed the nearby window. She could go out that way. Whoever was inside would never even know she'd been there.

She tensed when she heard a familiar male voice.

It couldn't be!

Tiptoeing closer to the door, she peeked out the open doorway. He was sitting in a corner chair peering out a front window. Although most of his features were hidden in shadows, Ashley instantly knew the identity of the man.

Blade.

He was the man who'd pleasured her during the ménage à trois with Colter. But why was he here? Had Colter done what he'd threatened to do? Had he called Blade to come and get her?

She wouldn't go with him. He couldn't make her. Damned if she'd let Colter get away with controlling her. She'd set that son of a bitch straight. The arrogant bastard. How dare he seduce her anyway? How dare he make her fall in love with him again.

No! No! No! She wasn't in love with Colter! She was in lust. That's all. Now was not the time to be freaking-out about it either.

"No, he hasn't shown yet," Blade was saying. She detected worry in his voice, a frown to his full lips. Gorgeous lips that had teased her body with sensual kisses while he and Colter had made love to her.

She blew out a slow breath as the memories tried to splash around her.

Two sets of hot lips sucking on her nipples. Four male hands roving her body, touching her, scratching her.

The fullness of their cocks deep inside her. The burn of pleasure-pain. The scent of sex. Skin slapping against skin.

Oh, God! Stop thinking this way!

Focus. She needed to focus.

"I'll give him another hour. He's probably got some sex slave trussed up and enjoying himself way too much to pay attention to his work. If I don't hear from him by then, I'll give you the call for backup. Pleasure Palace won't know what hit them."

No! He couldn't call for backup! He couldn't screw the conference!

"I know that would scrap the plan and Cheri will go back into hiding, but I won't screw him over again."

Again?

"No, I haven't told him about the other matter yet. The time isn't right."

What other matter?

Blade emitted a heavy sigh, the frustrated sound splashing through the silence of the room and wrapping around her own neck, making it hard for her to breathe. From this conversation and the worried frown on his face, Blade truly cared about his friend. It made Ashley feel just a bit better knowing this man had Colter's back in times of crisis.

"If that happens, we'll just have to find the cure another way. Like I said...Bev? You there? Shit! The bitch hung up on me. Too fucking bad. If she doesn't like what's going down, that's her fucking problem," he mumbled angrily.

Ashley heard the beep of the cell phone being disconnected and the sound of the chair creaking as he shifted his weight and pocketed the cell.

Now what? She was stuck. If she so much as moved, he'd see or hear her. Should she chance it? Or wait?

One hour. Blade's words rang through her mind. She had an hour to release Colter Outlaw or all her plans were shot. That is, if she were able to get out of there without Blade hearing her. But she had to chance it. Had to get back to the cabin and free her delicious sex slave before Blade called in the troops.

She was about to back away and head toward the window when the shrill sound of Blade's cell phone split the air, making her literally jump. Her frazzled nerves had her on the edge of screaming but she stopped herself cold.

No time to be skittish. Blade being busy with the caller was the chance she needed to get out of there.

Slowly she turned and hesitated by the open suitcase. The pretty comb gleamed up at her. Should she take it?

No! She shouldn't take it. It wasn't hers anymore. Despite her resistance, she found herself scooping up the comb and pocketing it.

She would keep it. As a reminder of what they should have had.

Heading for the window, she allowed her anger to spill free. Damn Colter Outlaw! When she got back to the cabin she needed to do some mighty fast thinking on whether she had to release him, and maybe some mighty fast talking too if she were to get him onto her side…even if it meant revealing the truth to him of why she was really there.

* * * * *

The instant Ashley entered the bedroom she spied Colter lying gloriously naked on the bed, his big cock half erect and apparently fast asleep.

Shit! She'd have to wake him. Tell him everything.

Anxiously biting her lower lip, she sat down on the bed right beside him. Before she knew what was happening he sat up and she felt Colter's cuffed hands slide up underneath her top and awkwardly cup her breasts.

She tried to pull away, truly she did, but his fingers had already found her hypersensitive nipples. Had already started tweaking and massaging, making her knees melt.

"Miss me, Starry Eyes?" The knowing humor in his voice pissed her off.

"Go to hell," she whispered, yet eagerly accepted the lock of his lips as his mouth slid over hers like a brand.

His kiss was greedy, leaving no doubt he wanted to make love to her again.

"We…can't," she said when he broke the breathtaking kiss and she tried to regain a small semblance of her senses. She had an hour. Maybe less. She should be talking to him.

Spilling her guts about why she was there. About why he needed to get back to his cabin and tell Blade he was fine.

"Sure we can." His head lowered and he kissed her nipple. Kissed and nibbled and tongued her until she wanted to scream.

Jesus. He was good with his mouth. But…

"Blade…your appointment…he's looking for you…"

He kissed a line of fire down her belly. The intimate feel of his lips sailing over her flesh just about drove her mad with desire.

"I called him," he whispered between kisses. "You forgot to take my cell phone with you. It was in my pants pocket. I told him I was…tied up for a while."

He'd used the phone and hadn't called for help? He trusted her that much? Trusted her to let him go? She found herself melting. Her earlier sadness vanishing, she found herself suddenly accepting the warm feelings of love she'd always harbored toward him.

His lips teased her belly. His moist tongue dipped into her bellybutton. His mouth tugged at her belly ring.

God. That felt so unbelievably delicious.

"I can see you still have your delicious belly ring, and I gather you like what I do to your innie?"

"It's my other innie that needs your immediate attention, Doctor."

"A quick satisfaction can be easily arranged."

He stood quickly. His eyes flashed heavily with lust. His cuffed hand dug the remote control from the tiny pocket of her jacket.

"Which button releases the cock cage?"

"This one."

She pressed the appropriate button and they both looked down to watch the metal cage click open. Urgency ripped through her at the sight of his engorged penis.

She moved quickly, removing his swollen flesh from the contraption, curling her fingers around the heated arousal.

He gasped. Swore softly. "The cuffs, the key." His breath came harsh and fast.

She hesitated only a moment. Even if she un-cuffed him, he couldn't go anywhere anyway. He still wore the collar.

She slid the key from between her breasts where she'd placed it.

He grinned. "Nice hiding place."

The instant the cuffs were off his wrists he grabbed her. She let out a yelp of surprise as he roughly turned her around and pushed her breasts and belly up against a nearby wall.

He grabbed her hands and pulled them to her sides.

"Keep them there," he ordered harshly.

The need to follow his order swirled around her and she did as he asked.

His force didn't surprise her. She'd been anticipating some sort of controlled aggression, especially at the way she'd left the vibrating cock cage running at low speed when she'd gone to his cabin. It had kept him on edge.

His hot fingers branded her skin as he lifted her short skirt.

She gasped as he entered her vagina. She'd expected him to penetrate fast. He didn't. He slid into her wet slit slowly, the hot sensation entering her like a silk-encased piece of hard metal. Her cunt muscles clambered around his thickness. Curved around his every ridge, his engorged thickness filling her so solidly she swore he was bigger now than he'd ever been.

He stayed there inside her, his cock impaling her, his hips pressing her into the wall. Her breasts were squished, her belly cool. Her back and ass, however, were so hot as his hard muscles splayed around her feminine curves. For a split second she imagined herself squeezed between Colter and

Blade once again, sandwiched between two tense soldier doctors, their desperate cocks plunging in and out of her in rapid rhythm.

She liked that memory. Wouldn't mind trying a ménage again. But she liked this better. One-on-one intimacy with the man she loved.

"Oh yes," she hissed as his fingers greedily he worked their magic. He played with her labia, pulled and pinched her swollen clit until pleasure burned through her.

She closed her eyes against the sensations beginning to peak. He began a fast, desperate thrust. Taking her hard and fast. Just the way she liked it.

His cock throbbed as it plunged in and out of her. The scent of their sex drifted to her nostrils. His ragged breath felt hot against the back of her neck. The slap of flesh against flesh as his powerful hips smacked into her ass over and over again sailed through the air.

"You're mine, Starry Eyes. Don't ever forget that," he hissed into her ear.

He flexed his hips harder and pushed his cock into her deeper than he'd ever been and she allowed the mind-shattering climax to shower her senses.

Chapter Seven

Ashley turned away from the entertainment set the general had made her watch.

Colter's and Blade's groans of arousal were still pounding through her mind and, despite her not wanting it to happen, her pussy was creaming wickedly as she remembered watching the video of both men slamming their cocks into her.

The general's dark chuckle from the couch on the other side of the room made red-hot anger push away her arousal.

"You videotaped us. Why?"

"Quite the entertainment, don't you think? I can get a lot of money selling that video on the Internet these days. Especially with so few women left alive. I could make millions with my little porn star. There's over forty-eight hours of it. No wonder you looked so wiped out every morning at breakfast."

Ashley bit back a retort that surely would have had her whipped. Instead, she tried like hell to keep her voice from shaking. She had to control herself, especially now that she was pregnant.

"I wanted you pregnant, Ashley. I knew even before you knew, that you would be. I so enjoyed watching you squirm for months, loved the fear glowing in your eyes of how you thought I would react at the news that my pleasure slave was pregnant by the man who saved my life."

Sadistic bastard.

"And I knew that my young soldier savior wouldn't be able to resist you if I left you two alone. It was simple to make the condoms in the mansion disappear. Very easy to replace your birth control with something ineffective."

Bastard! She felt sick. Used.

She'd been set up!

"Aren't you going to ask why I wanted you pregnant, my little pleasure slave?"

"I'm sure you'll tell me."

He chuckled and headed for the nearby bar.

"As punishment for getting pregnant by another man's seed I should give you to your stepbrother and his wife. The stepbrother whom you rejected when he wanted you. You should have agreed to sleep with him, to be his sex slave. He's not as bad a sadist as I am."

Asshole!

"Did you know his wife and he enjoy ménages with pregnant women…enjoy watching the horror shining in the woman's eyes when she knows she shouldn't orgasm, for if she does…bye-bye baby and maybe even her. It's a kind of Russian Roulette thing for them…quite addictive."

Ashley's legs threatened to give out at his softly spoken words. She knew all about Cheri and Blakely's sick, twisted fetishes and she found defiant words tumbling out of her mouth despite her fear of him. "You are a sick bastard."

"You seem to have forgotten your place, my sweet Ashley. I own you. I bought you from the government before they could send you to service the general soldiers. Aren't you lucky I purchased you? You should be grateful to me. Over the past year, you should have been on your knees, begging me to suck my cock in appreciation for what I've done for you. But all you've been doing is giving me grief every time I so much as fuck you."

He poured a tall glass of sherry, took a sip, smacked his lips and grinned smugly at her.

"According to Iraqi law, I can do anything that I want with you. You are merely property here. And if the rumored Claiming Law comes into effect, then when we return to the States, we'll be required to have a minimum four husbands for you and you'll be property there as well."

Oh, God! No!

To her shock his cold gray eyes twinkled and his nostrils flared wickedly. Instinctively she knew he could smell her fear. It always turned him on. He'd want to have sex with her. She'd be safe though. She'd never orgasmed with him. Had always faked it.

"Don't worry, my sweet slave. I have decided I don't want to lose you or the love child."

What? Was she hearing right? She forced the blade of relief from taking hold of her. Forced herself to remain cautious. To make sure he was serious and not just toying with her as he usually did.

"Blakely and his wife have a lab full of pregnant women to play with. They can amuse themselves with them. I can amuse myself with you after the baby arrives. You do know you will be punished for your behavior with the gyno. And for being aroused at the way he touched you. Do you know how embarrassed I was when you refused to name me as the father of your child? If he says anything, I could be the laughingstock of Iraq by not keeping a tight leash on my pleasure slave."

"I'm sorry," she lied. She'd never be sorry for something out of her control. It hadn't been her fault the gynecologist had purposely aroused her. The general had probably instructed him to do it just so he could watch her squirm.

"Oh you will be sorry."

A shiver or dread rippled through Ashley. The general's punishments were cruel. And he never left behind any scars.

"The next few months are going to be very pleasant for you, Ashley. Pure, sheer pleasure, but when that love baby pops out of you, life for you will become a living hell. Now return to your room and prepare yourself for me."

Ashley hesitated.

"You heard me, Ashley. Prepare yourself for me. Don't worry about pretending to orgasm…because the baby will know if you really do."

His laughter raged inside her head as she headed out of the room to do his bidding.

Ashley awoke in a cold sweat, the fear of the dream following her into the real world.

Hell.

She'd gone through it.

Whippings. Waxings. Bondage. Eventually torture.

She'd survived it. Survived everything the general had done to her. In the end, she'd paid him back, hadn't she? The bastard had pushed too far and he'd gotten his just reward.

Now she was free. At least she'd thought she'd been free until Colter had come back into her life and recaptured her heart.

She allowed herself the luxury of a heavy sigh and peered around the cabin, staring at the spot where Colter had taken her up against the wall.

That's how it had been between them in Iraq. Hurried fucks in the hallway by day and by night…long, tender lovemaking sessions.

Sessions the general had known about. Had planned. Had videotaped.

Bastard.

A silvery thread of moon glow splintered through the drawn blinds. The room was dark. Full of gentle shadows. Shadows that should soothe her, reassure her that she was safe there with Colter.

A quick glance at the nearby table revealed they'd been asleep for several hours. She let out a heavy, frustrated sigh. She simply had to stop playing these sexual games with Colter or she would never get that cure.

Beside her he stirred, felt his hand reach out and touch her bare arm.

"You all right?"

"Hmm. Just a dream."

She found herself cuddling against him, intertwining her fingers with his and holding on tight.

"You sure?" He blinked at her, a cute little furrow of concern wrinkled his forehead.

She was about to say she always felt fine when she was with him when she suddenly realized he wasn't wearing the collar…she was!

"Oh, God! I can't believe you've done this to me again!" She ripped herself from his embrace and tried to get up, but he grabbed her around the waist pulling her right back to his side again.

"Now don't get mad, Starry Eyes. The sight of you in the collar turns me on." He reached out and cupped one of her breasts, holding her swollen flesh in his palm as he leaned his head close to her mouth, his warm breath washing over her lips. "And it gives me the opportunity to show you how much I enjoy being with you."

"That's bullshit! You just don't trust me." She heard the hurt in her voice and couldn't believe she was allowing him to see her being so damn vulnerable.

"It has nothing to do with not trusting you—"

He cut himself off by greeting her to a scorching kiss. She felt his cock harden against her leg. Felt her pussy cream.

Sweet mercy. The man and his ferocious sexual appetite were going to be the death of her yet.

She broke the kiss and ignored his groan of disappointment.

"Stop it." She'd meant it as a command, but it came out in a hell of a husky whisper. "Blade's probably still waiting for you in your cabin."

Her warning didn't move him the least bit.

"How do you know he's in my cabin?"

"I was there. I heard him talking to someone named Bev on his cell."

He tensed, his eyes narrowing into alert mode.

Finally!

"Did he see you?"

"No, but he's suspicious. He thinks you have some gorgeous sex slave as a hostage."

"Wouldn't want him to think that now, would we? He might want to join us."

The soft way he said it made her think it would be something he'd be interested in trying again.

"What if he decides to call in backup?"

"Because I left the cell on and he hasn't called me. That is, unless I didn't hear it ringing when you so easily fell into my arms."

"Easily, my ass."

He chuckled in answer. "Did you find what you were looking for in my cabin…besides Blade, that is?"

"Wouldn't you like to know?"

"Actually not right now. I have better things on my mind."

He smiled and twirled a loose strand of her hair around his finger. Their gazes locked. There was no mistaking the sexual awareness in his eyes. The fast way he breathed or the awesome way his pupils dilated with hunger as he looked at her.

"Again?"

He nodded and clasped a leg over her thigh—the heat of his engorged cock scorched her flesh. She didn't like the way he made her weak in the knees at his simplest touch. The way he made her control melt and slip away. And she found herself wanting to kick herself for allowing his luscious lips to settle over hers again in the gentlest of ways.

But she'd chastise herself for being a fool later.

Much later.

Right now, she had better things to do with her time.

* * * * *

"I've sold your daughter to Cheri Blakely for her five sons."

Ashley could do nothing but blink and allow the shock to sear through her at what the general had just said. She couldn't believe what she was hearing. She had to be in some twisted nightmare!

"She said she'd enroll her in a private school for girls. They would teach her how to be submissive to her husbands."

He had to be kidding her. He just had to be playing another one of his sadistic jokes, but the way his cold eyes twinkled, she knew he was telling the truth.

"God! She's only a baby!" Her mind was screaming but her voice was barely a whisper.

"Babies grow up fast. She's four years old. She needs to be trained. She's valuable, Ashley. Extremely valuable. She's just not valuable to me. And you know I don't keep things I cannot use."

His words slapped against the hysteria claiming her senses. Her daughter was a thing? She was not valuable to him?

Although she hadn't been his child, the general had doted on her from the day she'd been born. Had been a most impressive father figure. Had given her everything a little girl would want, to the point where he'd spoiled her rotten. She'd thought her daughter was safe with the general. And now he was telling her Colette wasn't valuable to him?

"Of course, her youngest boy isn't much older than Colette and I'm sure Cheri will wait until Colette is of breeding age before she allows the Claiming."

"Oh, my God! You're insane!"

"And you're overstepping your boundaries, Ashley. Calm down or I'll have you punished. I know how you love to be punished."

The general smiled smugly at her as he lifted his scotch glass and sipped peacefully. Too peacefully. He acted as if he didn't have a care in the world. As if he didn't give two shits that her world was crashing in on her.

Hysteria nudged its way back into her mind. She clamped down on the urge to just scream and scream.

"I figure it's best to get rid of her now. Before she reaches her menses and contracts the X-virus. Cheri is willing to take a chance she won't die, and the money I'll get for her is hardly worth laughing at. I can put it to good use."

She could barely hear him above the roar in her head. She had to get away. Had to grab her daughter and escape. Escape from this madhouse. Escape from the general. She should have done it the instant she'd found out she was pregnant.

"At least let me say goodbye to her."

"Not possible. I know you would do something stupid if I let you see her. You will remain locked in your room until I can arrange for her to be shipped off to Cheri. Truly, Ashley, I don't know why you're so upset. She wasn't yours to begin with."

"I'm her mother!"

"I'm her owner. And I'm your owner. Seems as if you totally have forgotten that fact. I've been too lax with you over the years, Ashley. I'd wanted Colette to be brought up with a mother's nurturing touch so she'd be sweet and happy for her new owners. Your usefulness for her is over. It's time I had you bred again."

Breed? Sweet Jesus!

"I've already got a doctor lined up for the procedure. He'll be coming in the morning to start administering sperm washes containing only girls. With any luck, you'll be pregnant with another girl by the end of the week and I'll be rich when I sell her. Do you know the prices girls are bringing in? Men and their Claimed wives are willing to take huge chances, Ashley. They are having bidding wars for girls who are still too young to have a man's cock inside her. They purchase girls for their sons. They are willing to chance that their purchase won't get the virus. And when she does get it, they hope she'll live through it so they can become wives for their sons. These are desperate times. Lots of money to be made by breeding women and selling the girls to the highest bidder."

He grinned wickedly and her stomach hollowed out as if he'd just sucker punched her.

The general stood and chuckled. It was an arrogant sound. A sound that sliced her heart in two.

He held out his empty scotch glass to her. "Refill this, hon."

She could barely hear what he was saying as she obediently accepted the scotch glass and stumbled toward the bar. Tears burned her eyes. Tears that she knew when she released them wouldn't stop.

"You know, I don't know why I didn't think of this earlier. The price that Colette brings me will give me the opportunity to go after some more valuable art for my collection. Or maybe I can even bid on that X-virus cure Cheri Blakely has? What do you think? Art? Or the cure? Both would bring millions on the black market."

Ashley could hardly stand as she poured the scotch for him. Could barely contain her anger, could barely hold herself together as anguish threatened to rip her apart.

He was going to sell her daughter as if she were some item he owned.

"I won't let you do it," she muttered beneath her breath. "No way in hell."

"What did you say, hon?"

He was behind her now. She could feel the hard length of his cock pressing against her ass. Could feel his hands slide against her waist.

Ashley couldn't stop herself from stiffening.

"I've got some men coming over tonight. Can you feel how hard I am for them?"

She closed her eyes and fought hard to hold herself together. He'd just sold her daughter and all he could think about was having sex with his men?

"Get your hands off me."

The sharp, shocked inhalation of his breath made her realize she'd overstepped her bounds. She'd never pulled away from him before. Had always allowed him to touch her the very few times he'd been halfway affectionate to her. That's how starved she'd been for human affection.

This time he'd gone too far.

The rage came out of nowhere. Red-hot fury at what he wanted to do to her daughter.

His hands were still on her body. She wanted them off.

Now!

"I said get your hands off me!" Without thinking she pushed her body against him, so hard that they both stumbled backward…they both hit the carpet hard. She heard a grunt from him and then nothing.

When she managed to get her bearings she noticed the general had sprawled against the fireplace hearth. Noticed the odd angle of his neck. The unseeing stare of his eyes…

Realized now was her chance to grab Colette and escape.

A sharp pain to her cheek brought her out of the nightmare and she awoke to find hot tears streaming over her cheeks and drenched in a cold sweat. Her heart beat frantically against her chest and bitter bile was slipping up her throat. She quickly swallowed it, forbidding herself to be sick.

"Starry Eyes, are you okay?"

She felt Colter's warm breath whisper against the burning heat of what must have been a slap to her face. A slap that had thankfully broken her from the terror, the guilt.

She opened her eyes to find him staring down at her with furious concern. His face seemed too pale in the moonlight, his breaths too fast and too hard. The sight of him, the thought of him seeming so worried for her uncoiled some of the tension she'd accumulated from the nightmare.

"I'm sorry. I didn't want to slap you but you just wouldn't wake up. You were crying…are you okay?"

Such worry in his voice, such concern. For a fleeting moment she felt the old safety, the love and tenderness he'd once shown her so openly. She reached up a shaky hand to run her fingers over his sexy beard bristles. His face felt warm beneath her fingertips. Right then she just needed to touch him, to know he really was there and that she'd really finally escaped the general.

"It was just a dream. I'm fine," she whispered, trying hard to throw him a reassuring smile but it felt watery, false. A sudden chill slapped against her damp flesh and she drew her hand away, tugging the sheet around her nakedness, trying hard not to melt against his warm, safe body. He would be only a false security blanket. It was better she try to stay strong and focused, and not let the memory ruin what confidence she'd managed to gain over the past few days.

"Jesus Christ! You scared the shit out of me," he whispered hoarsely, and sank down onto the bed beside her. He closed his eyes and his chest rose and fell as he inhaled deep, slow breaths as if trying to calm himself.

For a few moments she thought he'd gone back to sleep but then he whispered softly, "What was the nightmare about?"

When she didn't answer, his weight shifted the mattress and he turned to face her. Confusion blazed in his eyes and suddenly she wanted to cry again.

"What's bothering you? What was it about? Tell me, Starry Eyes."

That familiar need to submit to his command seemed to swoop in over her again. God, was it already time to take her medication? She did a mental check and calculated that no, she had lots of time. Odd that her virus medication didn't seem to work around Colter very well.

"I…the general. It was about the general," she said in a surprisingly even voice.

Anger seemed to twist through his features at her admission. She sensed him pulling away, not physically but emotionally.

"What about him?" he asked tightly.

She was about to tell him everything when a sharp knock at the cabin door reverberated through the room.

The knock on the door frightened Ashley. Understandable since she'd just had a nightmare, but there was something she'd been about to tell him. Instincts told him it was something big.

"What should we do?" she breathed. The split second of terror in her gaze, the same look he'd seen when she'd first opened her eyes made nausea spill through his senses. Something horrible was bothering her and now it was coming out in her dreams. He'd have to get down to the bottom of it. Now was not the time. She was too edgy. Too upset for it to have been merely a dream as she'd Claimed.

"Here's your chance to scream and tell them I've been having my way with you for hours and hours against your will," he chuckled, trying to lighten her dark mood.

Her eyes widened with surprise and thankfully her shoulders slumped slightly as more of the tension left her.

"You won't try to stop me?"

"Only if you want me to."

The knock came again, more insistent this time. Why the hell didn't they just leave the food outside the door as he'd instructed them to do?

"How would you stop me?" her eyes twinkled. Thankfully her sense of humor was coming back.

"Hmm, perhaps with a ball and gag?"

She giggled. "We haven't tried that angle yet, have we?"

"I much prefer stopping you by a kiss or stuffing my cock into your mouth."

"I prefer those methods myself," she whispered, and finally she melted against him. Her hand slid around his shaft and she squeezed gently. Oh man, that felt good.

"Hello! I'm sorry to interrupt," came a man's curt voice from the other side of the door.

"What is it?" she called out then nipped playfully at his bottom lip with her sharp teeth.

There was a slight hesitation and the man's next words froze Colter's blood.

"I have a message from Cheri Blakely."

Oh shit! A hell of a way to rain on their parade. Before Ashley could respond, he slipped a hand over her mouth.

His heart clenched as betrayal splashed through her face. To his surprise she didn't so much as struggle.

"There's a meeting in one hour. Dungeon room 1. Will you be attending?" the attendant asked.

Ashley tensed against him.

"I don't want you near that bitch," he breathed quietly. He was a damned fool for keeping her there with him. Now she was in danger once again. "But I have no other choice. We have to keep up appearances until I can get you out of here. Tell him you'll be there. Is that clear?"

Anger sparked her eyes but she nodded. Slowly he slid his hand ever so slightly off her mouth, not quite trusting that she wouldn't scream.

"Yes, I'll be there," she called out.

Before she had a chance to say anything else, he slid his hand over her mouth again.

"Very well. I will let her know." The sound of his footsteps faded quickly away.

When Colter lifted his hand from her hot little mouth, he was instantly sorry he'd done what he had by covering her mouth.

"Damn you! I thought you trusted me by now. I should have screamed bloody murder. I should have told him you aren't who you said you are. I should have—"

He pressed his lips firmly against hers, cutting her off mid sentence. A split second later he felt the tension ease from her succulent body, felt her respond with an eager passion that equaled his own.

Spirals of lust circled his cock as her grip hardened. Although he knew she was pissed off at him, her touch built the familiar sexual tension, urging him to want to make love to her yet again.

But now was not the time.

It was hard to break the kiss, but they only had an hour before the meeting. There were things he needed to do to prepare her, to control her.

Naughty things she just might not like…at first.

* * * * *

Aside from Cheri, Ashley was the only woman there. Lusty grins and harsh frowns from the handful of male doctors greeted her as she walked into the conference room.

Colter followed closely, his freshly soaped body and his unique male scent titillating her senses, making her crave him, making her horny.

He was a dangerous son of a bitch, that's for sure. Covering all the angles of her possibly breaking his cover.

He'd even concealed an earphone in her ear so he could whisper instructions to her.

"Looks like we're the last ones." His whisper dripped with tension as they stepped into the conference room, but she didn't care. She was still pissed off at him for not trusting her. Angrier still when he'd outfitted her with clit clamps, nipple clamps, placed a concealed harness around her waist that firmly held a large vibrating butt plug in her ass. He'd also inserted a fleshlike, succulent strap-on dildo inside her vagina. A dildo, he'd warned, that would inflate and vibrate at his command if she so much as acted rebellious. With the touch of a button from a small, black remote-control box she'd seen him slip into his black jacket pocket, he now controlled her.

Or so he thought.

She hadn't even bothered to wear panties, because by the time he'd finished with the honors, her pussy had been creaming magnificently.

"Remember, Starry Eyes, you behave yourself or you will be punished right here in front of all these horny doctors."

"Go to hell, you son of a bitch," she muttered quietly, and tried to ignore the lusty looks of the doctors who watched her every move as she strolled into the room.

Colter's amused chuckle in her ear reminded her of the time he'd figged her ass with the ginger root. The memories made her cream harder.

He'd even laid out her pale, sky blue dress for her, the sexy one that enhanced the blue in her eyes. The thin velvet material hugged her every curve, gave everyone an awesome view of her cleavage and, of course, if the men looked close enough, they just might see the outline of the clamps clinging to her nipples.

She'd held her breath as he'd picked the combination lock on her suitcase, hoping he wouldn't find the pills that would give away her disease. Thankfully he didn't discover the medication, but he did find her slave jewelry and insisted she wear them.

Colter had taken great pleasure in tormenting her with his heated touches as he'd arranged the necklace around her neck then draped two tantalizing strands of chain, one attached to each of her clamped nipples, before leading them down and threading them through her belly ring. He'd then caressed her abdomen and mons with the jewelry before firmly attaching each strand to each of the pussy-lip clamps he'd placed on her.

Agreeing to his commands had been the only way to get that slave collar off her neck.

Silently she cursed him for the hundredth time as with each step the entire length of the delicate chain tightened and pulled gently. The intoxicating movements sensually chafed her clamped nipples and clamped labia. The erotic friction kept her highly aroused and, to her irritation, kept her mind on craving sex with Colter instead of concentrating on her desire to obtain that cure.

When she sat down, she was momentary thankful as the chains released the pressure on her pussy lips and nipples but she couldn't stop herself from wincing at the pleasure-pain gripping the intimate parts of her body as both the butt plug and the dildo sank even deeper into her hot depths.

"You look absolutely horny," Colter's whisper echoed in her hearing aid as he took a seat beside her. "I can't wait to get you out of here and fuck you all night."

She managed to keep herself from whimpering at the arousal in his voice, but couldn't stop her pussy from creaming warmly at his words.

"Now that all the parties are here, I'd like to give you a brief orientation about the product up for bid." Dr. Cheri Blakely said as she stood at the front of the room flanked by all her seven husbands a.k.a. bodyguards who impassively scanned the faces of the visiting seated bidders, probably making sure no one would make a move against Cheri.

Today the bitch wore a simple white lab coat that reached her knees. The coat was unbuttoned and open, allowing everyone a generous glimpse of a daring dove gray dress. A sheer dress that did nothing to hide the lush curves of the woman's braless breasts along with an unmistakable view of the dark hair covering her mons. She made no effort to conceal herself as she bent to pick up a pen she'd just dropped, giving the men an intimate view of her deep cleavage.

Ashley cast a quick glance at Colter who, as well as all the doctors, had his appreciative eyes riveted to the display.

To Ashley's irritation, a fissure of jealousy shot through her. She was about to elbow him in the ribs but caught herself as his gaze swung on her.

He grinned. A wickedly horny and knowing grin that sent a heated rush through her.

Bastard!

"As you know I've got the cure for one of the versions of the X-virus," Cheri continued. "What you don't know is I've decided when the time comes for bidding there will also be a live sample."

What exactly did she mean by "live sample"?

"The woman is currently being weaned off her drugs so she will be a submissive for the demo. I've called you here to let you know about it and also to tantalize you with a brief glimpse at how we came up with the cure as well as handing out more information for you to peruse until we can have that wonderful live demo. Please remember, I won't be revealing all the angles but only allowing a succinct glimpse. This will prevent those of you who are unsuccessful with the bidding from copycatting the cure unless the winning bidder wishes to share it. As I've already mentioned, the lucky doctor who bids the highest for the cure for their company will get it along with how to make it. Whoever wins the cure will be able to have it mass-produced within weeks. And now without further ado, I will begin my explanation." She paused for dramatic effect before grabbing a green marker off her desk. Turning to the white board behind her, she drew a large circle.

"This is the cure of all X-virus mutations, doctors. Embryonic stem cells."

Ashley's mind whirled in disappointment. That's it? Stem cell research? Governments around the world had given up on the stem cell angle after discovering it produced no long-term benefits and here was Cheri Blakely Claiming it could be done.

"That avenue was exhausted by all the major research companies who had billions of dollars to work with," she found herself blurting out. Everyone's eyes lashed onto her, including Colter's, which sparkled with anger at her outburst.

She found herself backing down at his gaze...but only a little.

"I mean why would Dr. Blakely continue work on stem cells when the world's top researchers hadn't been able to find a cure using that avenue?"

From beside her she noticed Colter slip his hand into the pocket of the jacket he wore. Obviously he was getting ready to keep her in line with that stupid remote-control box.

Well screw him! She had every right to ask questions, especially if she were about to bid millions, if not billions of dollars on a cure that may not even be valid.

"Yes, they wasted billions of dollars. But they also had stringent rules to follow." Cheri smiled smugly. "My husband was a renegade who followed no one's rules. That was how he was able to come up with a cure."

Your husband was an asshole! Ashley wanted to yell. An asshole who killed millions of women because he was a greedy son of a bitch in creating and then selling the X-virus to that fanatical group DogmarX who thought all women should be subservient and submissive to men.

"My late husband was a highly skilled researcher. A skilled craftsman if you will. As you all know, embryonic stem cells can be manipulated to produce replacement organs. Scientists have been able to clone the nerve cells using stem cells successfully and have eradicated certain diseases such as Alzheimer's, Parkinson's and even spinal cord injuries."

"But how was he able to get access to these embryonic stem cells? I mean certainly he wasn't stooping so low as to kidnap women and steal their eggs?"

Oops. Obviously Colter didn't like her question for the dildo inside her pussy inflated slightly, bringing a rush of cream down her channel. She felt the stickiness seep along her inner thighs and cradle her ass. The butt plug in her ass began a slow, erotic vibration, making Ashley bite her lip at the erotic sensations zipping through her ass. This warning from Colter had effectively shut her down.

For now.

"I have my own harem of virus-free women," Cheri said.

An excited mumble escaped the doctors at the table. Everyone knew that virus-free women were very rare and extremely valuable. Just as she had been rare and valuable for the general until she'd contracted the virus. Then he'd set her up with Colter and put another one of his money-making schemes into process without her being the least bit suspicious.

"For those of you who don't know too much about these embryonic stem cells—" Cheri glanced at her several husbands, obviously loving to show off how smart she was "—a cell begins to divide soon after it has been fertilized with a sperm. In a few days that cell is a minute ball of cells called a blastocyst." She began to draw again. This time a larger circle around the original one. "At this phase it is a hollow sphere consisting of an outer layer, in other words a shell. This is called the outer layer." She drew several smaller circles inside the original one as she continued to explain. "Attached to the inside of this shell is a cluster of around thirty cells called the inner cell mass. The outer layer will eventually become the placenta and the inner cell mass eventually becomes the embryo. But before it becomes an embryo, it is at the blastocyst stage. The inner cell mass has not yet developed into any specialized cell. It has no nerve cells, no kidney cells, no heart cells, etcetera... These cells at this stage are called stem cells. These stem cells when harvested and manipulated in different ways will eventually cure any virus known to mankind. The controversy of course lies right at this blastocyst stage. For when these stem cells are removed, the embryo is in effect destroyed."

Ashley's heart wrenched at her words. Thankfully the vibrator and butt plug stopped also. She glanced over at Colter and found him frowning as he watched Cheri's demonstration.

"Before he was murdered, my late husband Dr. Blakely had discovered the cure for one of the mutations. Hence, why I have summoned you all here to bid, so I can use the money to continue my husband's research and cure the rest of the mutations."

And line your own pocket, Ashley mused.

Through the general she'd learned of the hell her stepbrother Blakely and his wife put women through. She knew that because of those suffering women and Blakely's "research" Cheri's husbands had inherited mansions all over the world, many expensive cars and yachts and billions of dollars. She and her husbands were probably getting a wee bit greedy and wanting more money with this so-called cure.

She could barely contain her passion at the thought that if she played her cards right, she would have the cure and would make the drug available to the US government who could quickly develop a vaccine so they could vaccinate the young girls who would eventually be entering puberty and potentially falling ill to the X-virus.

"What is the rejection rate?" Ashley called out. "I mean surely you must have experimented on the innocent girls when they reached puberty? Perhaps even infected them with the X-virus so you could 'cure' them?"

The dildo started to expand inside her pussy again, making her clench her teeth at the erotic sensations gripping her. When she got Colter alone she was going to wring his gorgeous cock…or punish him in some naughty way that would make him think twice before he tried to control her.

"Actually yes. Girls have been used as lab rats. My husband particularly enjoyed that avenue of research. He had a fondness for his lab girls."

The smooth way she said fondness made her tense. Thankfully Colter came to her rescue by easing off on the inflating dildo and vibrating plug and asking the question she wanted to ask.

"You didn't say what the rejection rate is? Injecting foreign tissue into a person can ultimately lead to rejection by the recipient's immune system."

"That's the beauty of this particular cure. My husband has been able to manipulate the cell in such a way so that the cure is not rejected at all."

"Zero percent rejection," Colter mused. "How intriguing. But how do we know you're telling us the truth, Dr. Blakely? How do we know you won't take our money and leave us with a list of bogus tests that you say worked?"

Ashley felt her eyes widen in surprise at his direct question.

"As I mentioned earlier there will be a live demo, Dr. Van Dusen. It will answer all of your questions. Please, I wish for all of you to enjoy Pleasure Palace before I present to you the finale. Rest assured, you will not be disappointed."

"Every day that goes by more women die, Dr. Blakely," Ashley blurted out, barely able to conceal her irritation.

Anger flashed in Cheri's cold eyes. The back-off warning sign was on full tilt.

"Calm it down, Ash." Colter's voice echoed in her earpiece. Beneath the table, he squeezed Ashley's fingers so hard she winced.

"Dr. Blakely," another doctor interjected. "Some scientists have predicted in the past that with all these cures for Parkinson's, Alzheimer's and spinal cord injuries and others, there are still many gaps in the knowledge that can take decades to fill. Some scientists have even said these cures may not even be permanent. How do we know that say…ten or twenty years down the road your cure decides it isn't permanent and reverses itself? I mean, we have no way of knowing any long-term effects. Only a short-term. How long has your cure's success been? A few months? A year perhaps?"

"My husband covered that angle with computer projections. All of which prove this is a permanent cure. These projections are in the packages on the table beside the door. Please pick up a copy as you leave the room. Mull them over and then with the demonstration you can all make the best-informed decision possible. Are there any more questions?"

No one spoke.

"Good. Each of you will have a pleasure slave available to you, compliments of my husbands and myself. Simply put in your request at the front desk and feel free to share them or use them to your heart's content. I have an appointment I must be getting to. Thank you for all your questions."

Ashley couldn't help but sigh in relief. Thank God, the meeting was over. She still wasn't a hundred percent sure if she could trust Cheri. Perhaps after that promised live demo Cheri had mentioned, she'd be more willing to get her hopes up that her daughter's life would be saved.

As the seven husbands and Cheri Blakely straggled out of the room with the doctors, Colter's husky whisper slid into her earpiece.

"Make sure you follow me straight to your cabin, Ashley. And be prepared to take your punishment."

She found herself creaming at his husky words. Found herself eagerly following him from the room like the demure little pleasure slave he'd turned her into.

* * * * *

"Before we left, I asked you not to bring attention to yourself," Colter snapped when they entered her cabin.

"I'm sorry." Whoa! Where had that come from? She'd been prepared to let into him and inform him she was not just going to sit there and let him dictate to her, but she'd felt the rising anger drain away and merely submitted.

Why didn't her meds work properly around him?

He looked surprised at how easily she'd folded.

Dammit! She didn't want him to know she was infected. Didn't want him to feel sorry for her. And that's exactly what he was doing by the soft way he was looking at her, as if she were some helpless female.

"Don't worry, I will protect you from the general."

"I don't need your protection. I am quite capable of taking care of myself."

"We'll see about that. In the meantime..." He moved against her, his hands sliding intimately over the curves of her hips.

Her heart picked up a mad pace as his head lowered.

Scorching heat bruised her lips as his succulent mouth captured hers and he kissed her softly. So gently her head was spinning by the time he finished.

"Time to get undressed," he whispered. His warm breath caressed her cheeks, his long fingers left a silky trail of fire along the length of each of her bare arms. "And when you are finished, come into the bathroom for your punishment for defying my order."

She was about to tell him where to go when he grinned knowingly.

"Not a word, Starry Eyes. Get naked. Take off the slave jewelry and clamps. Leave everything else on. Do it now."

His command slithered over her, making her shiver with anticipation. Making her realize she was very eager to submit. She was definitely due for her medication. If she took the pill now, by the time she met him in the bathroom, it should kick in full force. Despite knowing that fact, she couldn't help but be curious. Medication or not, she still wanted to find out what form of punishment he would have waiting for her.

A moment later the bathroom door closed quietly behind him and he was out of sight.

For a split second she thought about hightailing it, escaping him, running away from the delicious punishment he wanted to dish out to her. And if she did escape, she knew he would only do something drastic like call Blade and have him kidnap her. It was best to do as he asked, which meant getting undressed and going into the bathroom.

But first…

She headed for her suitcase and her medication.

* * * * *

Despite his hatred for Ashley running off on Colter years ago, Blade couldn't stop his cock from engorging as he peeked through the slats of her cabin window. She stood there naked except for a leather belt, which he knew held a dildo up her sweet cunt and a butt plug deep inside her tight, curvy ass.

Colter had done well to keep her under wraps from him and the other S.K.U.L.L. members. For if Blade decided to tell his fellow members who Colter was once again associating with, they'd be a ticked off bunch of folks that's for sure. When S.K.U.L.L. had refused to help out Colter with his personal problem, they'd all been mighty pissed off at Bev. When it had been Blade's turn to do the weekly required sex with her, he'd shown her exactly how mad he'd been. Unfortunately the rougher he'd been with her, the more she'd enjoyed it.

Bitch!

Bev was nothing like Ashley, though.

Where Bev was cold and demanding, Ashley was sweet and so innocent of S.K.U.L.L.

Even now, as he remembered Ashley's soft, velvety flesh beneath his hands, the tips of his fingers burned with remembrance. He remembered kissing the hot contours of her freshly whipped ass cheeks before lubing his cock and entering her tight anal hole in one swift thrust.

God! She'd been unbelievably tight. Hot, tense, exploding like a volcano when both Colter and he had made love to her.

From the first moment he'd seen her, her shimmering baby blue eyes, cheeks flushed red with embarrassment as Colter had presented him to her while she'd been tied to the bed, he'd wanted her. She'd possessed the blackest hair he'd ever seen. Waves of it had spilled over her shoulders, concealing her heavy breasts.

He still remembered the morning Colter had come and gotten him, asking if he would join him at the general's mansion because he'd wanted to give the general's pleasure slave her ultimate fantasy, and then he'd said he wanted to try to persuade her to go with them. Her fantasy had turned out to be a ménage à trois.

At first he'd thought his friend was playing some kind of prank on him, but when he'd been ushered in the back door of the Iraqi mansion, into a luxurious bedroom and seen her splayed out, naked and tied to the bed, her wide, innocent look had just about made him come in his fatigues.

If Colter hadn't asked her to run away with him, he would have taken her for himself. A prettier creature and a better fuck there couldn't have been. No wonder the general, well-known for collecting expensive art and sacred objects, had kept her under lock and key.

Except that weekend things had been lax. Security practically non-existent. But he'd been too eager to participate in the ménage to pay his instincts too much heed.

Hindsight had been twenty-twenty. Obviously the general had used Ashley, whether she'd known it or not, she'd been the decoy to keep Colter and him entertained while the general had gone off to meet his elusive son, the man S.K.U.L.L. had ordered them to assassinate.

After the ménage, Blade had come back to his senses. Had realized the general had left the building, so to speak. They had managed to track down the general through Ashley's bodyguard. That man had a hatred for the general, and Blade had smelled it fast. He was good at that. Reading body signals.

Colter had been keeping an eye on him as well. He'd figured they could trust the bodyguard. When Colter had opened up to him that last night, the man had seemed to know why Colter and Blade were there to kill the son. He never spoke, but he'd led Blade to the restaurant where son and father were laughing. He could have taken the son right then and there, but there had been way too many bodyguards. It would have been suicide to kill him at that point and he hadn't been prepared to die.

He'd called Colter away from Ashley for his backup.

They'd lain in wait along a deserted stretch of alley just outside the building. Instead of assassinating the man, they'd been ambushed themselves. Only the bulletproof vests had saved them from serious injury.

He'd figured it had been the bodyguard who'd thrown them for fools. For allowing him to lead them down the garden path almost to their deaths. But he'd really sensed the hatred in that man for what the general had done to him. Had trusted him.

He'd get his time with the bodyguard S.K.U.L.L. had taken the other day. He'd show him that payback was a bitch.

After they'd managed their narrow escape, they'd headed straight back to the general's place to get Ashley where they'd left her asleep.

It had been deserted.

Except for that note and the prized antique brass comb Colter had given her sitting on the pillow. Even now, remembering the devastation on his face made sickness claw at Blade's belly.

Fuck! Had his friend gone mad? Did he want his heart ripped apart again? Did he want to blow his cover with that conniving bitch?

It was because of her that they'd screwed up that assignment. Instead of assassinating the general's terrorist son, they'd been fucking the general's slave.

Dammit!

He had to do something to make Colter see what a bad mistake he was making with Ashley, because there was no way in hell he was going to watch his friend hit rock-bottom again.

Chapter Eight

Ashley's heart pounded frantically as she stood in front of the closed bathroom door, her hands clenched at her sides.

God! She couldn't wait to find out what Colter had in mind for her. Maybe he would give her another ginger figging? Her ass had burned with arousal when he'd outfitted her with that ginger root. It had been an excruciating pleasure-pain but, now as she thought back, she'd drowned in it. Had loved it, especially afterward when he'd held her so tenderly in his arms.

She swallowed nervously, suddenly unsure if she were doing the right thing by being so subservient to him. But she needed to make him think she was on his side. He'd get the real picture when the bidding war began. By then, it would be too late for him to call in Blade to come and get her.

Boy, it sure was quiet in there. What was he doing?

Should she simply stroll in and accept her punishment? Or should she knock and pretend to fight him when he reached for her?

She opted for the latter and gave the door a firm knock to prove she wasn't the least bit afraid of him. No use showing him she was eager for punishment, either. He might change his mind if he knew she craved whatever he had planned for her.

"Come in, my beautiful pleasure slave."

She blew out a tense breath, thrust her shoulders back in defiance and stuck her breasts out as she'd been trained to do when she'd been sold into slavery.

"Here goes," she whispered to herself, and entered the room.

To her surprise, a blast of warm lilac-scented steam wafted against her as she pushed open the door.

"Come on in and close the door. You're letting the heat out."

What the hell was going on here?

The sound of splashing caught her attention and she found Colter practically drowning in a kaleidoscope of giant bubbles as he sat waist-deep in the enormous bathtub.

"How in the world…?" she asked as she shut the door behind her.

"I had a servant set this up for us while you were in the bathroom before our meeting," he chuckled, and held up a sparkling glass filled with red wine. "This is for you."

Wine? Her punishment was a seduction?

She eagerly accepted the glass, taking a tentative sip. Sweet pleasure burst over her taste buds.

"Very good," she said, and took a few healthy swallows of the delicious liquid. Lord only knew she needed it, she was so nervous.

Sweet heavens, her medication should be working for her. Should have given her the confidence to say no to him. Or at the very least make a show of not wanting him, despite the fact she did. Despite the fact she craved him from the bottom of her heart. Every inch of her heated flesh tingling at the lusty way he looked at her.

He was panting, his gaze touching and caressing her naked flesh. Desire shone bright in his eyes as he lingered on the belt that held the dildo and butt plug firmly in place.

He reached out a hand for the wine glass and she almost dropped it as flames licked her fingers as they touched.

She watched his Adam's apple bob as he swallowed, saw the wet, tanned muscles in his arms ripple as he placed his own wine glass on the nearby tray before leaning back comfortably against the tub.

"Dance for me, Starry Eyes," his voice was a harsh whisper, his eyes blazed with desire. "Dance for me as you did at the general's mansion."

She'd done more than dance for him and the general that first night. The way he was looking at her, she knew he wanted the rest of the show too. Now she understood why Colter had done what he'd done by inserting that butt plug and dildo into her.

My God! How could she have ever forgotten that night? Forgotten the general's instructions to her before his very important *guest* had shown up. Forgotten the hatred that had seared through her heart for the young soldier doctor who'd saved his life.

She remembered the slow tune she'd found comfort in during her years under the general's sadistic rule. A singer had once created it for a very important English princess shortly after she'd died in a horrible car accident. A song Ashley had later cherished as Colter and her's song.

Recognition flared in his eyes as she started to softly hum the tune, began to swing her hips in the erotic belly dancing way she'd been trained. She kept her eyes glued to his tanned face, to the half smile that made him just this side of darkly sexy. To the excitement flaring in his heavy-lidded eyes.

He looked just as he'd done that night when she'd strip-danced in front of the general and the young doctor.

She'd teased the handsome soldier by gyrating her hips all the while gasping at the sensual way the dildo moved within her and enjoyed the pleasure-pain gripping her ass.

Colter kept his gaze fixated to the way she massaged her quickly swelling breasts, to the way she pinched her nipples until they beaded and burned.

His breathing sounded raspy, his gaze riveted to her every move as she swayed seductively and slow-danced in front of him.

"That's it, Starry Eyes. Show me what I've been missing."

His words should have hurt, but they didn't. They only made her remember the tender way he touched her when they were together, the mind-blowing sex they shared and the astounding ménage à trois they'd had with his soldier friend.

By the time she'd finished her sexy dance and hummed her song, she could literally feel the sexual tension waiting to be unleashed from him.

"Remove only the dildo. Leave the butt plug in," he hissed through clenched teeth.

Without hesitation her hands slid from her aching breasts, her fingertips sliding slowly along her sides, down each rib, over the generous curve of her hips. Reaching down, she unclasped the hooks and exhaled her frustration as she slowly pulled the giant flesh-like phallus from her wet vagina, dropping it to the bathroom floor.

"Now step into the bathtub."

She could barely hear him above the frantic thumping of her heartbeat. Found it hard to breath in the misty air, it was so thick with sexual tension. He watched her as if she were his prey as she stepped into the warm water, the bubbles tingling against her flesh.

"Now lower yourself onto my cock and then I'll exact my punishment."

Oh sweet mercy! He wanted her to fuck him. Could she do it without losing her heart again?

"Did you hear me, Starry Eyes?"

She nodded, couldn't understand why she was so eager to have her heart broken, couldn't figure out why she needed to feel him inside her so badly.

Dark, dangerous desire swirled in his eyes. To her surprise, he held out his hands to her. She intertwined her fingers with his just as intimate lovers did. His knees rose from the bubbly depths, allowing her to orient herself, allowing her to spread her legs before his knees disappeared again and she felt his scorching ankles press against her own, preventing her from closing her legs—not that she wanted to anyway.

He held her hands tightly, almost as if he feared she would run away. Her head was telling her to do just that, but her heart and body craved his touch.

Heated blood screamed through her as she squatted. Bubbles tickled her pussy. Hard flesh pressed against her inner thigh.

Sweet heavens. It was his cock. Hard like steel.

Her vaginal muscles clenched with eagerness and she couldn't help but moan with anticipation.

He cried out and closed his eyes as she angled her hot pussy over his shaft, brushing her clit against the fat head until shivers of arousal pulsed through her.

"Impale yourself," he hissed. "And stay there. This isn't a fuck-fest. It's punishment."

Punishment? Confusion gripped her. The way he'd looked at her had made her think he was going to make love to her.

He yanked at her hands, guiding her quickly and efficiently until she felt the fat head of his cock press against her vaginal opening. Without hesitation he pulled her down, making her cry out as the thick, searing blade of flesh slipped inside her.

Oh, God!

He was so big. So blessedly big. Her vaginal muscles spread and clenched and sucked.

She found herself jerking, wanting to gyrate her hips as his hard length buried itself to the hilt. She was on her knees, blessedly impaled by the man she'd once loved.

He blinked back at her. His breathing sounded harsh, fast. Muscles twitched in his jaws. By the way his eyes shone with lust, she could tell he wanted her. Wanted her to make love to him—but his next words shot another bout of confusion through her.

"Now sit still. Don't move a muscle in that tight little pussy of yours."

He let go of her hands and turned to lift a white linen cover from a nearby tray where he'd set the wine bottle and glasses moments earlier.

What she saw there made her heart both skip in a bout of fear as well as insane excitement.

"It's a home nipple piercing kit," Colter explained as he pointed to the items. "Numbing cream, clamps, sterilized needles and pads, antiseptic cream and best of all..."

He lifted one of the rings and she couldn't help but inhale at the beauty of it. It was the same size as the ones he wore on his own nipples with one exception—it had the prettiest Austrian crystal teardrop dangling from it.

This was the latest rave among men. Having their Claimed women's nipples pierced.

"I've wanted to do this to you since we met. Your nipples are too beautiful to go without them. But I won't do it if you don't want me to."

"You're giving me a choice?"

"You sound surprised."

"You haven't given me any choices up until now."

Regret shone in his face. "You didn't give me any choices either when you threatened to blow my cover, Starry Eyes."

"I proved to you that you could trust me during Cheri's meeting. I could have easily started screaming my head off and cried kidnapping and rape."

"I trusted you wouldn't. The dildo and butt plug were just for my amusement, sweetheart."

"You son of a bitch."

He grinned at her soft whisper and put the ring back onto the tray.

"So? Would you like me to pierce you?"

"Why? Would it turn you on to see me in pain?"

That jab certainly wiped his grin from his lips.

"You won't feel any pain. The newly created antibiotic numbing cream lasts for days. It does however allow you to feel pleasure though, if that's what you're afraid you'll miss out on."

"And I suppose you're qualified to do this?"

He grinned and fiddled with one of his own nipple rings. "I can attest that having nipple rings greatly increases your nipples' sensitivity. Allows a greater pleasure when someone plays with them. Besides you don't have to be afraid—I am a doctor and I've done many of them. It's quite popular nowadays."

"And these women who have them done…do they want it? Or are they being forced to have it done by their husbands?"

His sharp inhalation made her realize she'd hit a truly sore spot.

"I'm the only physician for miles around. If I didn't do it, the men would do it themselves."

"That's noble of you."

"You'd do it too if you had to treat infected nipples and clits and all the other things that men are allowed to do to a woman these days."

He sounded angry. As if he cared about women. She found her anger disintegrating as she remembered the tender way he'd held her after the figging and the wonderful way he'd eaten her pussy.

"Do you want the nipple rings or not?" he asked rather gruffly. "It would be a pleasant surprise for the general."

"If I were to do it, then it wouldn't be for the general," she whispered.

His eyes narrowed. "Who would it be for?"

"Myself."

A spear of disappointment flashed across his face.

"And maybe for you," she added. "If you make love to me."

At her words, his cock thickened inside her. She fought back the urge to gyrate her hips.

"Oh I'll make love to you, Starry Eyes. Just not yet. Not until you tell me something."

"What's that?"

"Why didn't you tell me you're infected with the X-virus?"

* * * * *

Utter devastation flooded Ashley's face. She made a move to get up off him but he stopped her cold, grabbing hold of her arms and keeping her impaled on his cock.

"Let go of me," she whispered, her voice full of anguish.

He'd expected her to react this way. It's why he'd made her sink his cock into her. An intimate gesture to show her he didn't care if she were infected.

"Why are you humiliating me like this?"

She was red-faced now, avoiding his gaze.

"I'm not. And you have no reason to feel disgraced. It's completely normal for women to get infected. There's no reason to hide it from me. I'm a doctor. I've seen what happens to a woman's self-esteem and her confidence when she gets the virus."

"I want you to let me go. I want you to leave."

"Starry Eyes. Listen to me." He let go of one of her arms and grabbed her small chin firmly in his hand, forcing her to look at him.

Crystal tears bubbled in her eyes. She was fighting those tears of shame. Fighting against the need to break down and simply feel the anguish of him finding out.

"When did you get it? After us?" Surely he would have known if she'd acquired the illness before they'd met that first time, wouldn't he? But even before she shook her head, he realized he'd known. Somewhere deep down inside him, he must have known. Why else would she have been so submissive to him? Showing no embarrassment to an unknown soldier when she'd taken off her clothing and danced in front of the general and himself, and then all the things she'd allowed him to do afterward...including the ménage à trois with Blade.

"Yes, I had it before I met you," she admitted. Devastation rocked him.

He'd known it would be hard to hear the truth. Somehow he'd known having her warm pussy clenched around his cock would keep him grounded...literally.

"He wanted us to have sex," she whispered.

"Why?"

She tried to wrench away from his grip, but he wouldn't let loose. Pain shimmered in her pretty eyes. Pain and something else.

Secrets?

"I don't know why. He just did."

"You're lying. Tell me."

A command. Why wasn't the medication working? Or maybe she just wanted to tell him. Wanted to unburden herself.

"He taped us, okay? He got his kicks watching you and Blade fucking me. Don't you realize how much money he made selling our ménage à trois? Single men who will never have a woman in their lifetime are paying through the nose to be able to see two men fuck a woman, let alone one woman and one man."

She said it so nonchalantly that he wondered if maybe there wasn't more to the story.

"I'll hunt down the videos and destroy them."

"By now there are millions of copies. It's out of your hands," she said wearily. "Now please let go of my chin. You're hurting me."

Shit!

He let her go and cursed himself for the red mark he'd left behind.

"Starry Eyes, I want you to know it makes no difference to me that you've got the virus. I..." He wanted to tell her he loved her despite the damned illness. Wanted to tell her he would take care of her, protect her from the general, but there was still that little problem of the note she'd left behind.

She looked away. "You found the pills."

He nodded. "I was looking to see if you had any batteries for your vibrator...it seemed a little too slow for my liking. I searched the side pockets and found your medicine."

"I'm sorry. I guess I should have told you before you offered to take me away from the general."

"We had other things on our mind at the time, Starry Eyes," he said softly, and to his surprise, she threw him a wobbly grin.

He was about to ask her if the X-virus was the real reason she'd decided against coming with him when she leaned over, her hot, sultry breath washing against his face.

"Things like this?" She sucked his lower lip into her hot, lush mouth.

The sharp, erotic feel of her teeth nibbling on his flesh sparked a blaze inside his mouth and made his cock spasm inside her wet pussy.

"Or things like this?" she whispered. Her arms came up over his shoulders, her long fingernails digging painfully into his back as she clutched his muscles and began to gyrate her hips.

Oh shit, yeah, that felt damned good. She was the only woman who made him hot so fast.

"Trying to change the subject, are you?" he managed to ask when she let go of his lip.

She grinned. It was a breathtaking smile that lifted her flushed cheeks. Then she kissed him again. This time harder, fiercer. It was as if she were trying to forget that he now knew. He understood. He'd help her forget. If only for a short time.

Reaching down, he found her clit rigid and pulsing, engorged. Sliding the pad of his finger over the hot flesh, he groaned as her gyrations grew. The sound of water sloshed as she moved, intermingled with her sensual moans.

Wonderfully tight vaginal muscles clenched around his entire hard length. Tightened violently. Squeezing his cock. Urging him to spew.

He found himself bucking upwards, up into her hot, spasming cunt.

She wailed as she came.

Tremors rippled through her, her pussy wrapped tighter around his length and he soon became lost in the exquisite look of passion etching her face and the gut-wrenching spasms of her velvety come-soaked pussy milking his cock dry.

* * * * *

"Your nipples look awesome," Colter whispered.

They lay together in the king-size bed, the blankets turned down to their waists, his hands clasped behind his head, and she was thankfully without a collar this time as they surveyed her newly pierced nipples. Silver rings glittered there and from them Austrian crystals lay against her silky flesh, giving her breasts an unbelievably erotic look that really turned her on.

True to his word, she'd felt nothing when he'd pierced her nipples efficiently with the sterilized needles. The numbing antiseptic agent he'd used was new on the market. It cut off all pain centers but left pleasure ones working quite well so a woman could fulfill her sexual duties minutes after a piercing.

"Did you enjoy your punishment?" Colter chuckled as he snuggled his warm face into the crook of her neck and shoulder.

"If piercings and figgings are your way of punishment, I'll have to get you mad at me more often."

The corner of his lip curled up slightly as if he approved of her answer.

"Just don't draw attention to yourself the next time we meet with Cheri, Starry Eyes. I know you want the cure for the general but I don't want you in any kind of danger and—"

She smoothed her hand over the skull tattoo just above his hard cock, stopping his words cold. She didn't want to discuss the general or the real reason she was there. She trailed into his pubic hair, wrapping her fingers tightly over a tuft until he yelped in pain and tears welled in his eyes.

"Shit, woman! I didn't think you'd be this bad."

"Do I have your attention?"

"With a fistful of my sensitive parts, you got it."

She grinned impishly at him, feeling a surge of confidence. Confidence that seemed to be oddly lacking even after taking that last pill before she'd hopped into the bathtub with him and had her nipples pierced. "First of all, don't tell me what to do. Even if I am infected with a submissive disease, I am my own woman. I prefer to make the decisions about my own life."

He looked at her oddly. Probably not used to seeing her so bold. "Whatever you say Starry Eyes."

"Second of all, I want you to tell me about your wife. I heard you mention you had one to Cheri when you first arrived. Why aren't you using your real name? And who is this research company you're working for? How high are they willing to bid to get the cure?"

He frowned and said nothing. Not quite the answers she was looking for. She pulled at his pubic hairs a little harder, making him grimace.

"Ashley, you pull any harder and I may have to punish you again."

His stalling annoyed her. She tightened her grasp just a little. "Just tell me."

"Tell you what?"

"What I want to know." Or maybe she didn't really want to know about his wife. His arms came down from behind his head. His long fingers settling onto her wrists, most likely to prevent her from pulling too hard when he upset her, and by the frown on his face, he was definitely going to say something she didn't want to hear.

"Ashley…it's a really long story."

"So give me the short version."

He said nothing, but his fingers tightened on her wrists, keeping her hands immobile. If that wasn't an answer that he had a real wife, then she didn't know what was.

Oh damn, he'd been making love to her all this time and he had a wife at home. She really hadn't given it much thought during their time together. She'd been too busy being angry at him and aroused while he'd held her as his slave. But now that her anger was diminishing, she needed to know more about him. Maybe that had been the reason he'd left that note for her years ago. Why he'd changed his mind about taking her away from the general. Because of his wife.

"Do…do you love her?"

"No," he exhaled softly.

"Oh…" Relief splashed around her. He wasn't in love with another woman. It's the answer she'd been looking for but hadn't really expected him to say it.

"I care for her. It's an arrangement, Ashley. That's all."

"Tell me about it."

"Why?"

"Because I want to know who this woman is. How did you meet her? Why did you Claim her? What's this arrangement?" *And do I have a chance of taking you away from her? Taking you away with me?*

He chuckled and his abdomen rose and fell beneath her arm.

"Are you jealous?" he asked.

"I just want to know why you would Claim a woman you don't love?"

He frowned. "Like I said it's a long story."

"We've got time. Tell me."

"She was one of Blakely's guinea pigs."

Shockwaves curled through her. Blakely was notorious for having a harem of women to experiment on, sexually and otherwise. His wife Cheri was certainly no better.

"She's one of the women with a natural immunity to the X-virus. The government had her kidnapped and held her against her will for almost five years before turning her over to Blakely. He…" Colter hesitated for a moment before continuing. "He did some experiments on her. He drugged her, cut into her and took most of her eggs. I'm sure he had them fertilized possibly using the embryos to gain this cure that Cheri is talking about."

Ashley's tummy knotted at the thought of what had happened to the woman's eggs, her embryos, and the things that must have happened to the woman herself. "But none of these women who have been kidnapped have ever been seen or heard from again. She must have escaped somehow."

"She did. Then she hid out on Outlaw land. She was my brother Luke's fiancée before she was kidnapped."

Now she was beginning to understand this "arrangement".

"You Claimed her to protect her from the government and Blakely, didn't you?" She'd heard about the newest of the Claiming rules. A Claimed woman immune to the X-virus and its mutations was automatically protected under the laws from being legally taken by any other group of men including the government. According to the Law, a group of men's sexual satisfaction and the bearing of hopefully resistant-free females outweighed everything, including any Claims the government would have on a woman for experimental purposes.

"Do you have sex with her?"

Oh my gosh! She couldn't believe she'd just asked that question, but something deep inside her wanted to know.

"Yes. My three brothers and I did."

Four men? Of course! Claiming Law stated there had to be a minimum of four husbands to take a woman.

She felt a stab of envy for Colter's wife. She had four Outlaw men making love to her, protecting her, bringing her pleasure. If the others were anything like Colter…

She blew out an aroused breath. Four men making love to her? Have mercy, now wouldn't that be something!

Her bubble burst at his next words. "We had sex until we found out she was pregnant."

A baby. My God. He was already making a family with her and his brothers. How could he so easily have buckled to this new way of life? How could anyone accept this damned Claiming Law?

"It's Luke's baby," he continued. "We…he was the only one who took her vaginally. It seemed better that way since he's the one in love with her."

"Okay, I've heard enough." She let go of his pubic hair and pulled away from him, grabbing the blankets to cover her suddenly chilled flesh.

"I'm sorry, I shouldn't have told you all that."

"It's my fault. I shouldn't have asked. None of my business."

"It wasn't as if we couldn't not have sex with her. The Claiming is taped to ensure that each man…enjoys the woman…she did enjoy it too. You could say she became addicted to having sex with more than one man."

"Just shut up, will you?"

His low chuckle made her irritation burn higher.

"Wouldn't you like to have three or four men making love to you, Starry Eyes? I could arrange it."

Sweet Jesus! She was insane for even getting excited at his suggestion. Hated herself at the warm gush of cream sliding down her vagina at his softly spoken suggestion.

"I hear many women fantasize about ménages," he continued.

"Well, I don't," she found herself snapping, feeling guilty for wanting to indulge in sexual pleasures with Colter…and maybe his brothers as that other woman was doing. But it didn't mean she was going to do it.

"That's not what you told me during our time together in Iraq, or I wouldn't have brought Blade into our foray."

"The general must have withheld my medication…"

He grinned wickedly. "Even so, you did say a ménage à trois was your fantasy... Medication can't plant that idea in your head, and all I did was ask what your fantasy was."

"Shut up." She felt her cheeks warm up with embarrassment. "I think it's time we faced reality, Colter. You've got a wife waiting for you and three brothers who are depending on you to keep this Claiming shit legal. I'm not into casual ménages. I'm into a serious relationship with one man."

"You'd have to go into hiding. My brother Jude did that with the woman he loves. They took off on the *Outlaw Lover*."

"Outlaw Lover?"

"Our boat."

"The general has several yachts..." she found herself whispering. Found herself hoping Colter would suggest they take one and sail off together into the sunset.

He didn't.

"I suppose this means you and the general have discussed you and he going into hiding already?"

She didn't like the way this conversation was heading, nor did she like the odd need to tell him the truth about the general. Maybe if she could just tell him what was really going on and get him to help her...

No! She couldn't trust Colter. He'd proved it in the past by walking out on her.

"The general has his plans for me and only me. He doesn't go around fucking another woman just so he can Claim her," she lied, hoping to see jealousy rage across his features. A shallow inhalation of his breath was her only clue that she had made some sort of impact on him. Otherwise, his face remained impassive.

"He plans on taking me to Monaco. He's got a wonderful villa there fully staffed with faithful servants."

The villa was where she'd finally taken Colette when she'd escaped the general's mansion that night with the help of her bodyguard.

"And, of course, you'll be there to pleasure him anytime he wants."

"Go to hell," she snapped, suddenly wanting to get away from his knowing smile.

She'd climbed out of bed and was heading toward the bathroom to grab a glass of water when she spotted a shadowy figure through the open bedroom doorway in the adjoining room.

Before she could scream out a warning to Colter, he was pulling her behind him, protecting her from the pair of narrowed eyes peering at her.

A moment later Blade stepped into the light. Her heart froze at the sight of the lethal looking gun in his hand.

"What the fuck are you doing here?" Ashley couldn't believe the anger that laced Colter's words as he spoke to his friend.

"I could ask you the same thing, friend. Fucking the enemy on S.K.U.L.L.'s time—not a good thing. But then again, you always were stupid when it came to her."

There was no hint of friendliness in his voice or in the way he looked at her.

"What's with the gun, Blade?" Colter asked. She could see the muscles in his upper back flex with tension. As if he were preparing to fight.

"Consider it a hearing aid. We need to talk."

"So talk."

"Not in front of her. Get dressed. Meet me at your cabin." Having said that, Blade turned and disappeared into the darkness of the living room, leaving Ashley wondering if he'd been there at all. A moment later, the soft click of a door closing snapped her out of her disbelief.

"He looked as if he wanted to kill me," Ashley whispered, allowing the tremors of fear to grab a hold of her.

"He probably did."

"What? Why? What did I do to him?"

Colter didn't say anything as he quickly climbed into his underwear and gathered up his clothing.

"It's not what you did to him…" he said, and hopped into his pants, flashing her a rather serious look she didn't like. "It's what you did to me."

Before she could ask him what the hell he was talking about, he was palming a gun she never knew he had and was heading out of the bedroom.

"Stay here. I'll be back in a few minutes."

She found herself nodding as she followed him to the main door and watched his shirtless figure disappear into the moonlit night.

* * * * *

"Are you fucking insane?" Blade's voice slammed into Colter like a hurricane the instant he entered his cabin. He'd seen Blade pissed off only a few times since he'd known him. It wasn't a pretty sight. And it sure wasn't now.

"That bitch burned you and now you're getting right back in between her legs again like some stupid dog in heat."

At Blade's words, Colter stifled an overwhelming need to go for his gun and tell his friend to get the hell out of his face. Instead, he managed to keep his voice calm and cool.

"It's none of your business, Blade."

"The hell it isn't! She's fucking poison. She landed you in a hell of a lot of hot water when she split the way she did."

"You better back off, Blade."

"No! You're my friend, my S.K.U.L.L. partner and I owe you at least a piece of my mind, or at the very least to talk you out of going near her. S.K.U.L.L. finds out you're mixing business with pleasure, they won't be too pleased either."

"S.K.U.L.L. sanctioned me women—"

"Not of a personal nature," Blade snapped.

"They won't find out."

"They're already suspicious. You're not answering your pages. Bev's been trying to contact you. You didn't show up for the pre-arranged meet time with her. She wants details of that meeting you had with Cheri. How the hell do you expect to get the cure and get your brother safe while you're playing house with someone else's fucking pleasure slave?"

The words pleasure slave felt like a shard of glass grating into Colter's heart and he couldn't help but wince. Couldn't help but realize Blade was right. The assignment was in jeopardy because he'd been following his wrong head.

His friend must have caught his reaction because it appeared as if all the air flew right out of him and he ran a hand in frustration through his golden blond locks.

"I'm sorry I lost it. You're right, it's none of my business. You're out of S.K.U.L.L. now, but we have to get rid of her so you can do your job. We'll stash her until you two can pick up where you left off. I promise no one will harm her."

Tension coiled inside Colter. He wanted to say no. Wanted to tell Blade to go to hell, but he knew his friend was right. With Ashley around he couldn't think clearly. He needed her out of the way. They could pick up where they left off when she was safely out of there and away from the general and Cheri Blakely.

"Okay. But keep her safe."

* * * * *

Uneasiness slithered up Ashley's spine as she waited for Colter's return. He'd been gone only a few minutes, but without him she suddenly felt vulnerable, insecure, needy. Just like she felt when she was overdue for her medication. But that wasn't possible, she'd taken the damn pill. It must be her insecurities kicking in. He had a Claimed wife, another life. A baby on the way. Although he'd said the baby wasn't his, she knew he must feel a certain responsibility to his wife and brothers and the child.

Besides he'd left her once before…

Crud! Why did he have to make her feel like this? Wasn't love supposed to be based on trust and happiness? Not distrust and uneasiness and…

The twisting of the doorknob at the front door of the cabin made Ashley breathe a sigh of relief.

Thank God! Now they could pick up where they'd left off and he could tell her exactly what the heck she'd done to piss off Blade and why he thought she'd been the one who'd hurt him.

"Good evening, Ashley."

Her happiness froze solid as Cheri's crisp voice snapped through the open doorway of her bedroom.

"What are you doing here?" Ashley gasped as she grabbed her robe.

"Keep the robe off, Ashley."

My God! To her shock and horror she found Cheri's command smooth over her, felt her resistance melt away, felt her hands drop the robe, felt the familiar eagerness of wanting another command.

What the hell was happening to her?

"Your medication was switched when you first arrived, Ashley. While you were registering at the front desk. Actually during the mandatory luggage check all of Pleasure Palace's clients go through during the check in. The employee simply switched the drugs he found in the side pocket as per my instructions. The new medication does a very good job in masking symptoms as well as slightly delaying the onset of brain damage. Surely you must have noticed the gentle swings between confidence and submissiveness since you've arrived here? You've been taking another type of medication that masked your symptoms so you wouldn't become alarmed or suspicious. And I wanted you to be…shall we say…submissive when I came for you."

No, please this can't be happening! She must have fallen asleep while waiting for Colter. She must be dreaming. Please let her be dreaming! Cheri reached out and ran a cold finger along Ashley's arm.

Oh, God! This really was happening.

"What…what do you want from me?"

"First of all I want you to write Dr. Van Dusen a note. Tell him you got a call from me. Tell him there's a meeting. A demonstration about the cure. Down in dungeon room 3."

Cheri handed her a pen and a piece of paper and Ashley found herself writing the words, watching her hand write the note as if she were looking from outside her body.

When she finished, Cheri picked up the note and placed it on one of the pillows on the bed.

"There. Now let's get you prepared for the meeting, shall we?"

Cheri nodded to a couple of men who were now crowding around Ashley. Two of Cheri's husbands who watched her with lust in their eyes.

Oh, God! No!

When their cold hands smoothed over each of her wrists, part of her mind allowed them to lead her from the bedroom while another part screamed out for Colter's help. To her frustration, the men quickly ushered her out of the cabin and into the coolness of the night.

* * * * *

"You son of a bitch! You drew me away so you could take her!" Rage slammed into Colter when he discovered Ashley was nowhere in her cabin.

He saw red and turned on his friend. His fist slammed into Blade's face before he knew what was happening. Pain sliced through his knuckles and he heard bone crack, heard his friend curse.

"Where the hell is she?" Colter demanded as he grabbed him by his shirt lapels and slammed him up against the nearest wall ignoring the red splash of blood flowing from Blade's damaged nose.

"Dammit! I think you broke my freaking nose!"

"What the fuck did you do to her? You said I could at least explain it to her."

"I don't know. Shit! Take it easy, man. I was with you. How the hell could I take her?"

"You told S.K.U.L.L. They took her."

"No, man, I didn't. Come on. Maybe she just took off on her own again."

"Fuck!" He let go of Blade and ignored him when he slumped to the floor, cursing heavily as he cradled his broken face in his hands.

Heading toward the nearest window, Colter lifted the blind and peeked out into the moonlit yard. Maybe she'd gone out for a simple walk? No, she wouldn't be stupid enough to do that. Pleasure Palace was a secure area, but that wouldn't stop a group of male guests from taking her if they wanted her bad enough.

Nothing moved, and he found himself begging to see her silhouette standing out there watching the stars. Nothing transpired.

Had she taken off on him as Blade said? Had the general returned? Found out they'd been together?

"I found this note on the pillow," Blade hissed as he came up behind Colter. "You see? It's a simple explanation. Cheri's called the meeting. Now's your chance to get the cure and to free your brother. Don't blow it."

* * * * *

He didn't like the feel of this. Why hadn't he been contacted about the meeting? How had Ashley dressed and left so quickly? Why leave him a note? Why not just come next door and tell him if she wanted him to know? He'd been gone fifteen minutes, tops. Not to mention the handwriting on this note was all wrong. Over the past years he'd memorized her handwriting on her kiss-off note in Iraq. The handwriting on this note didn't even look like hers.

Tension clawed up his back as he walked down the narrow stairs that the clerk had indicated would take him to the sex dungeons.

He'd had to leave his gun and his knife with Blade because he knew they'd be frisking everyone entering the meeting room with a metal detector wand just as they'd done during the last one. Cheri Blakely left nothing to chance.

His footsteps echoed eerily as he walked down the hallway. It was quiet. Too quiet.

"Don't like the looks of it," he whispered so low he wasn't sure Blade could hear every word through the mike on the cufflink to his monkey suit.

"We're at your back. Just holler if there's trouble. We'll swarm the place," Blade's calm voice replied in the earphone he'd been outfitted with. The item was so tiny no one would see it unless he flipped his hair over his ears and they stuck their face right up against it.

His heart was beating a mile a minute as he spotted dungeon room 3. Instinctively he knew he'd calm down when he saw Ashley. That's all he cared about at the moment. Just seeing her and knowing she was all right.

Blade had been right when he'd lit into Colter about Ashley. She was his weak spot. He'd been enjoying himself with her while his assignment was going down the tube and his brother was rotting away somewhere waiting for a rescue. But it wasn't his fault Cheri hadn't put on the bidding war yet.

Now, however, was not the time to start thinking about Ty. He had to find Ashley and the cure. Once he had both then things would hopefully work out.

In front of him the thick wooden door redundant of the old dungeon doors in medieval England prisons and torture chambers swung inward. One of Cheri's husbands stepped outside, a metal detector in his hand.

"I'm clean," Colter replied as he lifted his hands so the man could run the wand up and down his body.

Cheri's husband said nothing and a moment later he nodded for Colter to go inside.

The instant he stepped through the doorway he realized three things. A quick scan of the room revealed the other three bidding doctors were already seated. He didn't see Ashley.

The second thing he noticed were the excited glances they were throwing to an area behind Cheri and her husbands who partially hid from his view what appeared to be a metal table with a white sheet draped over someone.

The third thing he noticed was the smug smile on Cheri's face.

Shit! He didn't like the feel of this at all.

"We've been waiting for you, Dr. Van Dusen." Cheri purred.

He didn't like the way she smiled. All cocksure and syrupy.

"Please have a seat with the others and we'll start the demo."

Where the hell was Ashley?

There was nothing he could do about it right now. He'd have to sit through the demonstration, make the bid and hopefully be able to get out and look for Ashley as soon as he could without arousing suspicion.

On rather unsteady legs he headed toward an empty chair then stopped cold as he cleared the doctor and her entourage.

Now he had the perfect view of the metal table and he didn't like what he saw, not at all.

Shock zipped along his spine as he recognized the woman lying beneath the white sheet.

Ashley.

Her long lashes framed her closed eyes. Her generous breasts moved up and down in a steady rhythm beneath the sheet.

She seemed to be sleeping. Totally at peace.

Drugged?

Sickness crawled into his belly at the same time anger soared through him. He fought it down. Hard to do when all he wanted was to start swinging his fists at these people as they looked upon Ashley's defenseless body.

"Doctors, I promised you an infected woman. Here she is. She graciously offered herself up for the demo. It was her way of being sure that the cure was the real thing. Her medication has been withheld for the appropriate time. Now let us get a good look at our guinea pig."

Cheri's hand reached out to grab the sheet covering Ashley.

"I was under the impression she was supposed to be in on the bidding?" *Easy does it, don't show her how freaked-out you are.*

Cheri whipped the sheet off Ashley, revealing her naked body.

Colter forced himself not to move. Forced himself not to react at the way the doctor and Cheri's husbands gazed longingly upon Ashley's lush nakedness. This was not the time to lose it.

"Not to worry, Dr. Van Dusen. She's still in," Cheri said as she ran a finger over Ashley's slightly rounded tummy.

Ashley whimpered, her eyes flickered open and she blinked. All evidence of the flashing, blue sparkling eyes was gone. Instead there was a blank stare to her face, a blankness he'd never seen before.

"She's in a fully submissive state now. She has reached the point where medication can never bring her back to her prior state."

Jesus, have mercy!

More than anything he wanted to scoop Ashley into his arms and carry her away from there, but he knew Cheri was right. Once a woman with Ashley's type of X-virus was withheld her medication for too long she fell into the phase of no return. Jesus Christ! There was no way in hell Ashley wouldn't have taken her drugs. Cheri must have done something. Maybe switched her drugs somehow.

"I shall demonstrate," Cheri said.

"This isn't really necessary to have her naked in front of us like this." Colter took a step forward, fully prepared to cover her with the sheet when two of Cheri's biggest husbands grabbed his arms, preventing him from doing anything.

"What's happening in there, Colter?" Blade's slightly worried voice whispered in his earpiece.

"Please, Doctor, have a seat," Cheri Blakely instructed. "It won't be painful at all for her. I think her participating in this demonstration is a small price for her to pay to get herself cured, wouldn't you say?"

"You've brought the cure?" Colter held his breath awaiting her answer.

She slid her hand into her pocket and pulled out a vial with pinkish fluid. "There's enough in here for two doses. One for my demonstration and one for the highest bidder."

An excited murmur rippled from the doctors.

"Are you sure it's safe?" Colter asked, resisting the urge to grab her by the throat and shake the truth out of her.

She looked honestly shocked at his question and he kicked himself for asking it. He was acting like a fool. Cheri wouldn't put on a demonstration that would ruin her chances at getting high bids.

"Since you appear to be so concerned for her wellbeing, you can stand at the foot of the table and watch."

The husbands let him go and he found himself moving to the end of the table where she'd directed him to stand. His heart beat a mile a minute as he looked down at Ashley. Her eyes were closed again.

"What did you do to her? Drug her?"

"Actually no. Her X-virus medication was merely withheld and replaced by another drug that would help mask some of her passive symptoms, but as all drugs react differently with different people she could have experienced bouts of submissiveness and-or bouts of defiance. She is, however, now in the natural submissive state that follows the withdrawal of the drugs. It happens when a woman with this particular strain of Virus doesn't take her medication within a certain timeframe. Surely you know all this, Dr. Van Dusen?"

Pull yourself together, man. "My apologies. I only wish for no one to get hurt."

Ashley looked pale. Too pale under the sickening light of the hot, bright white lights. Like some sort of helpless specimen about to be dissected by a sadistic scientist.

"Ashley, can you hear me?" Cheri said softly.

Ashley's eyes immediately popped open. She looked at Cheri and nodded.

"I want you to touch your breasts," Cheri cooed.

Jesus!

Without hesitation, Ashley did as she was told. Her fingers began to massage her luscious globes while everyone watched her.

Nausea clutched at his gut. This was sick!

"Pull on your lovely nipple rings. Arouse yourself."

Again Ashley complied, plucking and pulling until she was whimpering in pleasure.

He could only hope she wouldn't remember this abuse when they got out of there. And the only way out was to play Cheri's game.

"Keep one hand on your breast and use the other to play with your clit, Ashley," Cheri instructed.

Frustration crawled through Colter as he watched Ashley spread her legs. Her pale arm reached down, her fingers parted her pink nether lips, and she began to play with her plump clitoris. The doctors were now out of their seats moving in closer to watch.

Colter dug his nails into the palms until he felt pain and the warmth of blood. He needed to keep cool. Detached.

If Cheri gave Ashley the cure...she wouldn't have to be dependant on drugs. He could take her anywhere and not worry about the enormous medical costs of keeping her from being a submissive.

"Do you see how easily she can be persuaded to do anything you wish?" Cheri addressed the doctors who all nodded their heads eagerly. "And if I decided not to give her the cure she would remain submissive, her brain fried by the virus."

Cheri had said she had the cure, but could he trust her? He'd noticed the friction between the two women the first time they'd met. They detested each other. Yet here was Cheri offering to cure Ashley.

Why? And why the hell hadn't he thought to ask Ashley about why she'd feared Cheri when she'd first shown up at Pleasure Palace? While he'd been busy fucking her with sexual revenge on his mind, he'd been fucking up by not asking questions he should have been asking. Like why would the general allow her to come here with only one bodyguard? No man in his right mind would permit his woman out of his sight during these insane times. How the hell had he even been stupid enough to leave her in her room unprotected while he'd gone off to argue with Blade?

They had taken her against her will. She hadn't written that note just as he'd thought.

Maybe he was freaking-out for nothing. Maybe he was reading too much into this. Ashley was just convenient for them. There couldn't be anything sinister going on, could there? Cheri wouldn't be stupid enough to put her demonstration and the trust of these doctors into jeopardy. Not if she wanted to get those high bids from them.

He held his breath as Cheri produced a syringe from a pocket, flipped off a cap and jabbed it into the vial containing the pinkish fluid.

Instincts told him to swat the filled needle out of her hand. But what if Cheri were telling the truth? What if she held the cure in her hand?

Dammit! He had no other choice but to trust her.

Clamping down on his fear, he held himself steady. Prepared himself to rush to Ashley's side at the first sign of distress.

Ashley didn't even wince as the glittering needle penetrated the skin of her upper arm. She just kept playing with her clit as Cheri had instructed her to do.

The pink liquid disappeared quickly from the hypo needle as it entered Ashley's bloodstream. When the hypo was empty, Cheri withdrew the needle.

For several minutes he remained poised on edge, ready to come to Ashley's aid while the rest of the people in the room watched in silent fascination as she continued to play with her clit and massage her breasts.

Her eyes remained closed but the sounds of her arousal tore through him like sharp blades. Although she seemed oblivious of any shame, he felt the humiliation for her. Felt the fear rip through him that maybe this cure wouldn't work.

Then suddenly her finger stopped fraying against her clitoris. She frowned. Blinked in disbelief as she looked around at the doctors watching her. A rosy flush blossomed across her face. She was embarrassed and rightly so.

"Keep playing with yourself, Ashley," Cheri cooed. She took a step back and dropped the vial containing the rest of the cure into her lab coat.

Ashley shook her head, a defiant look slamming onto her face, her eyes suddenly sparkled with rage.

She bolted upright into a seated position.

Relief sliced through Colter and he quickly peeled off his suit jacket and stepped beside Ashley, tossing the jacket over her naked back. He grabbed her wrist, checking her pulse. It was a bit fast, but understandable under the circumstances.

"How do you feel?" Colter asked. Inwardly his gut twisted as he awaited her answer.

"I feel—" her eyes widened "—I feel different. Confident. Sure of myself. My God, what did she give me?"

"Play with your nipples, Ashley," Cheri ordered rather harshly.

"Go to hell!" Ashley spat as she shrugged her arms into the coat Colter had just draped over her shoulders. Her fingers trembled as she did up a couple of the buttons.

"What the hell did you give me?"

"The cure, my dear Ashley. Only because you will be…family."

Apprehension swept through him as Ashley's face paled. Family? What the hell was she talking about? For a moment he feared Ashley might collapse, and then she surprised him by reaching out and quickly ripping a gun from the shoulder holster of the nearest husband of Cheri's. Within a blink of an eye she'd rammed the barrel of the gun against the woman's temple, reached into Cheri's pocket and withdrew the vial containing the cure.

It all happened so fast Colter couldn't believe it.

Obviously neither did Cheri. She let out a blood-curdling scream.

Her husbands moved in on Ashley, but she pressed the gun harder against Cheri's temple in a threatening manner.

"No one moves! Or she's dead!"

Everyone froze.

"Jesus, Colter what the hell is going on down there?" Blade's voice echoed through the earpiece.

"Just relax. Everything is under control," he whispered it so lowly he wondered if Blade heard him, and he sure as hell wondered if everything were indeed under control.

"Have you gone insane?" Cheri cried out, her eyes wide with horror. "You wouldn't dare kill me."

"Try me," Ashley ground out as she dropped the vial into the pocket of her coat. "Now that I have everyone's attention…place your weapons on the metal table and sit down on the floor, cross your legs, foreheads against that wall…except you, Dr. Van Dusen. You'll be my hostage out of here."

Him as her hostage? He liked the sound of that.

"You won't get away with this," Cheri spat as she stood her ground.

Oh shit!

Ashley's lips twisted into a sneer as she eased off the table, not allowing the gun to move from Cheri's temple. "Get her toward that wall or I drop her."

"You'll lose your daughter."

Shock zipped through Colter. Ashley had a daughter?

"I'll hunt you down until I find you both and I'll make you and her sorry for the rest of your lives."

He noticed the flash of fear in Ashley's eyes. Oh come on, Starry Eyes, now is not the time to back down. He resisted the urge to move. To help her. Any movement on his part might spook her. Might make her actually shoot Cheri and eliminate their way out of there.

On top of that, it was imperative he keep what was left of his cover in case she fucked up. Besides he was still reeling about the news she had a daughter. She'd never mentioned she'd had a kid with the general. Christ! He really didn't know her at all.

"Who is the one with the key to this dungeon?" she yelled as she pushed Cheri away from her yet kept the gun aimed at the woman's head.

Ashley's eyes were now wide with anguish, desperation. The fingers holding the gun trembled just a little too much for his comfort.

No one spoke up.

She made a threatening gesture with the gun at Cheri's head.

"Give her the key," Cheri said shakily. "She won't get away with this."

"And the research papers and the disc for the cure," Ashley demanded.

"No, absolutely not," Cheri spat.

Cheri winced as Ashley's lips thinned with determination and her finger tightened on the trigger. "The file is in my inner lab pocket," Cheri said quickly.

"Don't move until I tell you," Ashley hissed as she grabbed one of the guns off the metal table, zipped off the safety catch and now aimed two guns at Cheri's head.

"One wrong move and your head is gone. Now get that file out of your pocket nice and easy. Give it to Dr. Van Dusen."

A moment later Colter had the file in his hand. Opening it, he noted a disc and papers then shut the file again.

"It's all there," he said.

"Now, Dr. Van Dusen, please grab all those guns and toss them out the door. Follow them out."

He didn't hesitate doing what he was told. Clutching the ends of the sheet closed, he hoisted the heavy linen clad with weapons over his shoulder. Once he cleared the doorway, he dropped the sheet and grabbed a gun.

Ashley was right behind him.

A quick jab of the electronic key into the slot of the dungeon door and it was locked.

He didn't think her face could get any paler but it did. She wavered weakly.

Colter wasted no time in grabbing onto her and steadying her.

"You okay?"

She nodded shakily. "God, Colter, I was scared shitless. I kept thinking something was going to go wrong."

"Do you want us to come in?" Blade's desperate yell tore painfully through Colter's ear.

"Hold on for a minute, Blade."

Ashley blinked at him with a mixture of fear and curiosity. "Blade? Where is he?"

"I'll explain later. Blade, tell S.K.U.L.L. we've got the cure and we're on our way out."

"Will do," came Blade's tense reply.

"Skull?" Ashley whispered. "What the hell is—?"

The harsh, ear-splitting sound of an alarm sliced through the hallway.

"There's the security alarm," Colter hissed. "I guess we forgot to get their cell phones."

"Shit! I can't think of everything." Ashley shook her head. Sliding one of the extra guns into the opposite jacket of where she'd shoved the vial, she headed for the stairs at the end of the hallway. "I got us the cure, now the rest is up to you, Outlaw."

"Damn woman, she's still never satisfied," Blade's calm voice chuckled into Colter's earpiece, and Colter didn't miss the sexual innuendo in his friend's voice.

"Shut up, Blade! We're coming out! Cover our asses."

"Will do...oh, and tell Ashley she's still got the cutest ass I've ever seen, will you?"

"Tell her yourself," Colter hissed, and then he swore softly as his friend chuckled into his earpiece. A split second later, the sound of gunfire erupted in the general direction of the exit.

"The welcoming committee?" Ashley grumbled as she jammed her other gun into the suit jacket pocket and began doing up the rest of the buttons on the coat he'd given her.

"You look hot in my jacket. Even hotter out of it." Colter grinned as he grabbed her hand and led her up the stairs.

"You'll get plenty an eyeful if you can get us out of here...alive."

"Ask her if I'm included in this eyeful, will you?" Blade chuckled into the earpiece.

"I won't ask her a damn thing for you, Blade. At least not until she explains a whole hell of a lot," Colter grumbled. "We're nearing the doorway to the lobby."

"Ask me what?" Ashley whispered as she pulled both guns back out of the jacket pockets.

"I think he's thinking of our ménage à trois," Colter grumbled as he carefully rolled up the folder, making sure the disc didn't get damaged then shoved the file into his jeans against the small of his back.

"Oh…" A pretty pink blush rushed to her face.

"She blushing by any chance?" Blade chuckled.

"Yes, she's blushing up quite a nice storm."

"She hasn't changed at all. Sorry I was so hard on her and you earlier."

"You can apologize later, Blade. We're at the doorway."

"Stay there a minute 'til we get in. They're putting up a hell of a resistance."

From behind them, they heard a loud crashing sound. The heavy sound of the dungeon door splintering quickly followed by shouts and running feet headed toward them.

"They're through, Blade. We don't have a minute." He turned to Ashley. "I hope you know how to use those guns because we're going to need them."

"I had a couple of older cousins who took a lot of survival trips into the wilderness. Sometimes they took me with them. They taught me everything they knew about guns. Said it would come in handy one day. Looks like they were right."

Colter nodded. "Smart cousins. Okay, Blade, we're making our move at the count of three."

Blade cursed wickedly then said, "Affirmative."

"Stick to me like glue, Ash. We're going out at the count of three. Okay?"

She nodded and pointed her guns at the door.

"Just don't shoot any of the S.K.U.L.L. men. They'll be wearing camouflage."

She nodded again and worried her lower lip with her white teeth while he snuck in one last look at her. Tangled black hair shrouded her cute face, perspiration scooted across her forehead, her face was pale and her blue eyes were wide as saucers and filled with fear. Her hands filled with guns. She looked like a regular warrior.

His gut clenched wonderfully as it always did when he looked at her. Without doubt, she was the most beautiful woman in the world to him.

He resisted the urge to kiss her and began the count.

At three he nodded to Ashley who returned his nod, her knuckles whitened as she tightened the grip around her guns.

Blowing out a breath, he pushed open the door.

Chapter Nine

Ashley had no time to think. Only react. Before she knew what she'd done she'd plugged two guards with bullets before they could get off a shot at her then they burst into the lobby.

Damn! Her reflexes were fantastic. Energy roared through her and she'd never felt so scared or so healthy in her life. Whatever Cheri had given her was working better than she'd ever expected.

While Colter locked the door behind them, keeping Cheri and her crew from coming through, they crouched behind a nearby marble lobby desk and Colter fired off another round of bullets into the door. A man screamed and then another—and then—silence.

"Blade, get your ass in here," Colter hissed coolly as he kept firing at the shadowy figures of security guards hovering around various points in the lobby.

God! They were everywhere!

From the corner of her eye she spotted movement at the lobby entrance and shot off another round. The entire glass door and window shattered with an ear-piercing splinter. A guard slumped to the ground.

Colter was busy firing at a couple of men who'd taken up residence in a side foyer.

"We'll go out the back way," he hissed, and nodded to his left. "You go first, I'll cover you."

"Not without you."

Anger blazed in his eyes. "Now's not the time to argue. Get your cute ass moving. I won't say it twice."

Maybe because she'd lived with the trained responses to commands compliments of the X-virus, but for a split second she expected the familiar submission fog to slip over her. To her relief, nothing happened.

Son of a bitch! She didn't have to do a thing anyone said. Not even Colter. But now wasn't the time to exert her newfound freedom.

She'd have plenty of time for her revenge against him.

Later.

When Colter raised his head over the lobby desk and set off yet another volley of gunfire, she made a run for it, plowing into the nearby hallway where she perched herself on her knees and zipped off retaliatory shots.

Jesus! There were so many guards shooting. One fired from behind the potted planter. Another one from a side foyer. Yet another one from the front entrance doorway replacing the fellow she'd taken down just seconds earlier.

Hysteria niggled at her as she watched Colter ready himself to come to her. Instincts told her he wouldn't make it.

She wanted to yell at him. To warn him to be careful. She had no time. He sprinted from the hiding place and she just opened fired at anything that moved.

Adrenaline roared faster as immediately from behind Colter she saw the basement door crash open. Cheri and her husbands piled out of the basement with guns in their hands.

Ashley swore softly. She should have hidden the rest of the guns and not left them outside the dungeon doorway as they'd done. It had been a stupid thing to do, but they hadn't had the time to carry them along.

The group fanned out to various points throughout the lobby.

Dammit! She couldn't hit all of them.

When they spotted her, they started shooting.

Her stomach sank as if she were on a runaway elevator.

Colter was in the crossfire!

Ashley knew the instant he got hit. He was in the process of diving through the air when she saw him flinch ever so slightly. He hit the ground hard right beside her then, to her amazement, he rolled into a crouched position and popped off some more rounds.

She spied a blossom of bright red bloodstain on the pink ceramic floor beneath him. Alarm zipped up her spine.

Shit!

"You're hit," she screeched. Her guts twisted in anguish.

"Get the hell moving down the hall out the back and head into the woods! I'll be right there," he hissed.

As if answering her question the glass door at the back of the hallway burst inward and a handful of men in camouflage fatigues came roaring in.

She sighed in relief when she spied Blade among them.

Blade zeroed right in on them while the others whipped past at lightning speed, opening fire on anyone who moved in the lobby.

"Got a car waiting just out back," Blade said as he crouched beside them.

"Hold on a minute, Blade," Colter answered. Perspiration glistened across his face and his eyes narrowed as he took a bead on one of Cheri's husbands.

Ashley jumped as Colter eased off a couple of rounds and the man screeched then dropped to the plush carpeted floor.

"Four down. Three to go."

"Nice job," Blade grinned.

It was then that Ashley realized Blade's nose looked twice the size as normal and was all black and blue.

"Here's the file outlining the cure," Colter said as he held up the file folder Cheri had given her. Blade reached for it, but Colter shook his head.

"You get the file along with a vial containing the cure once you get my brother's ass out of wherever he is."

"But Bev won't—"

"Fuck Bev. Tell her she does it my way or I sell the cure on the black market."

Blade nodded. "Will do. Where can we find you?"

"The Outlaw farm."

Blade's gaze narrowed slightly.

"Both of you?"

"Both of us," Colter replied.

"Together again. Like old times," Blade said. Even though the words sounded innocent enough she detected the sexual innuendo in Blade's tone, recognized the heat flaring up in his eyes as his gaze raked her form. For some reason his anger toward her had vanished. Why? Why was he looking at her with so much lust in his eyes? She found herself shivering at the intensity of it. It reminded her of the time she'd first met him. A scorching, open stare that told her he wanted to have sex.

That's when she realized she must look quite the picture wearing nothing but a man's jacket that barely covered her ass, allowing Blade quite the eyeful of her long, naked legs and probably a whole heck of a lot more.

Her face flamed.

Shit! Now was not the time to get embarrassed. She'd have plenty of time later when she could think of how she'd been laid out on the metal table in the dungeon fingering herself in front of all those people.

From the general direction of where Blade and his team had come inside, she made out the cracking sound of gunfire and then abrupt silence.

Suddenly Blade nodded affirmation as if he were listening to someone. That's when she noticed an odd device plugged into his right ear.

"Okay, S.K.U.L.L.'s cleared a path to the Jeep. I'll relay the message to Bev. Off you go, lovebirds."

Before she could thank him for his help Colter was yanking her down the hallway and into the warm night air. He pointed to a black Jeep with a man in camouflage.

"That's our getaway car. Come on!"

She noticed he was breathing heavily when they settled into the backseat of the Jeep. Noticed the tight grimace of pain around the edges of his mouth. The way his eyes fluttered.

And when his eyes rolled into the back of his head and closed, Ashley couldn't help but let out an agonizing scream.

* * * * *

"How is he?" Ashley asked, anxiety clawing through her as Blade opened the door of the bedroom they'd put Colter in and came out into the hall where she'd been anxiously waiting.

When Colter had passed out in the Jeep, the driver had radioed Blade who had quickly joined them. While the driver whisked them away, Blade had quickly located the bullet wound behind Colter's upper right thigh.

It was an ugly wound and Ashley had almost screamed again when she'd seen it.

Now as Blade quietly closed the bedroom door, she briefly spied Colter's very pregnant Claimed wife sitting on the edge of the bed running her hand over his forehead. Colter's eyes were closed but he sure appeared to be enjoying himself, a happy smile plastered over his lips. The tight knot that had been growing inside her stomach since he'd gotten shot suddenly became bigger.

"Come on. I'll tell you out in the living room with the others," Blade whispered as he led her down the hallway to where Colter's brothers awaited anxiously for the news.

The brothers, all three of them, who'd been pacing back and forth in various parts of the large living room, came rushing toward both Blade and her.

"How is he?" came a concerned Mack Outlaw's hushed whisper.

"What's the prognosis, Doc?" was Luke's immediate response.

"What the fuck kind of backup do you have letting my brother get all shot up?" was Cade's angry question.

"Hey, chill out, guys. Colter's going to be fine," Blade replied.

Ashley heard loud exhales of relief around the room, yet she felt no relief at all. In the Jeep when Colter had fallen unconscious, she'd thought she'd lost him. At the Outlaw farmhouse she'd seen how upset his very pregnant wife and brothers had been when Blade and the driver had dragged his unconscious body inside. Now she literally felt her heart dying inside. With so much love and devotion pouring out of these people for Colter, there was no way she could ask him to come away with her and go into hiding. It just wouldn't be right.

"The bullet didn't do any permanent damage, but he's going to be sore for a while," Blade explained. "At the moment we have a more pressing matter at hand." He turned to Ashley and her stomach twisted at the seriousness in his voice. "We're going to have to get you out of here before word gets out the Outlaws have an unClaimed woman on their hands."

"I'm not unClaimed," Ashley said quickly, her hand sliding into the pocket of the jacket Colter had given her, her fingers wrapped securely around the cool glass vial. If needed, she would use it to escape, just as she'd done at Pleasure Palace.

"Unfortunately, according to the government records, you are unClaimed, Ashley. I'm sorry, but I had to do a background check on you when I discovered you were with Colter. I know he also wanted you somewhere safe and protected until he could…deal with you. It might not be safe enough for you here, so you should come with me."

"She's not going anywhere," a woman's voice erupted from the hallway.

Ashley swung around to find Colter's wife holding her swollen belly as she waddled into the living room. She wore a rather firm scowl on her face and it was directed at Blade. Instincts told Ashley when this woman was pissed off, it was best to make a wide berth around her.

Obviously Blade didn't have the same instincts. He held his ground as she came and stood within inches from him and poked him none too gently in the chest.

"I'm sorry but you were obviously unable to keep Colter safe. That means you won't be able to protect Ashley, either. She stays here."

Having said that, Callie moved away and sat down on the nearby sofa, acting as if her word was law and there would be no argument.

Well, screw her!

"No one tells me where I can stay or not stay, especially not Colter or his wife," Ashley bit out.

The look of surprise on the woman's face struck a spear of regret into Ashley.

"Hey, she's just looking out for your best interest," the brother named Cade interjected. His dark gaze challenged her to say different. She certainly was going to speak her mind to this broody Outlaw whether he liked it or not.

"She's just looking out for Colter's best interest, not mine. I'm leaving with Blade." She headed toward the door. Going with Blade was the last thing she wanted. She'd much rather stay as close to Colter as possible. Besides, heading out with Blade would make it just that much harder to escape and get back to her daughter. So why was she being stupid enough in going with Blade? Probably because she didn't feel comfortable hanging around there with his gorgeous pregnant wife nearby.

Before she could grab the doorknob a strong hand wrapped around her upper arm, spinning her around. To her shock she came nose to nose with an ashen-faced Colter.

"Trying to leave without saying goodbye again?" Anger dripped from his voice and he glowered at her with such intense emotion that she couldn't stop the shiver of fear from zipping through her. Before she could stop him, his hand slipped into her pocket and he withdrew the vial containing the cure.

He handed it to his brother Cade. "Don't let it out of your sight."

Shit! Damn son of a bitch!

"What the hell are you doing? Give it back! I got the cure and I'm holding onto it."

"The cure goes to S.K.U.L.L.—as soon as Bev releases my brother. And you're staying right here on the Outlaw farm until I say otherwise. You've got some explaining to do too." Before she could utter another protest, Colter pulled her past the amused faces of his brothers, his surprised wife and a grinning Blade, and dragged her like a rag doll down the hallway and into the large bedroom where she'd seen his wife hovering over him only moments earlier.

The instant they entered the bedroom he turned, locked it with a key and deposited the key into his underwear.

"Oh for crying out loud," Ashley blurted. "If you think I'm going for the key, you're sorely mistaken."

"I'm counting on you not going for the key, Starry Eyes." Anger was still evident in his voice as he pulled her onto the bed with him. "I'm bushed and I need some sleep. And don't even think about trying to climb out one of the bedroom windows because I personally installed a high-tech security system and it will alert us if you try something stupid, so just get that jacket off and climb under the covers," he instructed.

"No way. I want out of here and I want out now."

"Why?"

His question came so unexpectedly it felt as if he'd socked her in the gut.

"I just want out of here."

"Why are you suddenly so claustrophobic?"

His fingers were branding her skin right through the jacket and she tried to yank herself free from his grip, but it remained iron hard, making her think he hadn't been as badly wounded as she'd thought.

"I want out, now. Or I'll start kicking that damn door down." Her nerves were strung so tight because of all the events that had transpired in such a short time she didn't doubt she would hurl herself at that door as she said she'd do.

To her surprise, he chuckled. "That would give the brothers and wife something to talk about."

"You're disgusting! How dare you have me under the same roof as your wife! Not to mention inviting me into your bed with her just in the other room. Don't you have an ounce of respect for your wedding vows?"

"Oh, so that's what's eating you. We can invite her into bed too if you like?"

"You're sick."

"Am I? Why?"

"She's pregnant for one thing."

"So? Pregnant women like to sleep too."

The tiniest tingle of a smile tilted his lips. The son of a bitch was toying with her.

"This isn't a funny situation for me, Colter."

"I'm sorry, Starry Eyes. But I just can't help teasing you. You look so cute wearing nothing but my monkey suit jacket."

Oh for heavens sakes! She'd forgotten about that.

"I must say it looks a hell of a lot better on you than it did on me."

She noticed the intimate way his eyes darkened. The way he leaned closer to her, the intense body heat splashing all around her.

She found herself moving away from him ever so slightly. Now was not the time to succumb to the delicious desires his hot looks created.

"I'm sure my brothers and Blade loved checking out your luscious long legs, maybe you even gave them a glimpse of your sweet ass or your pussy."

"Is that all you can think about? Sex?"

"I didn't mention anything about sex, Starry Eyes. I'm just wondering if my brothers were admiring you."

"We had a mad, passionate orgy while Blade and your wife were tending to you."

"Did you enjoy it?"

Oh boy! His eyes were growing even darker. She recognized that look. He wanted to bed her.

Sweet mercy, she wanted to be bedded too.

Her pussy heated at the thought of Colter touching her, kissing her, penetrating her, and with the others within hearing distance. Maybe even joining them?

Despite trying hard not to, heat flushed through her face.

"You're blushing, Ashley. Does the idea of several men making love to you turn you on that much?"

"You're insane," she whispered, noticing his expression was filled with lust. Noticed her pussy creamed with anticipation.

"Am I? You wouldn't have mentioned it if the thought wasn't already in your mind. Times have changed, Starry Eyes. Sharing women is the norm nowadays. My brother Tyler's woman is now married to four men. He'll probably kill all of them when he comes home and finds out. I know I would."

"You would?"

"Yes, I would kill your husbands, Ash. I would kill them to get to you. To get you for myself. Just as Tyler will do once I give S.K.U.L.L. the cure and they stick to our agreement and get him out."

"Is that why you were after the cure? To rescue your brother?"

Colter nodded.

Ashley swallowed at the shiver of excitement and fear crawling up her spine.

"Having a man love her so much, to kill the men she might possibly have fallen in love with after all this time just to get her, it could backfire. His…girlfriend might not be receptive to murder."

"It's not up to her, now is it?"

"What about Luke? Doesn't he feel that way about you and your brothers making love to Callie?"

Without warning he leaned closer and kissed her. A soft, sweet whisper against her lips that made her tremble with need. Made her want more.

"Callie and Luke are married only to each other in their hearts," he replied. "Yes, Luke shared her with us. And Callie shared her body with us, not her heart. Sex is just sex these days, sweetheart."

"Sex should be an intimate act between a man and a woman who love each other."

"No, Starry Eyes, that's called lovemaking. Sex, on the other hand, is enjoying each other's bodies. Hot, no-strings fun."

His warm breath washed all over her face, making the heat there burn so erotically she was close to swooning.

"You wouldn't share me again...would you?" She recognized the hope in her voice and mentally kicked herself for being so obvious.

"Only if you were willing."

"And if I said I was willing?"

Oh boy! What was she saying? Was she teasing him or was she serious? She wasn't in the least bit sure. Whatever was happening between them, it sure was turning her on hotter than a firecracker.

His warm lips brushed across her mouth again ever so gently and she found herself whimpering. Found herself helpless as he lifted both her arms over her head and kissed her again.

Deeper. Harder.

Oh yes, he sure did know how to kiss.

"Then I'd say we'd have to wait," his warm breath whispered softly against her mouth.

Ashley blinked. "Wait?"

"Until I was in top shape. Until then..."

To her surprise she felt a handcuff clamp down around her wrist and then the other. It was quickly followed by the clink of chains.

Shit! She looked up and saw the shackles. Fury gripped her. Anger at falling for this so easily.

"Colter! You bastard!"

He smiled smugly.

"There...now I've got you right where I want you again." He chuckled and got out of bed.

At the foot of the bed he lifted another chain. Cuffs dangled and clinked. Cuffs for her feet, no doubt.

She tried to move her legs away but he was faster. Capturing one and then the other, he had her clamped and trapped in no time flat.

"How convenient. Do you and your brothers do this to your wife?"

"Wouldn't you like to know?"

As a matter of fact, yes, she would like to know. Did his wife lie here in this bed, her arms and legs shackled while all the Outlaw brothers had their way with her?

Heated liquid pooled between her pussy lips.

She watched him stalk around the other side of the bed. Sympathy zipped through her when she noticed the thick white pad Blade had taped over the bullet wound on the back of his upper thigh. The bed moved as he wearily slipped beneath the covers.

The sympathy dissolved when he reached out and turned out the bedside lamp, dousing the room into darkness.

"Good night, Starry Eyes," he chuckled.

The bed moved slightly and then a moment later she heard the soft sound of his even breathing.

He was already asleep!

But what about her? His kisses had inflamed her. His talk of ménages had made her aroused. She needed relief or she'd be on edge all night long. How dare he leave her so sexually frustrated?

Screw him! She'd just have to find relief in her own way. Lifting her cuffed hands, she moved her arms downward and cursed softly when the chain stopped just short of its mark.

Damn him!

She couldn't reach her aching pussy, nor could she lift her legs or budge upward. He'd planned her capture very well and she found herself wondering if maybe his wife Callie had been in on her capture too.

* * * * *

A loud crash made Colter wince as he sipped his late morning coffee and watched Callie put the final touches of chocolate icing on the chocolate cake she'd baked earlier that morning.

"There goes that antique ceramic lamp I fixed last week. Sounds like she's smashed it against the wall," Mac grumbled from where he sat at the end of the kitchen table. Ever since Colter had joined them in the kitchen Mac had had his head stuck behind the weekly farm newsletter. He'd been searching for a used engine part to get their second tractor running but had come up with nothing. Their next step would be to pay an exuberantly high price through the black market, and if S.K.U.L.L. didn't come through with the money promised for getting the cure, they'd be right back to square one.

No money for tractor parts. No parts, no tractor. No way of getting the seed into the ground. No seed. No vegetables to sell. And no money to pay the mortgage.

But if S.K.U.L.L. came through, then things would really be looking bright.

Another loud bang echoed from somewhere near the back of the farmhouse.

"I think that's the bathroom door shutting. She must be going in for a shower," Cade's voice sounded tight as he sat opposite from Colter. His dark brown shoulder-length hair was mussed from the wind. His face unshaven and so tanned he could pass for a dangerous renegade Indian. Since before sunup he'd been out plowing the fields with their remaining rusty tractor. For the past few weeks—with the threat of foreclosure looming over their heads—all of them had been nervous, uptight and constantly working the farm. Sometimes one of them would suggest that maybe they should just give up the farm and let the evil Barlow brothers who owned the bank and their mortgage simply foreclose on them. But the thought of giving in to those bastards who'd Claimed Tyler's woman would always offer them an incentive to work harder.

"Good grief. How long are you going to keep her locked up in that stuffy bedroom?"

His three brothers chuckled at Callie's question as she waddled over from the counter, chocolate cake in hand, and heaved her pregnant frame at the kitchen table. She looked absolutely stunning this morning. Her cheeks were flushed pink, her eyes sparkled and she'd put her long shoulder-length hair into an updo with two curls drooping down on each side of her pretty face. They sure didn't kid around when they said pregnant women had a certain glow about them.

However, that's not what had his immediate attention. His gaze zeroed in on the chocolate cake she placed in front of them.

"Damn that smells delicious." He couldn't stop his mouth from watering at the heavenly aroma drifting beneath his nostrils. Nor could he stop himself from wiggling with excitement in his chair. A niggle of pain from his bullet wound to the thigh made him stop short. Not more than twelve hours after getting shot he was feeling a heck of a lot better thanks to the supply of painkillers and numbing cream he kept in his house office medical cabinet.

These days, having chocolate cake was a rare treat, especially with the skyrocketing cost of food since the economy had collapsed.

"You didn't answer my question," Callie said coolly as she began cutting some huge slices.

"I'll let her out when she settles down," he admitted.

"She doesn't strike me as the type who's going to settle down, bro. And she won't put up with too much of your shit, either," his brother Luke chuckled from his perch on the kitchen counter as he kept one eye on the chocolate cake and the other eye to the window and the driveway.

Blade had said he'd come as soon as he got any word about Tyler being released. Everyone was understandably on edge. They had no way of knowing if Bev would give in to Colter's demands of him not handing over the research papers and cure unless his brother were out of danger.

Anything and everything could go wrong. Especially where Tyler was concerned. Their baby brother had a knack for getting himself into trouble. He was the hothead of the family. Acting first and thinking second. It had gotten him into a lot of fights during his young life, and no one had been too surprised when he'd turned up missing during the Terrorist Wars.

"If anything, you denying her her freedom will only make her more mad," Callie replied.

"She'll be fine," Colter replied, not really believing what he was telling Callie. He doubted Ashley would forgive him easily for trussing her up as he had last night. But he'd been tired and weak, and with the help of Callie he'd managed to outfit the bed with restraints. He still couldn't believe how easily she'd melted against him when he'd kissed her, how quickly her anger had diminished and how easily she'd trusted him, enabling him to capture her yet again. It gave him a fragment of hope for their future together. First though, he needed his questions answered and he wasn't about to let her go anywhere until she answered them.

This morning when he'd awoken, she'd still been sleeping and before he'd snuck out of the bedroom he'd unlocked the cuffs from her wrists and ankles, all the while admiring her stretched-out luscious form. There had been an odd smile on her sleeping face. A smile that, if his instincts were correct, was anything but kindly towards him. Oh yeah, she was definitely going to be pissed off when he showed up and let her out of the locked bedroom. But he'd much rather deal with her when his stomach was full of that chocolate cake.

"She is a feisty one, isn't she?" Luke chuckled as he scraped a finger full of chocolate icing out of the empty bowl on the counter. "She sure didn't much enjoy you dragging her off to the bedroom last night. I'm sure she must be a spitfire in bed when she's mad."

Callie threw him a stern scowl. "You aren't helping, dear husband."

Luke winked at Callie, and Colter noticed her relax. She knew Luke was only kidding. Ever since Callie had come back home, Luke hadn't so much as looked at another woman…not that there were any women around there to look at, with all the groups of men keeping their Claimed women under virtual house arrest and not letting them go anywhere on their own. It was for a woman's protection to remain out of sight these days. Life for any woman was becoming increasingly dangerous, especially for the ones who still opted to live unClaimed and unprotected in the Maine wilderness and other areas throughout the States.

There were hoards of men who didn't have a woman to love. Men who were frantic to have kids of their own. To have a woman's soft touch on their skin. The warm, nourishing companionship of the opposite sex.

The water pipes began to groan and squeak, indicating Cade was right. Ashley was taking a shower.

Now would be the perfect time to go in and calm her down.

He eyed the chocolate cake…or maybe he should stay and enjoy that cake before his brothers wolfed it down?

Chocolate cake? Or Ashley?

It shouldn't be such a damned tough decision.

But it was.

Chapter Ten

Colter Outlaw slipped into the bedroom and tiptoed toward the bathroom. The shower was still running, but the door to the bathroom was locked. She'd been in there a long time. Probably getting herself off without his help.

He grinned.

A locked door never stopped him when he wanted something. All he needed was a credit card, which he just so happened to have. He slid it out of his wallet, slipped it between the crack and the door latch, and voila.

The doorknob turned and he walked into the hot, steamy bathroom.

The closed shower curtain moved back and forth with the breeze of the powering water. He stepped toward it and his cock pulsed with heated lust. In a moment he'd be able to see her lusciously nude body all wet and soft, and maybe, if she weren't too mad at him, she might let him bring her the relief he'd denied her last night.

Man, he'd sure been an asshole last night. Selfish and arrogant in grabbing her and embarrassing her that way by dragging her away in front of Blade, his brothers and Callie like she'd been a child instead of a stubborn, sexy woman. He'd tucked her into his bedroom just so he'd be able to sleep easier knowing she was right there lying beside him.

He found his smile widening as the moist steam from the shower seeped through the sides of the curtain and slapped against his face.

Déjà vu. He'd done the same thing back at Pleasure Palace, sneaking into the shower when Ashley had first shown up there. Then he'd barely kept himself from stepping into the shower stall with her. Had told himself he wouldn't get emotionally involved. His mission at the time had been purely sexual revenge. His only motive to sexually torture her and leave her wanting him just as she'd left him wanting her.

Things sure had changed in the course of a few days. Now he couldn't wait to mount her. Couldn't wait to figure out how they were going to get around this Claiming Law, because there was no way he could accept anyone being her husband except himself.

Having her being pleasured by other men was another story though.

He knew ménages were her ultimate fantasy and, truth be told, he'd truly enjoyed watching his woman getting pleasure at another man's hands. Watching Blade arousing her and pleasuring her back during the Terrorist Wars had been such a satisfying experience for Ashley, he'd seen it written all over her face when she'd been double penetrated.

Last night he'd seen a similar look on her face when he'd mentioned her being in Callie's position with his brothers pleasuring her. Her face had flamed with such a lovely hue of red he knew she wanted a ménage again, maybe with more than just Blade this time around.

The shower curtain was moist beneath his fingertips as he slowly slid it aside and— The stall was empty!

Before he could turn, he felt the cuff snap around his left wrist and heard Ashley's satisfied giggle as her soft, warm curves pressed against his backside.

"It's my turn now, Outlaw," she whispered in a sexy bedroom tone of voice that made his heart pick up an excited pace.

Her warm breath tingled against his ear and he found himself not resisting arrest, so to speak, as she tugged on the long chain she'd obviously retrieved from where it had been tangled through the headboard of his bed.

He noticed she wore his black suit jacket again as she leaned over and shut off the shower then led him out of the bathroom back into the bedroom. The suit enhanced her long, luscious legs and gave him an enticing peek of her deliciously rounded ass as she climbed onto the bed and looped the chain and other cuff through the bed spindles.

When she yanked on the chain a little he obliged and lay down on the bed, quite anxious to participate with this playful side of her. When she was finished looping the chain, she came to stand in front of him again. He didn't even think of resisting when she clamped the other cuff around his wrist.

Being her hostage this time around was only fair, and he found himself loving the lust glowing in her bright blue eyes as she stared down at him. She looked so damned cute with that satisfied smirk on her flushed face. Her long black hair was tangled and wet, giving her a seductive bad-girl appearance.

Although Colter had never personally used the cuffs with the attached chains on Callie, he knew Luke had.

Even though four of them had Claimed her, Luke was Callie's number one husband and Callie only allowed him to do the kinky stuff to her. Delicious delights he hoped Ashley would allow him to do to her someday.

"Thought you were in the shower," he said as he anxiously awaited her next move. Would she zip open his pants and take his engorged cock into her hot little mouth? Or would she strip him and do other naughty things to him?

"I was hoping you'd think that," she purred, and suddenly headed for the door.

Shit! He hadn't locked it behind him.

"Hey! Where are you going?"

"Don't worry, I won't run away."

She couldn't even if she wanted to. His brothers and Callie wouldn't let her go. They knew how much he wanted to protect Ashley, his stupid behavior last night had only shown them how much.

"Not when I've got you as my captive this time around," she tossed over her shoulder. "You know I really was expecting breakfast in bed. But I can see that isn't going to happen. So now that you've pissed me off, I'll just have to leave you here to stew over your rude behavior for last night and this morning."

Son of a bitch!

"Ashley! Get your ass in here and get these cuffs off me or there will be hell to pay."

Her answer was the bedroom door slamming shut behind her.

"You are going to pay, Starry Eyes. You're going to pay big time," Colter muttered beneath his breath as a slip of excited lust brushed aside his anger at being so easily duped by her. He'd give her breakfast in bed all right, but not the kind she was expecting.

* * * * *

"That sounds like the alarm clock smashing against the door," Ashley said cheerfully as a loud crash followed her into the sunny kitchen. She found herself thoroughly enjoying the shocked expressions on the faces of the Outlaw brothers and the woman named Callie when they gazed up from the scrumptious-looking cake they'd been devouring.

"Good morning," Callie said softly. "Would you like some breakfast?"

"Actually I wouldn't mind having some of that cake. The smell has been teasing me all morning long. I haven't had chocolate in years."

"Have a seat and help yourself. I'll make you some tea."

"Thanks," Ashley seated herself across from the Outlaw brother named Cade and a delicious shiver raced up her spine at the dark, agonizing way he was watching her.

Oh boy! This one looked like he was starved for sex. She snapped her gaze back to the delicious-looking chocolate cake.

"I warned Colter you wouldn't take any of his shit," the man she remembered as being introduced to her as Luke said.

"He should have listened," Ashley said as, without hesitation, she wrapped her fingers onto one gooey iced chunk of the cake and picked it up.

Damn! It sure smelled good!

Tasted even better.

She moaned and closed her eyes the instant the sweet, dark chocolate exploded against her taste buds.

"Absolute heaven."

When she opened her eyes, she found the Outlaw brothers staring at her. Interest and appreciation not to mention carnal lust brewed in Mac and Cade's eyes. She remembered Colter mentioning they hadn't had sex since they'd found out Callie was pregnant. The brother named Luke, on the other hand, was frowning at her and shaking his head.

"Cheri Blakely isn't going to give up until she finds you and Colter, you realize that, don't you?"

Leave it to an Outlaw to ruin her first experience with chocolate in one hell of a long time.

"I know. I won't be staying long." Just until she could contact Blade and have her bodyguard released, along with obtaining a guarantee she would get first crack at the vaccine for her daughter when it became mass-produced. While she waited, maybe she'd even exact a little revenge on Colter.

"Don't you men have something else to do with your time?" Callie cut in. "Luke, I need you to go and buy some sugar."

"Sugar? We've got enough sugar—"

Callie's firm look stopped him cold. "Okay, will do." He stood quickly, taking his wife's hint.

"And don't you two have a field to finish plowing?" she said to Cade and Mac, who were still busily staring at Ashley as she licked the sweet chocolate icing from her fingers.

"I think we get the message," Luke chuckled as he nodded to his two brothers who stood. In a flurry of movement they joined him and headed out of the kitchen.

"House alarm is set," Luke called out, and then a moment later the front door slammed shut.

Silence ensued.

But not for long.

From the rear of the house another loud crash followed.

"That could have been a chair being hurled against the wall or maybe it was the antique clock." Callie chuckled as she set a pot of tea and a cup down in front of Ashley.

"Neither."

"What do you think he threw?"

"Considering he can't reach anything except whatever is beside the bed..."

Ashley enjoyed the way Callie's eyes rounded in surprise. "You cuffed him to the bed?"

"That's right. Just returning the favor."

"Oh boy, he's going to be really pissed off if you leave him there."

"He's already pissed off," Ashley said as she licked the rest of the gooey chocolate off her fingers and grabbed the mug.

"Two spoons of sugar and some cream, just the way you like it," Callie replied as Ashley took a tentative sip and tried hard not to give in to the relaxing feeling she was getting around this woman.

No, she wasn't just a woman. She was Colter's wife. She'd do well to remember that.

"How'd you know that's how I like my tea?" she asked as she took a larger sip of the delicious tea.

"Colter told me some things about you."

She almost choked as the liquid went down the wrong way.

"Are you okay?" Concern splashed across Callie's face.

Ashley nodded and put down the mug. Suddenly she didn't want to eat the cake or have tea anymore.

"Exactly what did he say?" Oh sweet heavens, she couldn't believe she'd just asked that question. What in the world had Colter told his wife about her?

"Just that he was very upset at the way things were left between you two in Iraq."

Hmm. Colter had a guilty conscience perhaps? But that didn't make sense. He sure hadn't acted guilty when he'd snapped that collar around her neck, figged her and all those other naughty things he'd done.

"I'm sure we'll get along fine as long as he doesn't try to dominate me anymore."

"You mean dominate you outside of the bedroom."

Oh, my God! She couldn't believe Colter's wife was talking to her this way.

Callie laughed. Her eyes absolutely sparkled and Ashley decided she liked this woman.

"Listen, I don't want to stand in the way between you two. I know legally I'm Colter's Claimed wife but if he wants out to be with you, I certainly understand. It's just, well…we'd have to get a replacement husband."

"I can't believe you say this so casually."

Callie frowned. "It's the way it is now."

"But how can you accept this…this arrangement so easily? Doesn't it bother you to have four husbands forced upon you?"

"They weren't forced upon me. I came into the arrangement willingly. I suppose Colter told you that I spent five years incarcerated as a guinea pig?"

Ashley nodded.

"After being locked up like that and then escaping, only to discover the government invoked this Claiming Law, which forced me to hide yet again…well, I'm not one for living in fear and constantly looking over my shoulder like some of the women are choosing to do. I just wanted to settle down and continue my life, and so I allowed myself to be Claimed by the man I love along with three of his brothers. It's that simple."

"Wish I could see it that way."

"It's actually quite a lovely arrangement. The sex life was absolutely phenomenal. Having four men making love to you, pleasuring you, making you climax over and over again. Especially the Outlaw Lovers, they do know how to make a woman feel fabulous."

"Outlaw Lovers?"

"My nickname for them."

"Oh, I see. How…interesting." That's how she considered Colter. Her Outlaw Lover.

To Ashley's surprise, she didn't feel an ounce of jealousy that this woman and Colter had had sexual relations. Actually, she found herself rather envying Callie's casual attitude toward her circumstances.

"Leave me a piece of that chocolate cake! Or there will be hell to pay!" came Colter's shout from the back of the house.

"I could think of a few things I could do to him with chocolate cake." Callie winked, and Ashley couldn't stop herself from laughing.

* * * * *

"You're really missing a delicious chocolate cake by sleeping the day away."

At the teasing sound of Ashley's voice Colter opened his eyes and blinked. He didn't know how long he'd been in this bondage position on the bed with his wrists shackled because he'd fallen asleep. From the low slant of sunshine splashing through the windows, he'd say it'd been at least a few hours.

Moving his head, he inhaled sharply at the gorgeous sight of Ashley standing in the open doorway. She'd changed out of the suit jacket and now wore a provocative see-through pale blue floral teddy.

Oh boy, she looked so hot!

The teddy had luscious peek-a-boo side slits held together by flirty strings showing off the creamy curves of her generous breasts as well as her waist, hips and her silky thighs.

His cock swelled with appreciation.

With a low dipping V-neck, the teddy didn't have any cups to cover her breasts but the delicate material cradled the underneath of her luscious curves like hands, making her gorgeous mounds look almost twice their size. Star-shaped silver nipple shields allowed her recently pierced nipples to poke through the appropriate holes.

"You like?" she teased as she left the door open and held a huge, icing-covered, chocolate slice of cake in her hand. In the other hand, he spied a small sack as she came to stand beside the bed where she'd made him her hostage.

"Like is a hell of an understatement."

"You can thank your wife for being so generous with her things. She made this lovely outfit herself from a tablecloth. The nipple decorations, which I must add she has quite an assortment of, Luke makes from tin out in the barn when you and your brothers are working in the field."

"So that's what he's doing with his free time." Lucky dog!

"And these are homemade too…"

A surge of heat pounded through his veins when she lifted one leg and placed her foot on the side of the bed, giving him an erotic view of a skimpy thong and a breathless opening in the material at her crotch. He swallowed tightly at the sight of the puffy pink pussy lips stretching through the opening. Large silver-shaped star weights dangled on tiny chains from each clamped labia.

He blew out a breath. Was it suddenly getting hot in here or what?

"I've never seen this…outfit. I had no idea Callie and Luke were playing so much while we were working."

"I don't know if I should be pleased or angry that you had no idea these items existed."

"She only allowed Luke to…"

"I think I get the picture. No wonder you were so hot to try those delicious toys out on me back at Pleasure Palace."

She leaned over and placed the chocolate cake and the small bag she'd come into the room with on the nearby table. Then she returned her attention to him.

"I really didn't appreciate the way you tied me down last night. Teasing me with possibilities of ménages. Not letting me get my satisfaction from that gorgeous bulge pressing against your briefs."

"Would an apology suffice?"

Ashley smiled mischievously and shook her head.

Oh yeah, she was definitely up to something. "Didn't think so."

"And I didn't appreciate the way you pumped my nipples and figged me and left me all hot and bothered all those times back at Pleasure Palace."

"Kind of thought you'd enjoy that."

"Oh, don't get me wrong, Outlaw Lover. I did enjoy all those naughty things you did to me, but when you start something, you really should follow through the way a woman truly craves."

"Perhaps you should show me how I should follow through next time?"

"You're getting the picture," she giggled. Reaching into the bag with her chocolate-covered fingers, she dug out a pair of scissors.

"Um, do I want to know what those scissors are for?"

"To undress you of course."

Shit!

"Then what?" His voice sounded strangled, aroused.

"You'll see."

She leaned over him. Her succulent body heat lashed against him in such lusty waves it had him gritting his teeth and his heart beating a mile a minute. He couldn't help but tense when the cool blade of the scissors slid against his chest and she began to cut away his cotton shirt.

"That's my favorite shirt," he complained as she splayed the two sides apart revealing his chest.

"So, pay me back later."

"You bet I will."

"How about these pants? They your favorites too?"

"Yes," he lied.

"Good, double payback."

His belly quivered as she slid one blade of the scissors inside his pants and against his skin.

"Better watch out, Starry Eyes. Payback's a bitch."

She winked. "I'm counting on it."

A moment later, she peeled the tattered remains of his pants away.

"Careful down there," he warned as the blade slid against his swollen cock. The crunchy sound of her scissors cutting through his cotton briefs split the air.

"Very careful," she agreed.

He heard her suck in her breath as she peeled the underwear aside and his swollen, purple cock ran up at full staff. The angry scratches—compliments of Cheri—were lashed back and forth over the pulsing veins.

"Very nice," she whispered. He was surprised there was no jealousy in her voice as there had been the first time she'd seen Cheri's territorial markings on him. Instead, sparkling lust shone in her eyes and the pink tip of her tongue darted out of her slightly parted mouth as if she were pondering doing something totally delicious.

And he'd guessed right. A moment later she was smearing cool chocolate icing up and down his shaft and over the scratches. Her soft, sensuous touches made his balls tighten painfully, made him growl his appreciation.

"Feel good?"

He nodded, his gaze transfixed to the generous curves of her breasts as she leaned over. Warmth zipped through his flesh as she licked the chocolate-covered tip of his cock with her luscious tongue.

"It's going to get even better."

She reached into the bag and his eyes widened as he heard the sharp clink of metal.

"This Y-clamp cock strap is going to keep your nipples nice and taut and your erection strong and hard for me."

"Um, I don't think I have a problem with being hard whenever I'm with you, Starry Eyes," he chuckled.

She continued to drag out the chain. Eventually it divided into two chains with the nipple clamps on the ends.

"I will exact my sexual revenge and get some questions answered."

"Questions answered? What questions?"

When he saw the other end of the chain, spotted the chrome metal ring with the ball she'd used as the clitoral stimulator, he knew he was in trouble.

"Oh no, you don't!" he hissed.

"Oh yes, my sweetheart. And your wife has even given me her blessing. Not to mention we'll have until tomorrow all by ourselves to play, so you can make as much noise as you want because the house is empty."

"They wouldn't leave me here at your mercy." Even as he said it, he knew they would. His brothers knew how hard he'd fallen for Ashley back in the Wars and he wouldn't put it past them to have suggested this entire forced seduction to Ashley.

"Mac, Luke and Callie have left for the next state to pick up a part for the tractor. They'll stay overnight with friends. Cade was conveniently called away on a bounty hunting job, which leaves you totally at my mercy."

Shit!

"What about Blade?"

"He can join us when he shows up."

A roar of arousal pummeled him at the thought of watching Ashley squirm between the two of them again.

"As you said, revenge is a bitch, sweetheart," she cooed as she pulled a ball stretcher from the bag.

Double Shit! *Think fast, Outlaw!*

"I mean we have to keep an eye out for Blade. He'll be coming with word about Tyler. I'm going to have to give him the cure, the research papers."

"Everything is under control, my sweet. Don't worry about anything. Cade told me where he put the cure and papers."

"Cade's not one to trust easy. How did you convince him to tell you where the cure is?"

"Actually I had nothing to do with it. Callie can be pretty persuasive. Especially with the threat of withholding another piece of chocolate cake."

Colter chuckled. "We all have a major weakness for chocolate cake."

"So I've been told." Her gentle fingers branded him as she held his cock with one hand.

"What else did Callie tell you?" He breathed into the sensual sensations of having her fingers wrapped around his cock.

"Well…" she scooped a finger of chocolate icing off the cake and smeared it slowly around his skull tattoo.

"She said that you give out the cutest little moan just before you come."

His cock pulsed around the cock ring and his balls felt as if they were about to burst.

"I told her I already knew that from personal experience."

"You did, did you?"

"Yes, we had quite a nice chat over tea and chocolate cake."

"You did save some for me, didn't you?"

"Of course. There is one last piece and I had to hide it from your brothers or they would have devoured it…now just relax and let all your worries disappear, and rest assured I'll be gentle…for now. I know all about how a man's cock and balls are extremely sensitive and should be handled with care especially while aroused…and you certainly are aroused." Ashley grinned. Her warm fingers wrapped around his swollen testicles none too gently.

He winced as pain zipped through his balls and into his belly.

"Hurt?"

"No."

"Liar," she whispered as she gently pulled his scrotum downward and maneuvered the ball stretcher around each swollen ball and fastened the binding in place. He groaned at the erotic way his testicles throbbed from the pressure.

"Oh that looks absolutely delicious. Now, for the next step."

Her fingers trailed sensuous, featherlike brushes up over his abdomen and then up his belly until she reached his nipples. Index fingers from each hand looped through his nipple rings and she twisted and pulled and flicked until his nipples ached and became tender, hard beads. She snapped the clamps over each nipple and ring, engorging them both in a slow, erotic burn that sent a shiver of excitement pulsing through his cock and stretched balls.

"I've been dying to do this to you. To get the answers I've been curious about," she whispered. One hand wrapped around his penis and she gently squeezed him. "Nice and rock-hard. Just the way I want my cock."

"Getting a little possessive, are we?" he found himself chuckling as the cool clink of chains dribbled over his belly and lower abdomen.

"Very. Especially after what Callie said about you."

"Oh? And what's that?"

He expected jealousy to spark her eyes at his question. There was none. Obviously whatever hostility had been there last night when Ashley had seemed defiant against Callie was now gone.

"Ladies don't tell on each other." She grinned as she fiddled with something on the cock ring.

"Sounds like you two have bonded."

"She's a very nice lady. I can see why you would do her the favor of Claiming her."

"What are you doing with that cock ring?"

"This clit stimulator on it doubles as a screw. Twist it and it'll make the band larger to fit over your cock. Like this," she slid the cool ring over his engorged cock and nestled it close to his root. Then she started twisting the clit stimulator. The band grew tighter and tighter until just the tiniest burst of pain made him shift his hips nervously.

"Easy, Starry Eyes," he warned.

"What's the matter, don't you trust me?" her eyes glittered teasingly as she gave the chain a yank.

He gasped as sparks of pain zipped through both his nipples as well as the base of his cock. His cock turned a darker shade of purple.

"I know what I'm doing, sweet thing. Your cock and balls are safe with me...only as long as you cooperate and answer my questions."

Oh jeez.

The mattress shifted beneath him as she climbed on. She stood over him and spread her legs on both sides of his hips, giving him an awesome view of her luscious breasts as well as the stars dangling off her labia clamps. Her pussy lips were even puffier and pinker than a moment before. He watched as she ran her finger over her engorged clit.

Her eyes closed. Her lips parted.

His cock pulsed.

Oh man. What a freaking tease.

She moaned her arousal.

His heart picked up speed, furiously pounding against his chest.

Slurpy sounds ripped through the air as her finger dipped into her moist sheath. He found himself cursing as he pictured his cock disappearing inside her tight hole or her velvety vaginal muscles clamping around his throbbing flesh.

"Oh this feels so good," she whispered.

The sweet little bitch knew how to torture him. "Ashley..."

Another erotic moan shot fire through his veins. If his cock and balls weren't tied up, he would have come on the spot at the sound.

Her finger kept sliding over her red swollen clit then slipping inside her pussy. She rode her hand harder, faster, her hips swiveling with the arousal until she cried out her release.

Oh man! What he wouldn't do to join her.

For a moment, the only sounds were their combined rapid breaths bursting through the air. Her face was flushed a gorgeous pink and her full breasts rose and fell with her every inhalation, her nipple rings glistened in the late afternoon sunshine streaming through the windows. Her eyes flickered open and she gazed down at him with those intimate starry eyes he remembered so well.

"Now...that the appetizer is out of the way...let's get down to business, shall we?"

"How about giving me a little appetizer first?"

"Uh-uh. Answer my questions first."

Colter sighed with frustration. "What do you want to know?"

She sat down on his lap. Her long shimmering hair streamed down in front of her like a black veil covering her breasts from him. Her flesh was hot and wet on his thighs as she carefully avoided his cock with her pussy. He sucked in a breath as she reached over and scraped her nails along the knuckle-sized tattoo he'd had done after they'd denied him personal help to find Ashley. A tattoo he'd gotten as a reminder to never trust S.K.U.L.L.

"Who are these skull people?" she whispered, her voice full of curiosity as she leaned her head close to his chest.

His gut tightened at her question. "You don't want to know about them."

"A little information might get you a mouthful of that cake," her cute little rosebud mouth pursed over his left, clamped, ringed nipple. Warm, sweet waves of her breath washed against his chest as she parted her lips and sucked the tiny clamp, silver nipple ring and his nipple into her mouth, pulling to this side of sweet pain.

Oh shit, that felt good.

Too good.

"Tell me about them," she said after lifting her mouth away.

"I shouldn't, Starry Eyes."

"Please trust me. I really want to know everything about you."

"I quit them and they are out of my life. I want nothing to do with them."

"And yet you went into Pleasure Palace to get that cure for them and to help your brother. They must still be important to you. I could see how concerned Blade was when he found us together."

She let go of the ring and her hand snuck over the tattoo and headed for parts south. The instant her fingers cupped his vulnerable testicles he knew he would be telling her anything she wanted to hear if she decided to squeeze too hard.

"Maybe I should add some more scratch marks to your sac? I'm sure I could do more damage than Cheri."

"I'm sure you could, but would you want to? Pain would render me useless."

The tip of her pink tongue peeked out of her mouth. Such a beautiful tongue.

"Then perhaps you should participate in telling me?"

Her hand tightened around his testicles and she squeezed. None too gently.

"You could say I have you by the balls…literally."

Shit! Ouch!

"All right, you win. On one condition."

"Name it."

"I want to know your secrets. What's been bothering you? Why the nightmares?"

He swore her face paled a shade or two. Noticed her jaw twitch ever so slightly. His questions irritated her, but she barely showed her annoyance as she threw him a forced smile and tossed her head back to get her black bangs out of her eyes.

"You talk first."

The pressure around his swollen testicles eased as she loosened her grip and he found himself breathing a little sigh of relief.

"What does this skull stand for?"

Ah damn.

"I thought we just covered that."

"You covered it. I still want to know."

"It's a part of my past I'm not very proud of. You don't need to hear it."

"I'd never judge you, Colter. Please believe me when I say I would love you no matter what."

Oh boy. The love word. A fuzzy warmth sifted through him.

"Please trust me."

"If I tell you, you mustn't repeat it. It would be dangerous if word got out they exist."

She nodded and said sadly, "I'm very good at keeping secrets."

"I'm counting on you telling me yours, Ashley."

"I will. I promise. I will tell you everything...but first you have to answer my questions."

There appeared to be a desperation about her. A need to know more about him. It seemed as if she might be testing him. Maybe she was checking him out to see if she could trust him with her secrets?

"Okay…S.K.U.L.L. stands for Skilled Kill Undercover Liaison Links. They are a secret US Army Intelligence agency that uses men and women in the medical profession. People who have excellent shooting skills and who know how to kill."

Ashley drew a lazy circle around his right nipple and acted as if this newest tidbit didn't bother her. But it did. He could tell by the cute little worry wrinkles marring the area between her eyebrows.

"An assassin, like the general told me."

"You both knew who I was?"

"No. The general didn't know anything until that last day. And he told me long afterward…after you and I had parted. He told me someone tipped off his son that there was a hit out on him. While you, Blade and I were…together that last night, the general was at a restaurant meeting with his son. He had guards secretly stationed outside the building…they saw Blade…and then they saw you when you showed up and one of them recognized you. That's when they realized you were an assassin. He told me you'd just used him and me as a cover to get to his son."

She shrugged her shoulders and inhaled a shaky breath.

So that accounted for all these questions she was throwing at him and why they'd known Blade and he were lying in wait that night. It also proved she hadn't been a knowing decoy as Blade had once suggested. These tidbits of information certainly made him feel a whole hell of a lot better.

Suddenly she peeked up at him. "Doesn't that go against your oath or something? Killing people."

He repressed the painful memories of the people he'd had to kill during the Wars. His life back then had been out of his control. The unleashing of the X-virus. The mutations that had followed. The helplessness he'd felt when he'd watched his mother and sister die horribly from a deadly mutation of the virus. The deaths of so many women he'd known. It had just been so overwhelming.

Anger had followed. Red-hot rage that had persuaded him and his brothers to join and fight against the bastards who'd killed so many women. The fight had spread and ultimately included any country who had insisted on placing women as second-class citizens or non-persons.

He'd always been the best shot when his dad had taken them hunting. The Army had noticed. Seen his potential. Had sent him to S.K.U.L.L. for training.

He'd been part of a large military machine and fighting for his country. Simply following his orders and fighting for all the women who had died.

Over the years he'd become an expert at keeping his focus directly to the present and keeping the past in the past…keeping everything in the past…except Ashley. She'd been the one person who he'd never been able to forget. Probably because he'd thought she'd been a sweet and innocent victim, dragged unwilling into the mayhem of the Terrorist Wars.

"When I was ordered to join S.K.U.L.L. that oath was abolished," he admitted.

"So you had to go undercover to kill people…terrorists?"

"Anyone the US Army wanted out of the way. On either side. I used my medical skills as a doctor as my cover."

He held his breath as he let his words sink in. More wrinkles, this time in her forehead.

"On our side too?"

"That's right."

"You had to kill our own people? Why?"

Oh shit! She'd said she wouldn't judge.

"There were traitors…high-ranking officers who fed information to the terrorists for money. And then there were officers like the general whose son had left the US Army to join the terrorists. S.K.U.L.L. worked it so the general believed I'd saved his life in some controversial brain surgery. They'd hoped he'd be so grateful that I'd put my career on the line to save him, that I must be trustworthy. They anticipated he would thank me by taking me into his home as his personal physician."

The lazy fingers smoothing over his skull tattoo got a little tenser.

"What would have happened if you'd refused to join S.K.U.L.L.?"

"Not following orders would have gotten me into the brig. I couldn't practice my profession in the brig…so I did what I was told. I did the assigned kills and I was allowed to use my skills out in the field between assignments."

"And Blade? He's what?"

"He's my backup. My partner."

"And why did you bring him to the general's villa…was he part of the cover or…"

So that's what she was angling at. She'd wanted to know if he'd used her for his friend's benefit.

"It was nothing like that, Ash. I wanted to give you your fantasy and I needed his help in taking you away with me."

"But you never did take me away. I woke up and you were gone."

"We came back. But the note and the comb you left me on the pillow—"

She tensed, gazed at him. Anger sparked her eyes. "I never left that comb on the pillow and I certainly did not leave you a note. You left me one. You said you changed your mind. That you were only acting out a fantasy with me."

He stilled. "I never left you a note, Ash."

Her confused gaze unsettled him. "The only one I ever wrote was the one Cheri made me write to you the other night."

Colter closed his eyes as everything sunk in around him. She'd never left him. The concept of it wrapped snugly around his heart. She'd never written that note. She'd never left the comb on the pillow for him to find. Christ! All this time he'd hated her, wanted her, planned to walk away from her once he'd had her.

"Fuck!" she whispered harshly. "That bastard! I should have known he was involved. Should have known!"

Colter swallowed hard as memories of searching for her burst behind his eyes. He'd read that note. Hadn't believed it. Had wanted to hear it from her own lips.

He'd put his life in jeopardy asking around about the general. He'd discovered the general had vanished with Ashley. The Army wasn't giving out the details. He'd known the general had connections. Had probably paid off the higher ranks to find him a cushy job somewhere else until Colter forgot about her.

He'd counted on S.K.U.L.L.'s help. He'd been pissed off beyond belief they'd refused his personal request. Thank God for Blade. He'd tried to help him find Ashley but he hadn't been successful either.

Colter had spiraled after losing her. Hit rock-bottom. Somehow, Blade had gotten him out of it. Had kept him busy with assignments and Colter had vowed he'd get his revenge. Had nurtured his anger toward Ashley. Had planned his revenge against her and when the opportunity had presented itself, he'd put his assignment in danger because of her.

No, because of what the general had done.

He fought down the anger churning inside him. Now was not the time to be pissed off. Now was the time to get answers from her.

He snapped open his eyes and found Ashley staring at him. She looked lost. Afraid. Devastated.

He wanted to reach out to her. To hug her to his chest, but there was no more time to waste. They had to pick up the pieces of their relationship, but first, he needed to hear her secrets.

"Your turn," he said simply.

She nodded.

Chapter Eleven

Anxiety tightened in Ashley's chest. She couldn't believe she was so surprised in learning the general had somehow gotten someone, probably a member of his staff, to put that horrid note on her pillow pretending it was from Colter. She'd had no reason not to believe it was from him. She didn't know his handwriting. Had assumed it was his.

The general had somehow found out about the comb, probably had videotaped Colter giving it to her. He would know how important the comb had been to both of them.

Of course Colter would assume the items would be from her.

And there she sat. In bed with the man she'd trusted, the man who she'd thought had betrayed her and all she could think of was how he must have hated her. Hated her for something she'd never even done.

Now everything made sense. His anger toward her. Blade's anger toward her.

And now he wanted her to tell him her secrets.

She made a move to loosen the ball stretcher she'd wrapped around him. It must be hurting by now.

"Leave it for now, Ashley. Quit stalling. Why didn't you tell me about your daughter? Why are you here with only one bodyguard?"

"I'm here with only one bodyguard because I escaped the general. He's dead. I killed him a couple of weeks ago at his Utah compound where he'd taken me after the collapse of the Terrorist Wars. My bodyguard helped me to cover up his death. He made it look as though the general had suddenly gone out of the country on business. He also helped my daughter and me escape. When I had her in a safe place he helped me to come here to bid on the cure."

He blinked at her but said nothing. It was as if he hadn't heard her confession. Or maybe he had and he was just trying to figure out what to do about the fact he'd been fucking a murderess. Suddenly the need to explain simply broke from her. It all just started spilling out in a horrible rush.

"We were fighting about our daughter. He'd sold her to Cheri. He was going to send my innocent baby to that evil woman, and he said he was going to breed me again. He was touching me, and he made me feel so furious, so dirty and worthless...so helpless... I tried to push him away...we both fell and he broke his neck when he hit the fireplace mantel."

Now besides her trusty bodyguard, only Colter and she knew what a terrible thing she'd done.

He was shaking his head and rubbing his chin with puzzlement as if denying what she'd said.

"So that's why you were so scared when you were talking to Cheri when you first arrived. You thought she'd find out about the general?"

"Yes. Mike forged the letter, bribed his way for us to get here so I could bid on the cure. I wanted to give the information to the government, to make sure they would create the vaccine for my daughter and all the young girls but now..."

Now she was at the mercy of Colter for the cure. At the mercy of S.K.U.L.L.

A sob escaped her and he reached out and grabbed her, pulled her against him. She sank against his welcome warmth. There were too many emotions to sort through at the moment, and the strong feel of his hard body against hers made her feel safe. Safe enough to finally allow the tears of rage, the humiliation of being a sex slave, the fear of what would happen to her daughter, everything to just flow out of her in a wave of endless tears.

She snuggled closer to him. Tried to bury herself into his power, his strength as he softly caressed her hair and whispered to her. His calm voice magnetized her. Centered her, and after a while she was able to pull herself together.

But she stayed in his embrace, awaiting his next questions. She didn't have long to wait.

"You said he wanted to breed you again…who did he breed you with before?" His voice sounded hoarse, strangled.

He knew the answer. She could feel it in the tense way he held himself.

"He put drugs in your food. It only allowed the sperm that would create females to reach my womb."

"You said you were on birth control."

"They were placebos. He told me everything afterward…after I found out I was pregnant with your child…your daughter. He knew we were together. It's why he brought you to the mansion. For us to produce a girl for him to eventually sell." An odd silence filled the room.

She'd expected him to be angry. He wasn't. She'd expected him to curse the general. He didn't.

"I have a daughter?" he finally whispered. His voice was thick with emotion.

Ashley nodded and found herself stroking his skull tattoo again. For some reason she seemed drawn toward it. Maybe because she realized if he hadn't been assigned to this S.K.U.L.L. team, then she would never have met Colter and never had Colette.

Just thinking about her pretty little daughter made a wonderful happiness bubble through her entire being.

"She's what…four years old?"

"Yes. Her name is Colette and she's absolutely adorable."

"Who does she look like more? You? Or me?" Typical father question. Ashley couldn't help but smile.

"Both of us. She has your hair color and my eyes."

"Starry Eyes just like her mother, her beautiful mother. I'm so sorry I've been such an asshole with you."

"You were angry. We both were angry."

"I'm not angry anymore. I just want to make love to you. Feel myself inside you…now."

She felt the same way. They needed to bond. Needed to forget. If only for a few minutes.

She moaned as he leaned down and took her mouth in a wickedly delicious kiss. Closing her eyes, she savored the carnal sensations showering her. She was unsure of their future together, but there was one thing she knew for sure. She wanted this man. Wanted her Outlaw Lover with her very being.

He chuckled after breaking the kiss. Then he grabbed her hands and maneuvered her on top of his lap just like the way she'd done earlier. Earlier before her whole world had changed.

She still couldn't absorb it. They'd been used, manipulated and duped horribly by the general and she couldn't decipher the feelings swamping through her.

It would probably hit her later.

But right now…

"Oh my gosh! What are you doing?"

He'd grabbed her by the shoulders and pushed her backward until her head was lying on top of his ankles.

"Just enjoy, Starry Eyes," he chuckled, and maneuvered both her legs to each side of his shoulders. Firm fingers gripped her hips and he pulled her upwards, dragging her ass over his captive cock, his hard belly, his damp chest until she giggled when his hot breath slammed against her pussy.

Tease!

Using his teeth, he managed to unclip one of her clamps. Fiery pain roared through her labia and Ashley couldn't help but grimace. Thankfully, the hot flush of Colter's tongue slowly pacified the ache, replacing the pain with soothing pleasure. He did the same with the other clit clamp. He maneuvered her higher and she cried out again as her pussy lips were parted by his nose. He moved back and forth, using his nose to smooth over her ultrasensitive clit. She could feel her flesh hardening, pulsing with arousal.

His unshaven face raked wonderfully against the delicate insides of her labia, arousing her to new heights. Her breasts felt heavy, so swollen as they jiggled with her every movement.

Just when she thought she just might climax, he maneuvered her off him.

"God, Ashley," he gasped, licking his lips. "You taste so damn good…but my cock is going to explode."

His big chest heaved with his every ragged beat and she couldn't help but giggle.

Positioning herself over his lower half, she bent her knees onto both sides of his hips, being extra careful with his wounded thigh, she quickly twisted the clit ring that doubled for the release screw.

She popped off the ball stretcher.

He groaned as the blood roared into his balls. Easing herself down, she couldn't help but inhale as his delicious thickness sliced into her, his huge size filling her wet channel.

Colter's eyes were now closed. His nostrils flared. His cock pulsed inside her vagina. Squeezing her muscles around his pulsing cock, she held it tight for a long time, watching the gorgeous way he closed his eyes tighter. She was an expert at keeping a man aroused with her vaginal muscles. The general had made her do pelvic exercises every day while he'd watched. He'd even stuck his finger or his cock inside her to make sure she was tightening properly. Thank God, those horrid days were over and she could hopefully go on with life as a free woman.

Moving her hips gently, trying hard not to hurt his cock because of the overlong bondage, she slowly brought them both to the sultry edge of climax.

She watched Colter's mouth open in a sensual gasp.

"You like?"

His answer came as an erotic moan.

Oh yes, he was enjoying himself. Now might be a good time to present her final question.

"Colter?"

"Mmm?"

His eyes remained closed.

"Do you…want to…?"

He must have heard the seriousness in her voice. The need for him to pay attention to what she was about to say for his eyes popped open.

She allowed her vaginal muscles to relax around his rod. Maybe this was the wrong time to bring it up. But her time was running out.

She hadn't told Colter, but while he'd slept, Blade had come back with the cash S.K.U.L.L. had promised. It had been a goodwill gesture on their part. The Outlaws had been ecstatic, but their happiness had been short-lived when Blade told them S.K.U.L.L. was having difficulty locating Tyler. The rescue team had broken into the small, private prison Tyler had been housed in. It had been abandoned.

But the members were tracking down the several guards of the prison. Blade felt confident it would only be a matter of time before they had Tyler, if he wasn't dead. It was information the family had asked her not to share with Colter until he'd recuperated and she had agreed.

Before Blade had left, she'd asked him to release her bodyguard and bring him back there. Once that happened, she would have to leave with him immediately.

"I need to return to Colette."

A flash of hurt splashed across his face and then it was gone. "That's understandable."

"I want you to come with me. I can't bring her here. I can't risk her being registered or taken away for the Claiming Law."

"She's only four! No one is going to touch her!"

Ashley smiled and sighed in relief. He'd turned into a fierce, protective father already. She'd expected this, but not quite so soon.

"All girls in the countries that have adopted the Claiming Law are being registered despite their ages, and many are already being sold and placed with their prospective husbands long before they reach marrying age. Men are so desperate, they are willing to take the risk and dish out thousands and thousands of dollars for purchasing a girl even before she's infected. It's a chance they are willing to take. One I'm not. I have had her removed from this country."

"But I've heard the entire world is adopting this Law. Are you sure she's safe? Where was she born?"

"She was born in Iraq. After leaving you…we moved continuously throughout Europe. About four months later he was assigned back to Iraq where we stayed until she was born and then we were moving around again. After the collapse of the Terrorist Wars he brought me back to the States, to Utah. I was lucky because the general had connections to exempt me from the Claiming Law but Colette…"

"We've got to hide her from the government."

"There are a few smaller countries who've vowed to never adopt the Claiming Law. The country of Monaco is one of them. I have her there with a trusted friend. Once I leave the

States… I won't be coming back. I won't bring her back here, at least not until women have rights again."

"I don't want her in this type of world, either."

"Before you give me an answer, there is something else you have to consider."

"What's that?"

"Callie."

He cursed softly. "We'd have to find another man to take my place. I doubt Luke would go with that idea."

"There's another way. We can take Callie and your brothers with us. I have more than enough money to secure their voyage…"

"I don't know, Starry Eyes."

Devastation rocked her at his words. She thought she'd been prepared for him to say no. Thought she could handle it. But now she realized she really hadn't realized that Colter might not come with her. He had responsibilities. The farm they'd worked so hard to keep. Callie. His brothers and Tyler hopefully coming home. His entire world was here. Aside from this magnificent sexual attraction they shared, he really didn't know her all that much either.

"It should be up to them individually if they want to come with us. I can't speak for them, sweetheart."

"Us?"

"Of course. I want to be with both you and our girl. I want to protect you and I'll do it with my life if I have to."

"Your life is already in too much danger as it is with Cheri—"

"S.K.U.L.L. should do a good enough job at covering my tail, at least long enough for us to get out of the country."

"Speaking of tails…" She clenched her vagina around his pulsing rod again.

He groaned. "I'll get even with you, I swear, Ashley."

She laughed and tweaked her pierced nipples in front of him and gently moved her hips at the same time.

"I can't take much more," he warned.

"Are you going to come with me?"

"Yes, I'm coming," he hissed between gritted teeth.

"To Monaco?"

"I'll come inside you in Monaco too, Starry Eyes."

An almost hysterical happiness swelled through her at his answer and she giggled wildly, unable to believe her luck. Her Outlaw Lover would come away with her. She gyrated her hips harder, quicker. The suctioning sound of her cunt devouring his cock intermingled with her whimpers of enjoyment and she headed straight into a wonderful climax intermingled with his hoarse groans of fulfillment.

* * * * *

Colter couldn't stop himself from grinning as he watched Ashley standing at the stove scrambling eggs and frying bacon for him for breakfast. They'd made love far into the night, and at first light they'd woken and made love again.

Shit!

He couldn't get enough of looking at her. She wore a plain brown skirt that hugged her shapely ass and a peasant-style white blouse that allowed him just the tiniest glimpse of her dark nipples when she occasionally turned around to talk to him about their plans to go to Monaco.

And he was still trying to come to grips that he was a father. It gave him a hell of a new perspective on things. He had a little girl and a woman to protect against the Claiming Law. Now he understood why fathers were so defiant against the Law. Why they sent their daughters into hiding. He'd do the same. No way in hell would he ever let anyone touch his little girl.

God! He hadn't even met her and already his emotions were on a roller coaster, and he was planning her future. She'd go to college. Maybe even go into medicine. Or maybe she'd be an artist. But he wouldn't allow her to go out with just any guy. He'd demand she bring home any prospective suitors to allow him to interrogate them. He'd make sure the guy was scared stiff. Enough so he wouldn't make any wrong moves on his daughter. Yeah, and he'd even show the boy his shotgun just for good measure.

"What's so funny?"

The cheerful sound of Ashley's voice snapped him back to the present. While he'd been daydreaming she'd spooned a heap full of scrambled eggs and pea meal bacon onto his plate along with toast and jam.

"I've been thinking," he said as he forked down delicious mouthfuls of the fluffy eggs.

Man! She was a good cook too!

"Maybe we should try to give Colette a brother. A protector."

"Oh for heaven's sake, Colter. That's not a reason to have another baby."

"He'd be there for her when we're gone. Maybe we should give her several brothers." Yeah that would be even better. Colette would need a strong family to support her in this crazy world.

"Easy, big guy. One baby at a time, okay? And don't be planning our daughter's future for her, either. I want her to do what she wants to do and not think that she needs to do this or that just to please us."

"An independent woman, just like her starry-eyed mother. I just hope she's not as headstrong and as stubborn as you are."

Her eyes widened in mock anger and a flutter of excitement shot through him.

"And let's hope she doesn't have your flair for living on the edge by accepting assignments that put her life in too much danger."

"I told you, I'm finished with S.K.U.L.L."

"Until the next time they show up and make you an offer you can't refuse."

Colter shoved a crisp piece of bacon into his mouth and held up his fingers in a Scout pledge.

"I promise. I won't accept another assignment from them. No matter what. Besides, I'll be too busy bouncing all those baby boys on my knees."

"You'll have to catch me and pin me down before you get that wish, big guy."

"If I wasn't so damn hungry, I'd take you right here on the kitchen table, woman."

The pink tip of her tongue poked out of her mouth and she wiggled her eyebrows at him. "I'm hungry, but not for food."

"Blade was right, you are an insatiable woman."

Suddenly he wasn't so hungry for food anymore, either. He stood and came around to where she sat.

Her eyes were twinkling with that breathtaking starry look she only reserved for him. A wild fluttery feeling whipped through his lower abdomen and he inhaled sharply.

"What's wrong? Is your wound hurting you?"

"No, it's...nothing." How in the world could he ever explain to her the intense joy he felt every time she looked at him like that? There just weren't words to explain it.

"It's just you're so beautiful. All the years we've wasted."

She grabbed his hands. They were soft and feminine—her fingers branded him. Oh man! The things she'd done to his cock with her fingers. He pulled her off the chair and hoisted her onto the table.

"Don't think about what the general did to us," she whispered. She held tight to his hands as if trying to reassure him everything would be all right. "It was out of our control. Now we're back on track. Back in control. We have our future. We have our girl to protect. We have to stay safe for her."

He could read the uncertainty on her face, the cute little frown burrowed between her eyes, the tight smile. He sensed she was giving up control. Leaning on him now. Trusting him to protect her.

Damned if he would let her down.

"Don't worry, Starry Eyes. We'll be safe."

The sound of a car's engine rumbled through the partially opened kitchen window and her eyes widened.

"Colter, someone's here."

The fear in her voice made adrenaline shoot into his very core.

Three short, sharp blasts of a horn settled him down.

"It's okay. That's Cade's signal. He's back."

He hoisted her off the table and led her to the window where they watched Cade's pickup truck roar into the yard.

"Blade's with him," Ashley whispered. Worry etched her face and her hand tightened even harder against his palm.

"Must be bad news if they've hooked up and come back together," Colter found himself saying.

As he watched the two men saunter toward the house his guts wrenched into a tight knot. Ashley's bodyguard wasn't with them. He didn't know if that part was good news or bad.

That wasn't his main concern, though. His brother Tyler wasn't with them, either.

* * * * *

"You want the good news or the bad news first?" Blade asked as he stomped into the kitchen.

Ashley couldn't stop herself from biting her lip as a grim-faced Cade came sauntering in right behind him. Whatever had happened, it didn't look good.

"Just spill it, Blade. Is Ty safe or not?" Colter asked tightly.

"That's the good news. He's been successfully extracted."

Thank God!

"The bad news?"

"He caused a bit of trouble for S.K.U.L.L. Refused to leave with them unless they took his cellmate. I have to tell you, I've never heard a S.K.U.L.L. member swear so much like Bev when she talked about someone."

Colter chuckled. "That's Tyler. Always a handful. That's not the bad news though, is it?"

"He's in rough shape. He and his cellmate have been hospitalized. Seems they've been through quite the ordeal. They have broken bones… A lot of torture was involved. He's an angry young man. He won't be coming home for a little while. There's the debriefing…"

Colter frowned, looked at her. She could read the indecision in his face. Should he stay there for his injured brother or go with her to Monaco?

He turned back to Blade. "Where's Ashley's bodyguard?"

"He didn't want to come back with us."

"Oh, my God! No! He knows all the people to pay bribes to—he has control of the finances! He was the only man in the general's empire I could trust." Never in a million years had she expected Mike would turn his back on her.

"Easy. He's taking care of things for you. We've stashed him at a hotel out of state. He's being guarded by S.K.U.L.L. Bev is calling it extra insurance until she gets the cure into her hands. He wants you to come to him and then you can leave the States."

"You're leaving?" It was Cade. He looked a bit pissed off at her. Obviously he thought she was running away from Colter again.

"We're leaving together, bro," Colter interjected, and she noticed the obvious surprise flash on Cade's face. "That's something we need to discuss with the family. I'm going to have to get a hold of Tyler too."

"I've already talked to him on the phone," Cade replied. "He's really pissed off. He hates hospitals. Says he's fine. Wants to head back to his place…and he says he wants to get Laurie."

"You didn't tell him she was already Claimed, did you?"

"No. It would kill him."

"Or make him kill," Colter said quietly.

"I hate to break the mood, guys," Blake broke in as he eyed her untouched plate filled with breakfast. "But Bev says she wants the cure and the research papers."

Ashley noticed Colter's quick nod to Cade.

"I'll get it," Cade said, and disappeared.

"You're welcome to help yourself, Blade," Ashley said. She hadn't even finished her sentence and he'd already taken the seat and started wolfing down the food. Obviously the man had been so busy getting everything organized he'd forgotten to eat.

"I was wondering if I could crash here tonight," he said between mouthfuls. "I'm in no hurry to get the stuff back to S.K.U.L.L., and making Bev wait an extra day will truly piss the bitch off."

"Stay as long as you need," Colter said. The sound of Cade's footsteps echoed down the hall and he entered like a bullet. He handed the cure and papers to Colter.

"Hey! Is there any food for me? I'm starved," he asked as he rubbed his hands together with eagerness.

Ashley made a move to prepare something for him but Colter's hand snaked around her waist holding her steady against him.

"In the pots on the stove. Help yourself," Colter said quickly, and turned his attention to Blade.

"You cleared it with Bev that our daughter will be the first one who gets the cure when the vaccine is out?"

"Your daughter?" Both men looked utterly shocked as their gazes went back and forth between Ashley and Colter.

"She's mine, not the general's," Colter acknowledged. "I want her to be one of the first ones who get the cure or vaccine or whatever they're making when it gets produced."

"I'll deliver it to you myself. You have my word. But you have to realize there are still the mutated versions she might get when she comes of age."

Ashley's stomach dropped at the horrible reminder, and Colter gave her a reassuring squeeze.

"I'm sure the scientists will come up with something before my kid gets to that point," Colter said calmly. Too calmly. She wondered if he had in fact forgotten that the cure they'd taken from Cheri was only for one form of the X-virus, and he just wasn't allowing himself to think their daughter might die or become submissive when she reached puberty if she contracted the X-virus.

She watched as Cade headed to the table, his arms laden with the pots and frying pan containing breakfast.

"He didn't even warm up the food," Ashley complained, and made a move to do just that, but Colter held her steadfast with his powerful hand.

"Don't worry, he'll like it cold." He lowered his voice. "Are you sure you're okay with this agreement with S.K.U.L.L.?"

"I have to trust them. Blade said he'd bring us the vaccine when it was produced. I have to believe it. But I'll only hand it over to him if you agree."

He hesitated, and for a moment she read indecision in his eyes. "Protocol dictates we don't use S.K.U.L.L. for personal gain," he explained. "But since you got them the cure and made this arrangement with them, I'll have to trust them."

"I can understand if you'd rather stay here and wait until the vaccine comes out…maybe come and join us later, or maybe I can stay longer."

"No, the longer you stay, the more dangerous it is for you. We'll leave as soon as I can talk to Luke, Callie and Tyler."

"But what about your other brothers?"

"The most important person right now is you, Starry Eyes. Don't worry about my brothers. I highly doubt they'd leave the farm. Not unless they had their own women to protect. I'm sure Luke and Callie will be coming with us. But there is a favor I need to ask you."

"Anything."

"I have another brother, Jude and his woman Cate. I know for a fact they would love to take you up on your offer."

"How can we contact them?"

"Last I heard they were in the secluded Florida Everglades."

Ashley nodded. "My bodyguard can send someone down. He may not speak but he has a knack for getting messages to people in other ways. He's got a wonderful Internet connection and knows a lot of people and he is unbelievably reliable."

"This bodyguard sounds like a mighty handy guy."

"He has been," Ashley giggled. She tried hard to ignore the fact that her face was heating up at the curious way Colter gazed at her. If he only knew how handy her bodyguard had been for her when she'd been late in taking her medicine and needed immediate relief until the meds kicked in, her bodyguard just might be a dead man.

"He's castrated. No tongue. What can he do?"

"Fingers. Long, delicious fingers." She clasped Colter's hands and brought them up to gently kiss each of his knuckles. "His fingers did the talking."

"I don't know if I like the idea of this bodyguard letting his fingers walk and talk on my woman. If I ever see him or some other man near you without my permission…"

Her response to his words surprised her. She'd expected to be angry at his possessiveness, she wasn't. Instead, her breath caught in her throat and her breasts suddenly felt larger, her nipples tighter and her pussy quivered with liquid heat. Nerve endings she never knew she had sparkled to life as his fingers intimately caressed the length of her jaw.

"Jealous?" she prodded, welcoming the heat of his body washing against her.

"I don't think you ever want to find out, Starry Eyes."

She fought for breath as his strong hands left her face to skim down onto her hips and then behind to cup her ass. She moaned as he massaged her ass cheeks and shivered at the big bulge pressing into her lower abdomen. Felt her resolve disintegrate as his hot mouth nipped at her lower lip.

She heard a kitchen chair scrape. Her heart picked up speed. Hammered violently against her chest. She had forgotten Blade and Cade were in the room.

"The others…" she warned, expecting him to let her go. He didn't.

"Let them watch. Or they can join us. It would be the perfect going-away present. A ménage just like I promised the other night."

Sweet mercy!

His hands continued to massage her flesh with deep strokes and then one hand was lifting her skirt. She wasn't wearing any underwear. A habit acquired during the Terrorist Wars while serving the general. She moaned wantonly as his finger shocked her sensitive clit. Hot liquid gushed down her vagina.

She sensed movement from behind her. Knew Blade and Cade were close. Could hear their breaths, heavy and aroused.

"Just like old times," he whispered against her mouth. "Let us make love to you, Ashley. Three of us this time. Let us fulfill your fantasy. Show you what we did with Callie."

She could barely stand the sultry sound of his voice, the excitement grabbing at her knees and weakening her. His hot, moist mouth played with her lips and he slowly kissed her into submission.

She felt a hand at her waist, hot yet reassuring and gentle. Was it Cade's hand or Blade's? The hand at her waist was busy. She felt eager fingers working the clasp at the back of her skirt. A moment later her skirt dropped to the floor with a whoosh. Her breath backed up as mild air breezed against her naked ass.

Her cunt felt so hot, so on fire, so eager for their touches. She cried out as a pair of hands curved over her ass cheeks. Her breath quickened. Her pussy moistened, preparing her. Lust flared in Colter's eyes as his fingers cupped her chin.

"You okay with this?"

Her eyelids felt heavy and she could barely see him.

She nodded and he let go of her chin, his fingers working the buttons on her blouse.

"Just relax, Starry Eyes, and let us do all the work."

Work? He called this work? This was heaven.

Her heart pumped faster as her blouse was removed from her body and soft air brushed her nakedness.

Colter swept a gentle, possessive kiss across her lips. It was an exquisite contrast to the wicked hands kneading her buttocks. Calloused hands that massaged her flesh until she cried out at the wonderful sensations.

She found herself kissing Colter back. Crushing her mouth against his, sucking his lower lip into her mouth and nipping his flesh until she tasted blood.

He pulled away, his tongue soothing the tiny cut she'd given him. His look one of surprise and just a little bit of shock.

"Consider it my brand on you, Outlaw Lover. Know that you alone belong to me."

She could barely get the words out, her breath came in such huge gasps.

Calloused hands pried her legs apart. She wanted to look back, see who was there when Blade appeared behind Colter. Lusty eyes blazed back at her. Her panting increased. Her thighs tightened with need.

Colter grinned knowingly and moved slightly aside, allowing Blade to come in closer. Blade, who wore absolutely nothing but a hell of a good-looking erection. His plum-shaped head appeared smooth and red. His nine-inch shaft rigid with arousal, and stuck straight out, ready to impale her.

Sweet mercy! She'd forgotten he was just as big as Colter.

Speaking of her lover…he'd managed to ditch his clothing in one heck of a hurry and now stood in front of her. His gorgeous cock also fully erect, his perfectly shaped balls pulled up tight against him in full arousal.

She swallowed at the erotic sight of two naked men standing there, their heated gazes raking her nakedness while a third man tended to her ass.

Colter looked back at her with fire in his eyes.

Fire. Arousal. Love.

So much love!

"I love you, Starry Eyes," he whispered softly.

She wanted to answer back, to tell him she loved him too, but she couldn't speak, could barely see through the sexual haze as both men's heads lowered.

One brown-haired. One golden-haired. Both mouths opened in unison and she gasped as two hot brands latched onto each of her pink nipples. The powerful force of two mouths sucking her flesh jolted her. The erotic sight of two succulent lips at her breasts made her tremble. Made utterly delicious sensations envelop her.

Her breasts felt swollen, twice their normal size, as the men's sharp teeth nipped, causing delicate pain then quickly laved it away with their wet tongues, leaving behind a trail of delicious fire.

Slurping sounds ripped through the air. She could smell the scent of her sex as Cade's fingers continued to rub her ass cheeks in a deliciously rough way, dipping a finger into her hot little anal hole, teasing her, tormenting her.

When a hand sawed between her legs from her front, her knees weakened. She reached out, her hands settling onto two sets of muscular shoulders.

Against her breast, Colter chuckled. "Thought that would get your attention."

She groaned in response.

He pinched her aching clit, making her wild. Then he alternately stroked lightly. She closed her eyes and moaned as the primal sensations wrapped tightly around her, driving her toward a climax.

The two mouths upon her breasts continued to suckle and nip, stroking nerves that drove her pleasure even higher.

Cade's teeth scraped painfully against the tender curves of her ass and he followed up by soft strokes of a tongue that soothed the burns. Her hips swayed back against him, her ass demanding more.

In answer, a cool, generously lubed finger slipped inside her anus. She moaned at the zip of pleasure-pain. Another calloused finger slid in, stretching her.

Oh yes! More!

Another lubed finger! God! That felt so good.

He began a slow, erotic thrusting, a gentle driving that sent slurping sounds through the air and had her gasping.

At each of her breasts, the men were now also massaging her mounds, their fingers soothing and kneading while they sucked at her aching nipples. Their hands were hot and tender, their mouths eager and moist.

Colter was rubbing her clit. His caresses unleashing the tasty sensations she so craved. Her legs weakened. She could barely stand!

He must have sensed her rising agony for he let her nipple go with a loud pop and she barely heard him whisper, "She's ready."

Oh, she was more than ready. She wanted all of their swollen cocks! And she wanted them in her now!

Blade's mouth left her breast. Cade's fingers left her ass.

"The bed," she heard Colter growl. "Get her to the bedroom."

She could scarcely walk as they hurriedly led her down the hall. She could barely stand as she watched Colter lay down on the bed. His balls were so engorged, his cock so swollen it stood straight up like a silk-encased steel rod.

The sensual sight sent wicked sensations screaming through her.

Gorgeous muscles in his arms rippled as he reached out to her. She went to him eagerly. Coming over him in a missionary style, gasping as his thick rod pierced her slit in one mad thrust. His cock stretched her, filled her easily, compliments of the tending of her three lovers and her well-juiced vagina.

Their lips immediately clashed, melting together in a frantic kiss.

Her mouth slanted over his and she tasted his sweet flesh, smoothed over his teeth until their tongues dueled, bringing delightful flutters to her vagina. She heard Colter groan beneath her as her muscles quivered around his thick cock.

The bed moved. The other two men had joined them. Her heart fluttered with excitement. Her ass ached to be filled and her pussy once again clenched tighter around Colter's cock.

He groaned into her mouth and broke the delicious kiss.

"Damn, woman, you kill me when you do that with your cunt."

She grinned, kissed him again and quickly broke the kiss. "You just relax, and let us do all the work."

She giggled at his surprised look as she echoed the same words he'd said earlier.

"Work, woman? You call this work? I got this fucking aroused just by sucking on your breasts."

She laughed again, and from the corner of her eye, she discovered Blade's gorgeous mushroom-shaped cock head only inches from her face.

Her mouth watered at the sight. He was so huge! And she wanted to devour him!

She parted her lips and licked the underside of his rod. He was scorching and so solid as his cock pulsed with a life of its own against her tongue.

He groaned as she lapped at him, and her pussy clenched at the erotic sound. Beneath her, Colter hissed into his arousal.

Blade's cock head felt so smooth and she quickly lapped at the salty pre-come. He groaned again and his fingers tangled into her air. She opened her mouth and he came inside, filling her beautifully.

He had an impressive size. Hot, swollen flesh and oh so deliciously hard. He tasted clean, of lust. Old memories surfaced of the two of them. Blade and Colter, their thick cocks pummeling her, arousing her, making love to her.

And now there were three.

She gasped around Blade's cock as her buttocks were pried apart. Moaned as Cade's thick, hard, generously lubed cock penetrated her anus gently yet forcefully. She felt the ring of sphincter muscles give way as his hard length came inside. She gritted her teeth and inhaled into the sweet bite of pleasure-pain.

"Oh man, you're so fucking tight," Cade hissed as her ass clenched around his thick rod. Gripped him. Welcomed him.

She grimaced around Blade's shaft as Cade's thick rod drove deeper. She loved the snug way he fit up her ass, enjoyed the feel of three silky cocks inside her.

Colter's moist lips kissed the curve of her neck and shoulder, creating intimate sensations as Cade's calloused hands held her hips. He held her steady as he began pumping her. Slow, easy thrusts—almost too slow—as if he might be afraid of hurting her. She wanted to call out to him. Demand he fuck her harder. She wanted to tell him she'd had worse under the general's reign and his caring thrusts were just not hard enough. She wanted a harder bite of pleasure-pain.

For a fleeting moment she wondered if maybe the general had turned her into a masochist who enjoyed pain with her sex, but then remembered she'd always enjoyed a little bit of pain with her pleasure, especially when she'd been with Colter in Iraq.

Blade's fingers curled tighter in her hair. His cock slid easily in and out of her mouth. She allowed him to go to the back of her throat, even down it. She was an expert at deep throating. Knew how to relax the throat muscles so as not to gag.

Keeping her lips tight around his shaft, she moved her tongue against the underneath of his pulsing flesh and scraped her teeth along the top of his cock, creating a delicious friction for him as he thrust in and out.

"You're so damn good, Ashley," he growled.

She could see the sweat on his chest, heard his harsh gasps, saw the muscles in his neck tighten as he bore down on her. His hips thrust quickly, passionately, making her tremble with lust.

The pleasure from the three cocks was exquisite. Carnal sensations deep in her belly blossomed. Perspiration flourished over her heated flesh.

With every fierce thrust of Cade's hips, he pushed her pelvic bone harder against Colter's, causing friction against her clit. In reaction, her pussy contracted wonderfully around his pulsing cock. In this way, she gave her captive Outlaw, as well as herself, delicious pleasure. She found Cade lifting her hips, allowing Colter's cock to sink in and out of her cunt like a piston, creating a wonderful friction against her G-spot. Friction that teased and tormented her toward the climax she craved.

Suctioning noises and the slaps of flesh against flesh intermingled with the sultry masculine groans and her own whimpers of pleasure as all three men continued to fuck her.

All of them plunging so deep, in perfect rhythm, she felt as if each rod touched muscles and nerves that had never been touched before. Nerve endings that sizzled to life and took over her body.

She shuddered as the first pleasure wave hit her.

Cried out as the second slammed through her.

And then she was lost.

Lost in the release. Lost in the spirals of pleasure as the three cocks plunged in and out of her in utter perfection and fulfilling her ménage fantasy.

Chapter Twelve

Afterward Colter cradled her in his strong arms and gently stroked her silky cheek as she slept soundly. Her bared breasts heaved up and down with each deep, relaxed breath. Dark eyelashes framed her closed eyes and her lush lips curled into the sweetest, dreamiest smile.

His gut clenched with warmth as he watched her.

It had been an unbelievable fuck-fest. It had happened so quickly. So naturally.

His brother and Blade had watched as he'd kissed her. Their dark gazes riveted to his hand as he'd slipped it beneath her skirt. Hunger and desperation had brewed in their eyes.

When he nodded to them, and then vocalized to them about pleasuring Ashley, he'd seen the surprise, the thanks and the knowledge he trusted them not to hurt her.

And they hadn't.

They'd treated her like the sensual woman she was. A woman that he loved. They'd taken the time to pleasure her even if it had meant subduing their own sexual gratification. He knew Cade hadn't had sex for at least several months and had no idea when Blade had entertained a lady.

The three of them had fucked her in every conceivable way most of the day. Teasing her. Pleasuring her. The three of them grinning at the cute way she screamed every time she orgasmed, which had been often.

He smiled. Oh yeah, she'd been a screaming bundle of ecstasy and he'd seen every minute of the enjoyment splashed on her face. The tender sight had only made his heart burst with love.

She was unbelievable. Absolutely fantastic. And he bet Blade and Cade wouldn't soon forget her.

But forget her they eventually would, because fulfilling her ménage wouldn't be an everyday occurrence as it had been for Callie at the beginning of her Claiming. He had no idea how a divorce worked these days because he wanted to marry Ashley. Marry her the old-fashioned way. One man. One woman. Unfortunately, it didn't look like the laws were going to change any time soon though, so they'd just have to wait.

Until then, he'd protect her, love her and take care of their daughter and any kids that might come into the picture down the road.

He held her tighter against him. Felt the hot curves of her body kiss his hard planes, loved the way the silkiness of her black hair streamed over his chest and teased his skin.

And she smelled so damned good. Smelled of sex and woman and just plain love.

He gazed around the room, committing it to memory. Soon, he'd leave here. Leave the Outlaw farm, the only home he'd known. The only time he'd been away was to fight in the Terrorist Wars and then he'd come straight back. Back to the place he thought he'd love and would live on forever. The home he'd lived in since his mom had brought him home from the hospital. All his brothers had lived here all their lives. Except Tyler who'd gotten his own place shortly before the Terrorist Wars had broken out.

At the thought of what might have happened to Tyler at the hands of the terrorists and then the Barlows made a blade of anger rip through him. He hated the idea of leaving his little brother back here in the States. Hated to know he'd react real badly to finding out his woman had been Claimed by the same sons of bitches who'd kept him imprisoned after the Wars had finished. He could only hope and pray Tyler would somehow survive the anguish of Laurie's betrayal and not do something really stupid like get himself killed when he went after her.

Without a doubt, he would go after the woman he loved. He'd do the same thing. Would have done the same thing if he'd found Ashley. Hell he'd even have helped Ty get his woman away from the richest men in the state—but now Colter had a daughter to think about. A sweet little girl who needed his protection.

He had Ashley back too. Back in his arms.

And there was no way in hell he would ever lose her again.

A soft knock at the open door made Ashley shift in her sleep and Colter looked up to find Blade standing there fully dressed.

"Just wanted to let you know Cade's been called away on another bounty-hunting job. He just left." He lowered his voice as he caught Ashley sleeping. "Just wanted to thank you for all you've done. And thanks to Ashley for showing us a good time. She's a very sensual woman and very special. Hold onto her. Hold her tight."

"And I'm going to hold you to personally delivering that vaccine when it gets made," Colter whispered back, wanting his friend and ex-partner to know just how important it was to keep his daughter out of danger.

He was no fool, though. He knew this vaccine would take care of only one mutation of the X-virus. There were several others around. But it was a start. Maybe the medical profession would be able to glean the information from the research papers they'd taken from Cheri. That's what he hoped would happen, and he had to stick to that thought or he would surely drive himself mad just thinking about his daughter turning into a mindless submissive, or dying, or worse.

"S.K.U.L.L. has made the arrangements already. I'll bring it just as I promised."

"I never asked her why and how S.K.U.L.L. got involved in this gig in the first place. I mean they're Army. Top secret. Why take on this assignment?"

Blade shrugged.

"Either you don't really know or you're just not a liberty to say," Colter mused.

"Consider the latter. Besides, I'd think you wouldn't give a shit anymore, especially when you get entertained whenever you like by a beautiful woman."

"Or whenever I like," Ashley purred, and snuggled against Colter.

"Sorry we woke you." Blade grinned.

"You don't look too sorry," she countered.

Blade chuckled. "She's back to her feisty self again. Just like old times. Oh and here. One of the guys picked this up before they left Pleasure Palace. You must have dropped it."

Blade reached into his pocket and tossed something onto the bed.

"Oh, my God!" Ashley cried out, and grabbed the little Victorian comb Colter had given her in Iraq. The comb he'd found with the note he'd thought had been from her. He'd carried both the comb and the note with him wherever he'd gone. Reminders of his need for revenge against Ashley.

She clutched the item to her chest and Colter could instantly tell by the way her eyes sparkled she was truly grateful to have his mother's comb again.

"I'm so glad you got it out. Thank you so much, Blade."

She turned to Colter. "I'd taken it from your suitcase when I searched your room," she said quietly.

"And you wanted it back again after all this time? Even after you thought I'd betrayed you?"

She nodded her head. "Because I love you. I've never stopped loving you."

Emotion clogged his throat and warmth flooded through him as he felt the sheet covering his waist move slightly. Hot, feminine fingers wrapped around his cock and he grew hard instantly.

"Yep, just like old times," he agreed with what Blade had just said moments ago as her fingers began to stroke his length, invoking memories of Ashley never getting enough of touching him back in Iraq.

"Oh yeah, definitely like old times," he whispered hoarsely to the suddenly empty doorway.

* * * * *

After making love to Colter, he'd muttered something to her about Blade leaving soon. She'd insisted they get dressed and at least say a proper goodbye. They were doing just that, her stopping Blade near the front door while she'd sent Colter to the kitchen to grab and wrap the last piece of chocolate cake she knew Callie had hidden in the back of the fridge. The least she could do was send Blade off with something sweet as thanks for all he'd done for them.

That's when the shot shrieked through the living room window.

It was a loud blast. The glass shattering made Ashley literally freeze with shock. To her horror, Blade crumpled to the floor. Redness blossomed at the back of his upper right shoulder. Before she could even think of what to do, she heard Colter swear as a loud crash came from the kitchen area.

More shots!

Icy fingers of terror gripped her and instinctively she dove for Blade's prone figure. He had a gun in his shoulder holster, but he'd fallen in such a way that it lay beneath his heavy body. For a panic-stricken moment she wondered if he'd fallen onto the vial, shattering it. Should she go for the research papers?

She heard footsteps on the front porch.

Shit! No time!

Grabbing Blade's shoulder, she ignored his soft outcry as she struggled to turn him over. He rolled onto his back. His eyes fluttered open and he stared unseeing.

Oh God! Was he dead? No time to find out.

Clutching the pistol, she undid the safety and, in a crouch, she headed toward the kitchen.

She heard voices. One of them belonged to Cheri Blakely. She recognized the anger, the triumph in her voice.

Cheri must have caught Colter. Her blood froze. A strangled scream hovered in her throat.

Suddenly the front door burst inward.

Ashley reacted quickly. Spinning around, she shot at the figure in the doorway. The man let out a cry of pain and went down in a tangled heap. Another man appeared. A bullet whizzed too close to her ear for comfort and from the corner of her eye she noticed the white cotton fluff everywhere like snow as the edge of the sofa blew away.

She aimed and fired.

Without a word, the man dropped like a stone and lay still.

A woman's evil chuckle sliced through the air behind her. Dread filled her. She sensed she was in deep trouble. She wasn't wrong.

"Drop the gun, bitch, or your man dies."

"Don't do it, Ash!" It was Colter's voice, strangled with a tinge of fear.

She was about to spin around, about to start shooting but the sound of a gun cocking made her stop cold. Terror tangled in her chest. She struggled to remain as calm as possible.

"Just drop the gun, Ashley, and then turn around. Slowly."

Shit! If she dropped the gun, she was screwed, but if she didn't, then Cheri would take out Colter. Devastation rocked her and she came to her decision quickly. She allowed the gun to drop from her trembling fingers.

"That's a smart little sex slave. I told you you wouldn't get away. Now turn around."

She did as Cheri instructed. Her heart leapt into her throat the instant she spied one of Cheri's husbands holding a gun on Colter and Cheri aimed her gun at Ashley's midsection.

"You know why we're here. Give me the cure and the papers."

"You let him go and I'll tell you where they are."

Cheri shook her head. "I'm not in the mood for negotiating, you stupid bitch. I want what's mine and I want your daughter's whereabouts. I purchased her fair and square from the general. She belongs to my sons now."

"You'll never get her," Colter hissed. The anger, the coldness with which he spoke made Cheri wince but she kept her icy gaze on Ashley.

"I will kill him if you do not give me what I want."

"You'll kill him anyway," Ashley pointed out. Her knees were trembling so hard she thought she'd fall down or maybe even pass out.

"Yes, that's true." Cheri's red lips thinned into a satisfied smirk and she swung the gun around to point at Colter's head. Now he had two guns at his temples. Ashley couldn't help but cry out in protest.

"A quick death…or—" she pointed the gun at Colter's thigh "—or a slow, agonizing death. It's entirely up to you."

"Dammit! Tell her nothing, Ash," Colter warned.

"Shut up!" Cheri yelled. "Tell me! Or he dies!"

"Okay, okay. I'll tell you." *Just don't shoot the father of my child!*

Suddenly she felt lightheaded, disoriented. She noticed Colter's gaze skim slightly to behind her, to the living room where Blade had fallen. Did he know that Blade had been hit? Was he looking for help from him?

Oh, God! Didn't he know they were on their own?

Blade had the cure on him somewhere. But from this angle they wouldn't know he'd been hit. Wouldn't know he lay sprawled on the other side of the couch with the research papers inside his jacket, the vial most likely in his jacket pocket. Maybe even shattered, the precious fluid leaking into the carpet.

And if they found Blade, helpless, sprawled out and still alive…they'd kill him.

Dammit! What should she do?

"It's in the bedroom. Last door to your right," Colter said tightly.

"Good. He's smart, isn't he? After you, Ashley." She motioned her gun for Ashley to start down the hallway.

Every muscle inside her tensed as she cautiously moved in front of Cheri and her husband who still held the gun to Colter's temple. She could tell as she passed Colter that the way his hands were clenching and unclenching he was either frustrated or ready to make a move.

Most likely the latter.

She allowed her survival instincts to envelop her as she walked slowly down the long hallway. Behind her, she could hear three sets of footsteps following her. She tried to visualize exactly who was closest behind her. Was it Cheri? Her husband? Maybe Colter?

She couldn't make a move until she figured out everyone's positions.

"How did you find us, Cheri?" she called out.

"That's easy. When Dr. Van Dusen was nice enough to allow me to scratch his deliciously large cock and balls, I caught a glimpse of a skull tattoo on his belly. Mind you, I know that men have strange fetishes and so the skull intrigued me. Perhaps you could say it even made me suspicious. And me being the paranoid, I did not remember a mention of an identifying feature on the doctor. In my line of work I can't afford to be the least bit careless so I made sure to scrape some of his cells beneath my fingernails while I had him by the balls so to speak. Later I had the cells sent to check for DNA. I must admit the cover was very well laid. My connections, however, kept searching and were able to tap into the high-security government database and voila, your doctor lover's real name and his address."

"My mistake," Colter said coolly.

Okay, so Cheri was at the end of the row and Colter in between her and her husband. That meant her hubby was right behind her!

"That accounted for the delay while I tried to figure out who the intruder was," Cheri said. "Imagine my surprise when I discovered he was just a local farm boy turned doctor, turned S.K.U.L.L. member. And that he's the son of a bitch who killed my first husband. Now I do have this insane need to kill your man, Ashley. And I will."

Shit!

The burst of anger she needed to push aside her fear propelled Ashley into action. Ducking, she swung her arm out and grimaced in pain as it connected with bone. The gun went off, the bullet screamed past her ear. Too close for comfort.

Blurred movement from the side of her face made her realize Colter had also sprung into action. It was as if he'd been anticipating her move. She heard the sharp slap of flesh against flesh as if someone were hitting someone.

"I've never hit a lady before, but you sure aren't one," Colter growled.

Cheri howled. "You bastard! Unhand me!" Another slap.

Before Ashley could get to her feet, she felt pain rip through her scalp. She screamed at the red-hot agony searing through her. Hot tears blurred her vision. Cheri's husband had grabbed her by the hair and was pulling at her to stand up.

God it hurt!

She screamed.

The sound was quickly followed by a loud crash and a cry of pain from Cheri.

Gunshots rang out. The intense pain on her scalp disappeared as he let her go.

Suddenly there were hands all over her, helping her up.

"Sweet Jesus, Ashley! Are you okay?" Colter's voice trembled with concern.

"I…I think so."

Her legs quaked and her teeth chattered as she gazed upon the two bodies in the hallway. Cheri lay on the ground sprawled lifeless. A pool of blood gushing from her neck and her husband had a hole in his forehead. She looked up to see Blade swaying behind them, a gun in his hand.

Then everything went black.

* * * * *

"I never pass out," Ashley replied defiantly as she laid on the bed where Colter had carried her after she'd passed out, and where he'd forced her to stay for the remainder of the day.

Callie, Luke and Mac, along with Cade, had all returned and now they stood around the bed with Colter and Blade, who had his arm in a sling.

Gosh, it was kind of embarrassing with everyone fussing over her. She just wasn't used to all this attention.

"I'm just glad you're all right," Callie said softly as she hoisted her very pregnant self onto the side of the bed. "And I'm very grateful for your offer to take Luke and me with you, but I just can't leave my sister behind."

"Then we can take her with us."

"She won't leave. I've already asked her," Blade's deep voice cut through the room.

"You?" Callie asked looking shocked and confused and asked the same question as Ashley had just been thinking. "Why would you ask my sister?"

"Because I'm her fourth husband. I Claimed her a few days ago with the Barlow brothers."

"Oh, God!" Callie and Ashley both gasped in unison.

"What the hell are you talking about?" Colter growled. "Are you fucking nuts?"

"I should have told you right from the beginning. But I felt it would compromise this assignment," Blade said.

There was a round of swearing from the remaining Outlaw brothers.

"You're the one who fucked us up?" Disbelief etched Mack's voice.

"We were the only ones who knew she didn't have the required fourth husband anymore. We were using that fucking fact to blackmail the Barlows and to try to gain Tyler's release," Cade growled.

"Why the hell would you Claim my brother's woman? When he comes back, he'll kill you to get to her," Colter hissed. "Do you have a fucking death wish?"

"I'll fucking kill him right now!" Cade spat, and made a move toward Blade.

"Relax! All of you!" Callie shouted. "Please, I want you all to leave the room, except for Colter, Ashley and Blade."

There was a murmur of protests but Callie's stern look made all her husbands fall silent. They stomped out of the room, slamming the door shut behind them with so much force it sounded as if a gunshot had gone off.

"What's going on?" Colter asked between gritted teeth. "If I didn't think you were up to something, I'd kill you right here and now with my bare hands."

Blade took a deep breath and exhaled. "Okay, I can't tell you much. It's a S.K.U.L.L. assignment, and for Laurie's safety I need for you all to keep that fact under your hat."

"Laurie's life is in danger, isn't it?" Callie whispered. Ashley's heart almost broke at the tears spilling from the soft-spoken woman's eyes. She obviously cared very deeply for her sister.

"She's fine. Not to worry. She is a very strong, determined woman. She has her reasons for not leaving her husbands." Blade reassured her with a smile. "I will take care of her."

"And who the hell is going to take care of you and the Barlows when Tyler comes home, Blade?" Colter growled. "He won't give up Laurie easily."

By the way he stood with every muscle in his entire body tense and coiled, she knew Colter was pissed off. Probably more angry than he'd ever been at her.

"Tyler won't be hurt by me. Rest assured, Colter. I'll keep an eye on him. You and Callie and Luke are free to go Monaco. Laurie wants you to go. For you and the baby to be safe."

"Are you certain my sister is safe?" Callie asked, her hands still knotted in anguish on her swollen belly.

"If Blade says she's safe, then she's safe," Colter said softly. "She's lucky to have a member of S.K.U.L.L. as her husband."

Ashley held her breath as Callie looked at Colter and then at Blade again. Her shoulders slumped with apparent relief.

"And you won't hurt Tyler when he returns?" she asked. "My sister really loves that man and she doesn't even know he's alive."

"I promise I'll keep an eye on him. Now you best get packing. You leave first thing in the morning."

"Could you say goodbye to Laurie for me? I know she's not allowed to visit here without her husbands in tow and—"

"I can arrange a meeting between the two of you tonight. Alone. You can say your goodbyes then. I'll come for you a little later on."

"Okay. Okay. I'd like that," Callie whispered. To Ashley's surprise, a watery smile lifted the woman's full lips. "Well then! I guess I'd better hurry and pack."

Ashley watched as she lifted her heavy frame off the bed and waddled off to do her packing.

"I've got another piece of news for you," Blade said as he waited for Callie to close the door behind her.

Oh, God! Please not bad news.

"Ashley's bodyguard contacted me earlier. Jude and Cate have agreed to come with you to Monaco."

"Thank God," Ashley breathed. Some good news for a change.

"As a matter of fact, the two of them will be meeting you at a prearranged meeting place day after tomorrow. But we're going to have to work hard to pull this off. Once word gets out that the general is dead, Ashley's life could be in danger. Men he once knew might want to Claim her."

"Colter can take on the general's identity. I'm sure we can pass through the checkpoints without any problems if he wears a disguise and produces the proper ID." *Why in the hell hadn't she thought of this earlier?*

"The general can just simply disappear off the face of the Earth once you leave the States. I can set an alternate paper trail to cover your asses," Blade said thoughtfully.

"By golly, I think we've got ourselves a plan." Colter chuckled. "Let's get our butts in gear!"

Epilogue

Monaco

Three days later…

Colter couldn't believe how perfect his four-year-old daughter looked as she played in the sandbox amidst a backdrop of craggy rocks in the tiny villa's backyard that overlooked the azure-blue Mediterranean Sea.

Her short pigtails glistened in the Monaco sunshine, a smudge of dirt sat on her cute button nose and her chubby tanned arms worked diligently on a sandcastle as she was totally oblivious to her parents who stood only a few feet away watching her.

"She's so unbelievably beautiful," he found himself whispering, totally mesmerized at the intense way such a tiny creature could capture his heart and unleash such a powerful bout of protectiveness it almost hurt.

There was no mistaking she belonged to him. He could tell by the stubborn tilt of her jaw as she concentrated on placing a miniature Monaco flag in the center of her sandcastle. Nor could he deny she possessed the exact same color of hair as his.

Sweet Jesus, he had a daughter.

"Want to meet her?" Ashley asked from beside him. Pride shone in her starry blue eyes as she watched their girl.

A bout of panic gripped him at her question. Would Colette like him? Would she be scared of him? Would he make her a good father? Or would he blow it?

Despite all his doubts, he found himself nodding. Yes, he wanted to meet her. Touch her. Hug her.

He found himself tensing with anxiety as Ashley called out to her. The little girl looked up and when she saw her mamma, her eyes lit up like a kid who'd just discovered a thousand presents under the Christmas tree.

Without hesitation she flew across the yard, short, chubby legs chugging like crazy and her pigtails flying wildly as she flung herself into Ashley's open arms. She lifted the girl with ease, hugging her and spattering her face with kisses and whispering I love yous and I missed you so muches.

Her little arms wrapped around Ashley's neck and she held tight, kissing her mother back and giggling with glee.

Then suddenly she became aware of his presence and disentangled her arms from Ashley's neck. She peered at him directly with the same starry-blue eyes Ashley possessed. Her little brows were scrunched together with curiosity and her chubby cheeks were pink with excitement.

"Hi," he found himself saying.

"Are you my daddy?" she asked point-blank. "Mommy says my daddy is very handsome and he has the same hair color as me. You must be him."

At her sweet, innocent voice, something warm unleashed itself inside him. It was an almost indescribable feeling. Something he'd never felt before in his life.

"Yes, sweetie. I finally found your daddy. He's finally home."

Both of them smiled at him and Colter knew Ashley was right.

He was finally home.

Also by Jan Springer

eBooks:

Christmas Lovers

Claiming Hannah

Colter's Revenge

Edible Delights

Ellora's Cavemen: Legendary Tails II (*anthology*)

Heroes at Heart 1: A Hero's Welcome

Heroes at Heart 2: A Hero Escapes

Heroes at Heart 3: A Hero Betrayed

Heroes at Heart 4: A Hero's Kiss

Heroes at Heart: A Hero Needed

Holiday Heat (*anthology*)

Intimate Stranger

Jade

Kiss Me

Outlaw Lovers Dossier

Outlaw Lovers: Jude Outlaw

Outlaw Lovers: The Claiming

Peppermint Creek Inn

Tyler's Woman

Sexual Release

Sinderella

Sweet Heat

Zero to Sexy

Print Books:

A Hero Betrayed

A Hero's Kiss

A Hero's Love

A Hero's Welcome

Bad Girls Have More Fun (Pocket)

Ellora's Cavemen: Legendary Tails II (*anthology*)

Holiday Heat

Jude and Luke

Overtime, Under Him (Pocket)

Peppermint Creek Inn

White Hot Holidays Volume 3 (*anthology*)

About the Author

Jan Springer writes on four acres of paradise tucked away in the Haliburton Highlands of Ontario, Canada. Past careers include Accounting, Truck Driving, Farming and Factory work but her passion for writing won out in the end. Now Jan writes full time and is a part-time caretaker. She enjoys kayaking, hiking, photography and gardening. She is a member of the Romance Writers of America and Passionate Ink (RWA–Erotic Romance Chapter). She loves hearing from her readers.

Jan welcomes comments from readers. You can find her website and email address on her author bio page at www.ellorascave.com.

Tell Us What You Think

We appreciate hearing reader opinions about our books. You can email us at Comments@EllorasCave.com.

Why an electronic book?

We live in the Information Age—an exciting time in the history of human civilization, in which technology rules supreme and continues to progress in leaps and bounds every minute of every day. For a multitude of reasons, more and more avid literary fans are opting to purchase e-books instead of paper books. The question from those not yet initiated into the world of electronic reading is simply: *Why?*

1. ***Price.*** An electronic title at Ellora's Cave Publishing and Cerridwen Press runs anywhere from 40% to 75% less than the cover price of the exact same title in paperback format. Why? Basic mathematics and cost. It is less expensive to publish an e-book (no paper and printing, no warehousing and shipping) than it is to publish a paperback, so the savings are passed along to the consumer.
2. ***Space.*** Running out of room in your house for your books? That is one worry you will never have with electronic books. For a low one-time cost, you can purchase a handheld device specifically designed for e-reading. Many e-readers have large, convenient screens for viewing. Better yet, hundreds of titles can be stored within your new library—on a single microchip. There are a variety of e-readers from different manufacturers. You can also read e-books on your PC or laptop computer. (Please note that Ellora's Cave does not endorse any specific brands.

You can check our websites at www.ellorascave.com or www.cerridwenpress.com for information we make available to new consumers.)

3. ***Mobility.*** Because your new e-library consists of only a microchip within a small, easily transportable e-reader, your entire cache of books can be taken with you wherever you go.
4. ***Personal Viewing Preferences.*** Are the words you are currently reading too small? Too large? Too... ANNOYING? Paperback books cannot be modified according to personal preferences, but e-books can.
5. ***Instant Gratification.*** Is it the middle of the night and all the bookstores near you are closed? Are you tired of waiting days, sometimes weeks, for bookstores to ship the novels you bought? Ellora's Cave Publishing sells instantaneous downloads twenty-four hours a day, seven days a week, every day of the year. Our webstore is never closed. Our e-book delivery system is 100% automated, meaning your order is filled as soon as you pay for it.

Those are a few of the top reasons why electronic books are replacing paperbacks for many avid readers.

As always, Ellora's Cave and Cerridwen Press welcome your questions and comments. We invite you to email us at Comments@ellorascave.com or write to us directly at Ellora's Cave Publishing Inc., 1056 Home Avenue, Akron, OH 44310-3502.

CPSIA information can be obtained at www.ICGtesting.com
227024LV00001B/4/P

9 781419 960758